I0593487

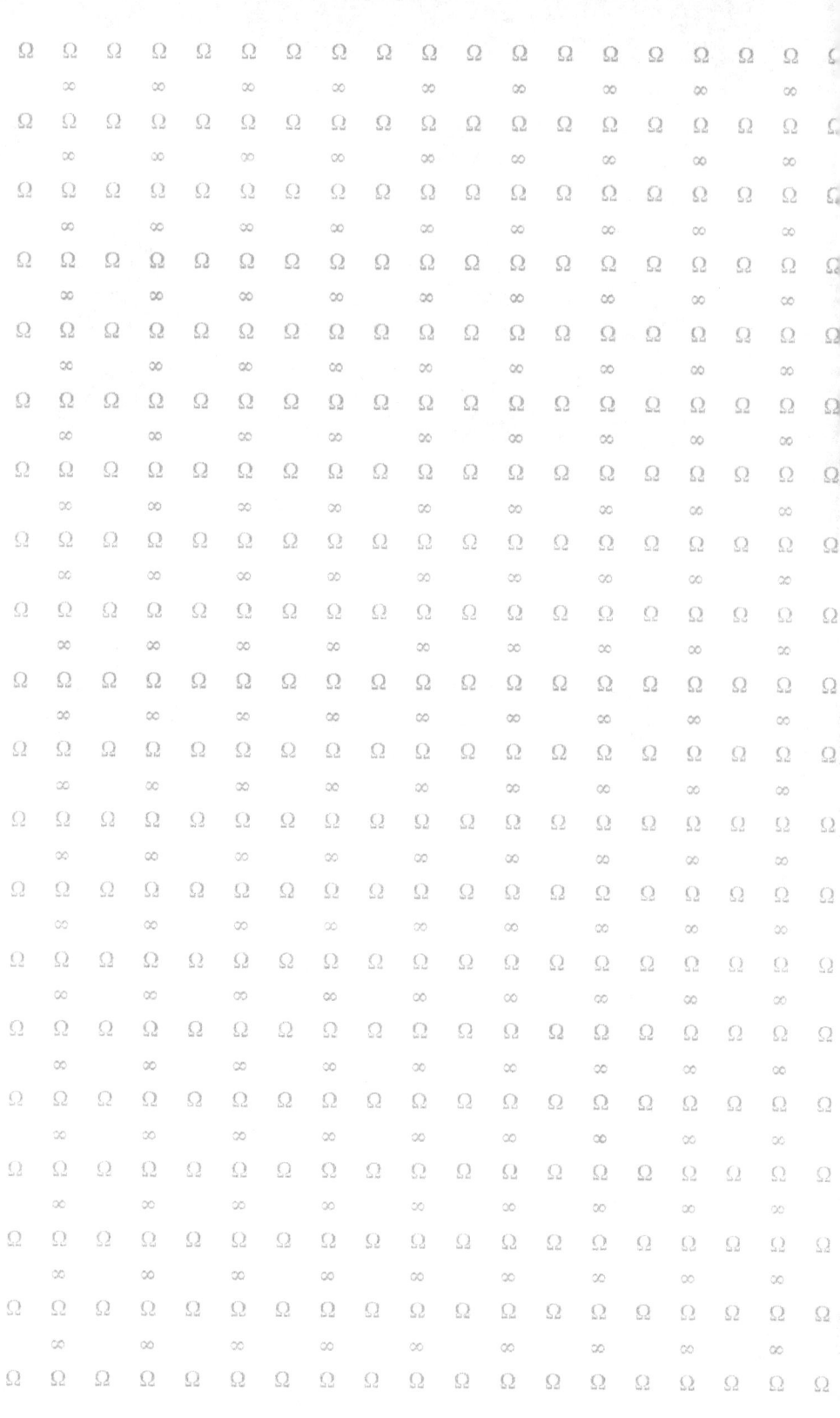

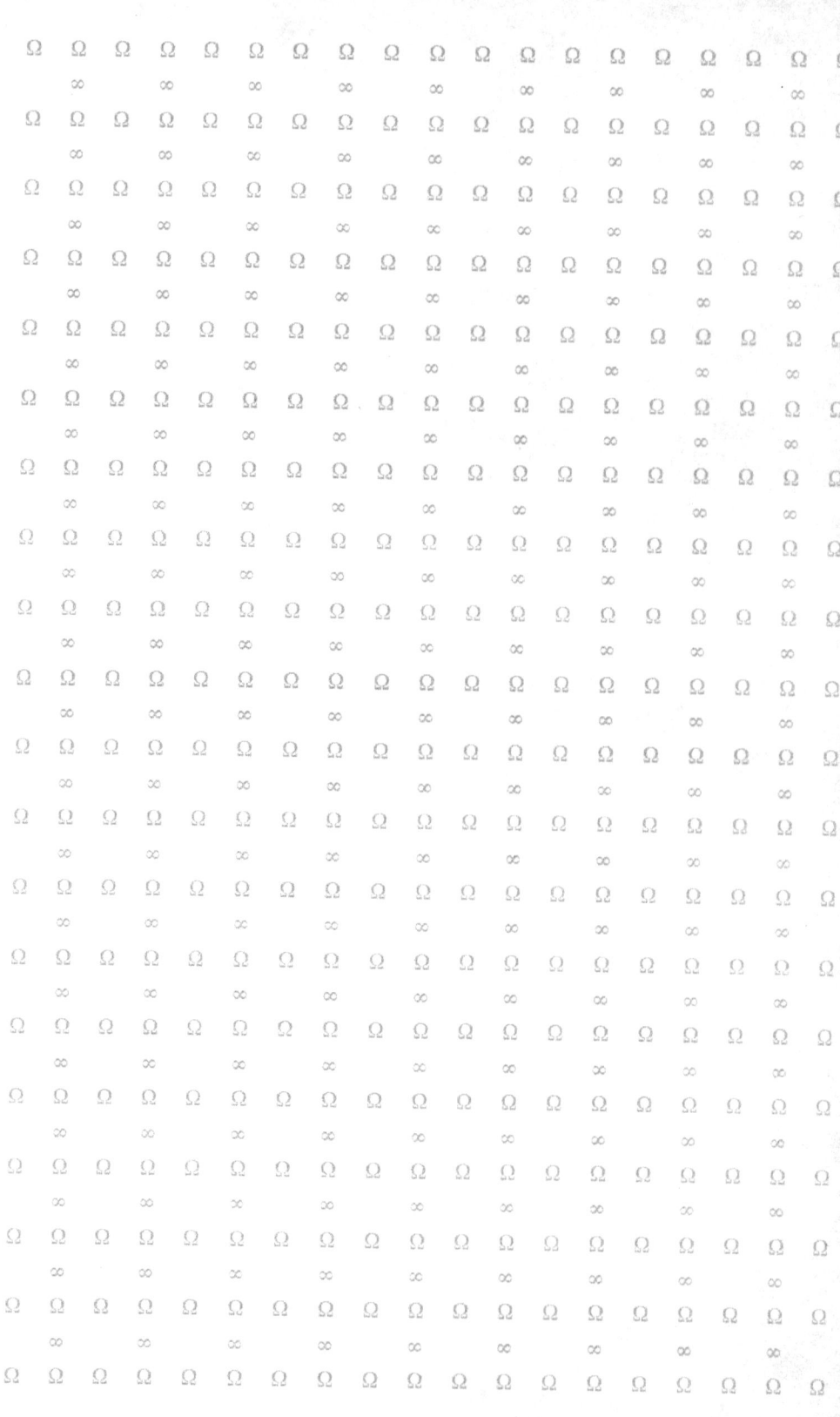

Last Time Around
A *novel in three books*

in case of emergency press
We are proud to acknowledge the Traditional Owners of country throughout Australia and to recognise their continuing connection to land, waters, and culture.
We pay our respects to their Elders.
We support recognition, reconciliation, and reparation.

Last Time Around

A *novel in three books*

Will Clattenburg

in case of emergency press
https://icoe.com.au
Travancore, Victoria
Australia

Published by **in case of emergency press** 2022

ISBN 978-0-6451280-8-6

Cover and Title Page Photo:
Oleg Onchky on Unsplash

You burn with the fiery passion of youth.
I can't be satisfied.
You read it in literature, so it must be the truth.

You certainly know how to have a good time.
I can't be satisfied.
I had some fun about eight, but I was all right by nine.

Talulah Gosh,
"I Can't Get No Satisfaction, Thank God"

Table of contents

Acknowledgements

I would like to thank the following people for their help and support with this book:

Lee K. Abbott, Lily Hoang, Connie Voisine, Elizabeth Horodowich, Rus Bradburd, Barry Pearce, Emily Cook, Alex Hallwyler, Gautam Emani, and Howard Firkin and the team at in case of emergency press.

Dedication

For Amanda

Last Time Around

Book One

Maggie knew something about beer and had just been talking to us about top and bottom fermentation and yeast fermentation and I don't know what, I just deferred to her general wisdom, her long-running appearances at Munich's Oktoberfest, and personal anecdotes about breweries of the world, when she was like "Did I tell you about Preston?"[1]

I was like "No. What about Preston?" I exchanged glances with Sean and he just shook his head like he didn't want to get involved (of course, he probably knew all about it anyway and was staying quiet so Maggie could tell her own story).[2] He

---

[1] Until today, Preston and I sat on either side of a cubicle, separated by a carpeted wall. I knew for a fact Preston did nothing all day—and not just because I didn't do anything either so I had the opportunity to listen to him. Our boss used to complain openly about Preston's laziness. She'd grumble into the phone to Velma two cubicles down: "That's Preston's job! That's Preston's job, isn't it?" I'm not sure if she always knew what Preston's job was, his job was so nebulous, and no one had the time to trace his actual job responsibilities, which would have required archival research. "All right, he needs to get going," our boss would rant, "I'd like to see what he's done by the end of today. There's some urgency here." And then she would delegate the responsibility of lighting a fire under Preston's ass to Velma who was the kindest, most soft-spoken lady in the entire office and about the worst enforcer imaginable. Preston, it just so happened, was running late to the beer garden where we all were, but was due to arrive any minute.

[2] Women tended to confide in Sean, there was just something brotherly and harmless about the guy. I'll admit, I'd been on the gab with him more than my share of odd nights at Hibernian, or

almost touched his nose to his stein, folding himself against the table in the attitude of a passive listener. Maggie hadn't wanted to sit outside on account of the humidity, not that it was any better where we were, even with the French doors unfolded to the street where the heat had been rising like blown glass, distorting the view of apartments, bodegas, fire hydrants, and here and there a wreckage of urban plant life. The room at this German place was filled to capacity, the tables and benches wedged tight as a mess hall, with people bumping into you all the time, swiping their rear-ends across your back like boats at a dock as they negotiated the aisles. We were sitting in the center of the room at a small square table flanked by a decorative wood beam. On the table were two empty beer steins, one of them Maggie's, one of them mine.

Maggie was like "So, you know how Preston has that thing where he can make a CD with one-hundred songs, like one of those big memory CDs?"

"Sure," I said, not knowing anything about a big memory CD, but figuring it was an incidental part of the story and pretending I knew it anyway, just as I still pretend to know words like "metaphysical" and "facetious."[3]

McSorley's, or just in the office kitchen while he cleaned the coffee pot. I think Sean liked hearing a predicament all the way through··· at least that's what I told myself.

[3] Add "redolent" to the list. My first time reading that Nick Amante book (*Inferno*, Volta Press, 2006), I couldn't help sneering to Rebecca Fershleiser, my roommate, "You know he didn't even use the word redolent correctly." Fershleiser was like "How did he use it?" (Despite her trumpeting Amante to the high heavens, I don't think she ever read *Inferno* herself, or she might have modified her opinion of him, re: male/female relations). I was like "He used it to mean like smell. Something like redolent of summertime, mown grass, etc. When it's more of a metaphorical word type thing." Fershleiser was like "No, Ian, it can mean smell too. Even if it's also sometimes a metaphor type

thing, like you're saying." "Oh, come on," I said. "Can't you back me up here?" Fershleiser was like "He used it correctly, what do you want me to say? He's right. You're wrong." "What do I know?" I said. "You're probably right. I've just never heard it used like that." "Have a drink later, and I'll quiz you," Fershleiser said. "I'll print out some SAT flash cards." Then she lightened up. "He's reading at my fundraiser," she said. "I forgot to tell you. It's happening the week before Thanksgiving." I was like "Super."[3A]

[3A] Not super. I wasn't the least bit thrilled about Amante's reading, even less because I knew I'd be forced to go. I'd known Amante in college, he was more an acquaintance than a friend; I was told we looked similar, and though that wasn't too unusual—I've been cursed with a face that has been duplicated and facsimiled throughout the four corners of the earth—I kind of resented Amante for resembling me so distinctly. Not only that, he was always *around*. He was one of those people who couldn't be avoided and I had my reasons to be on guard (see notes 115, 117, generally). Even still, we were always cordial when we were together. I'd kept tabs on him sporadically ever since *Inferno* came out—to some fanfare. He was at the height of his success the fall and winter of 2006, when I was living in Soho with Rebecca and her high school BFF Lizzie Lieberman. But *Inferno* wasn't enough to make Amante a household name; it's been pretty much back to obscurity since. The night of the reading, I arrived almost on time, which meant I was sitting in one of those fold-down auditorium chairs in the middle aisle, just waiting for half an hour, before anybody bothered to come to the microphone and say hello. Then Fershleiser, who was kind of like the MC, appeared in a black cocktail dress and started announcing the first reader, and I settled back. That's when I first saw Amante. I'd been scanning the room for him, expecting him to be backstage or standing in the aisle, or chatting with Fershleiser or some other luminary, but instead he was sitting in the cheap seats, just a few rows in front of me. I waved clumsily and he sort of nodded. He was looking behind

"We were talking and stuff and I was like 'Hey, can you make me a CD?' Because, you know, what else is there to do at work? And he was like 'Yeah.' And I came in one morning and he was already there and he said, 'Check out your desk,' and I went over and there was the CD on my desk. So, I didn't listen to it right away. I put it in my computer at home and it was all love songs. It was like fifty love songs in a row; the first song was 'Alone Together' by Daryl Throbhart.[4] I was like 'This is freaking

---

me when our eyes met, peering through his dark rectangular glasses as if he expected someone else; even then he looked a bit anxious. And then I saw her—this like Swedish model in a camel hair jacket and a scarf that looked like it was made out of an otter. She glided in, with this effortless presence of mind, like she was accustomed to making these sorts of entrances, no doubt aware of how everyone had stopped listening to the reader and was staring only at her. Amante stood to help her out of the jacket, a real gentleman, and then she settled into the seat beside him. To be honest, I didn't hear much of anything at all after that, until Amante himself read; all I could do was stare at the coiffed head of that Swedish model—her hair was arranged in some sort of chic, fashionable, fishtail braid or the like, scooped up and turned around, and fitted into a humungous ponytail, an ultrablonde color that grabbed up all the light. "So," I thought, "the tables have turned" (see note 119).

[4] Also included were: "My Lil' Dumpling", "Ain't No Surprise", "Too Many Nights in Reno (Not Enough Days in School)", "Put a Little Shine in My Pan", "Nookie", "Gumbo and Prawns", (a bluegrass number), "My Pleasure Ship", "Itty Bitty Hips", "Married, With Lovers", "She Don't Know Me Like You (Know Me)", "Bikinis, Bikinis, Bikinis", "Accidental Kiss", "Show Some Skin", "As Nature Intends", "God, You're Hot", "Skip the Smalltalk", "Mile High But Going Down on You", "Robots in Love", "Reboot in 5", "What We're Doing Can't Be Legal", "Baby Making Blues", "Down Home Romping", "Come Natural", "I'd

weird, Preston's married.'[5] I kind of ignored him for a few days, because it was super awkward and I didn't know what to even say. So this one morning, I was in the lunchroom getting a coffee and Preston corners me. He's like 'Hey, what's up?' and I

Die for Loretta, But Live for Bobby-Jean", "Whoopie Pie", "Skinny Dipping, Whisky Sipping", "Lotion and Fuzz", "I Want to Get This Right", "Learning the Ropes", "Maybe Tomorrow?", "I Can Wait An Hour", "Been Too Long", "Won't Wait Forever", "Lazy Sunday All Week Long", "My Mind's Made Up", "I'll Be Your Back Up Plan", "Would You Do It For the Thrill?", "Sloppy Seconds", "Love Can Never Be Premature", "I'm Aging Gracefully, & Falling in Love", etc. "Lazy Sunday All Week Long" was the only other Daryl Throbhart entry, so far as Maggie shared with us.

[5] It was no secret Preston's relations with his wife were strained. Whenever his wife called, his voice changed and became automatic, brusque, and snippy. Come to think of it, sometimes I had to get up and leave the cubicle when his wife called, it got so awkward. Preston fielded two types of calls from his cubicle, calls from his buddy Rick back home in Kentucky, who called to talk about Louisville, and calls from his wife. I could immediately tell who was calling by the tone of his voice. More often than not, his wife called at quarter to five to remind Preston of what to pick up from the store. I guess Preston didn't like stopping at the store for his wife because he sounded as if she were asking him to put more fiber in his diet, or start using Rogaine or go to ten showings of *The Nutcracker* in a row to support his ballet dancing niece, or switch allegiance from Louisville to University of Kentucky and burn in effigy a Rick Pitino doll followed by the team mascot and any other bobbleheads he'd collected over the years going back to the golden era of sports. He mumbled "Mmmhmm⋯ alrightmmmm⋯ I've got to get back to work. I have work to do" which was the worst, since everyone else around him knew he was lying through his teeth, and probably his wife did too.

was like 'Nothing.' And he's like 'I noticed there's something up with us, like it's gotten weird or something, you don't come over and talk anymore. What's the matter?' and I was like 'Oh, gee, Preston. It could be the CD you gave me with fifty love songs.' And he was like 'I didn't mean anything by that. What are you talking about?' and I was like 'Uh, dude you're married!' and he was like 'It's totally unintentional, what you're picking up. You're totally reading into it.' And I was like 'Yeah, right, man. Whatever. You've got some issues to work out.'"[6]

I was on the verge of saying something like "Jeez" or "Wow" or "No way" or "Holy shit" except my phone started buzzing and—because I can only really engage with one thing at a time—I pulled it out and open and read Olivia Walsh, technically my ex-girlfriend though I was never too sure, had just messaged me: HEY.[7]

---

[6] Now in all fairness, I was kind of surprised by Maggie's reaction. I mean, Preston was always going over and talking with her and laughing, telling jokes he'd already partly told to Rick on the phone previously, or to George so-and-so in the office; he even ran through his entire joke-line with her in the morning first thing, standing by her desk with his belly tilted against the wall of her cubicle, his hair freshly moistened from hair gel and the sweat from riding his bike into Manhattan, threading his way through the dense stop-and-go traffic of Manhattan City Hall like a 270-pound Floyd Landis, and well··· you know how that goes. And hadn't Maggie *asked* him to make a CD? To Preston that had to seem at least a little like flirting, or reciprocating his advances. I mean, the two of them were always getting drinks after work by themselves and never inviting anyone else. I guess I just didn't buy that it came out of nowhere is all.

[7] A significant overture—I hadn't spoken to her in at least two weeks, and the last time I'd seen her had been at her twenty-third birthday party, last March, out at her house in Clinton Hill or whatever that neighborhood is called sandwiched between

Fort Greene and Bedford Stuyvesant—a party I'd arrived at like a doofus, only about an hour or so late, with the party in full-swing, and about three of her ex-boyfriends gathered around and socializing while her current boyfriend, Anton Kolnikov (see notes 201, 225), argued jocularly with his ragtag ensemble of Russian friends about something or other musical-related—one of the Russians was a bass guitar player or thought he was, I couldn't be sure, I don't speak Russian. Had I known about the guest-list and the exact ratio of ex-boyfriends/current lovers to regular partygoers, I might have partaken of my roommates' vodka stash myself before departing on that excruciatingly slow train to make the switch to the G at Bergen—but what made the whole deal even worse, the crowning glory of the night so to speak, was that Olivia with her usual impulsiveness decided that this night of all nights was the best and most opportune occasion to tell me that whatever sort of weird on-again off-again relationship we were/had been having was finally kaput, but of course we were still going to be friends. "I'm with Kolnikov now," she said. "No shit," I mumbled too low for her to hear above the squall of their amphetamine-powered Europop. Olivia was like "What did you say?" "I said," I said, "I don't trust Russians." But she was like "Come on," taking me by the hand and making me spin her around even if the music didn't call for it, "Don't be such a poopy-face" and we waltzed and/or sidestepped clumsily over the lintel into her roommate's barebones room where the speakers were set up and the DJ—another Russian—was sipping melon-colored coladas out of a see-through Dixie cup while jerking her entire torso up and down with a painful seizing that was shockingly catchy. I was like "I can't do this," I.E. I didn't feel like boogie-ing in front of all the exes. So I moped off to the shared living room with its large yellow couch draped in soft, flannelly, Snuggle-scented throw blankets which had absorbed the sweat and sexual fluids of God knows how many Russians, among others, and an abundance of succulents in the window creating a Cretaceous silhouette from the street level should anyone from the Lafayette Gardens

Sean was shaking his head, like he could add one or two insights into the whole Maggie/Preston debacle if he wanted to, but it wasn't worth his while. I closed my phone, nodded, gave Maggie a pinched look, and drank a little off my stein, which was number three for me, a lighter beer this round. "Unbelievable," I said—this was the best I could come up with, what with the phone distraction.

"What? Shouldn't you answer that?" Maggie said, narrowing her eyes.

"Oh no," I said. "Nope."

I was going to let the whole thing play out with Olivia, at least wait until she texted again, otherwise I'd just chalk her message off as a drunkdial or some accidental, inconsequential salutation.[8] I was like "I just meant *unbelievable*: Preston and his CD. Bold move, wouldn't you say?"

Housing Complex happen to glance up at the house. "There you are!" Olivia said, after a while, although she'd been standing in the doorway talking to one of her exes for at least forty-five minutes, during which time she had to have seen me pulling long faces and nearly dozing. "What's the matter?" she said. I turned to her and shrugged, but my arms were too tired to lift into a real shrug, and that gesture—that pathetic, dweeby little half of a shrug, almost brought tears to my eyes. She slipped into my lap and draped her arms around me and started kissing me all over the face. "Ian. I will always always love you," she said, serious too, and then she got up and told me not to drink anymore and she'd be back. Of course, she never came back.

[8] I mean, it would take a while to wash away the memory of that Russian—since he was the last dude I saw her with on that same memorable night when I departed surreptitiously without even saying goodbye and let myself out into the rain, which come to think of it, was kind of an accompaniment to our entire "relationship", (see the end of note 15, note 107), not that I put much significance into that meteorological detail, it rains pretty regularly in NYC.

Maggie was like "He has problems."

"Sounds like he has a real thing for you," I said. I settled on my bench, a bit rocky, and propped my chin in my hand.

"Thank you, Captain Obvious," Maggie said.

"You're welcome," I said.

"I wasn't really thanking you."

"Got that."

"I feel like I'm talking to a kid," Maggie said. "How old are you again?"

Sean was like "Ian's legal."

"Let me see your ID," Maggie said. "Do you have one of those vertical ones?"

I shrugged and passed Maggie my wallet. "They wouldn't let you in with that," I said.

"You're the same age as my brother Jake," Maggie said. "You're just a baby."

"How old are you anyway?"

"Thirty-three," Maggie said. "Thirty-four this August. Don't look so friggin' shocked." She handed me back my ID.

"I don't look like anything."

Sean traded looks between the two of us and laughed.

Maggie was like "I'm sorry. I don't want to blow your cover." She stared at me hard, her mouth all sour. "Go ahead and answer it," she said.

"Answer what?"

She raised an eyebrow, her trademark move. "The phone."

"I'm sorry," I said, patting the phone into a snug position in my pocket (nothing escaped Maggie's vigilant eye), "before that... you were saying?"

"Look at you, Mr. Popular."

"Not at all," I said. I'd rolled up my shirtsleeves, but I was sweating nonetheless, no help for it, and the heat from the kitchen and those globe lights ensconced along the walls weren't exactly cooling things down. The tag on my shirt collar had started to itch my neck.

"You don't date much, do you?" Maggie said.

I was like "No. What about you?"

"EHarmony," Sean said.

Maggie punched him. "Kind of hard when you live with your friggin' parents." She'd almost finished another beer, which was impressive, considering each beer was like a tankard. I'd been matching her drink for drink until now, out of collegiality, or camaraderie, or pride, or something, but I couldn't keep up with this renegade pace—not if I wanted to remember anything the next day. I was kind of hoping that tonight wouldn't be one of those nights where I ended up passed out on Sean's futon, my broken sleep interwoven by some hypnotic, melodically gorgeous, if lyrically vacuous track by Phil Collins (Sean's go-to mood music), which would haunt me the rest of the following day.[9]

"Move," I said.

Maggie went "Great advice. Why didn't I think of that?" She shook her head, her face frozen in a smug, half-hearted smirk.[10] "No," she said. "I'm saving money. It's really not that bad."

"It is what it is," Sean said.

I smoothed a crease in my jeans. "How's that hot girl?" I asked him, to get off the phone business with Mags.[11]

---

[9] As in note 177 "when I woke up… "

[10] Similar to the smirk former president George W. Bush excelled at, which for him was completely natural and maybe not even half-hearted but a normal facial expression which he couldn't control, but for Maggie, in this instance, was just an expression of exaggerated disbelief.

[11] I wasn't so oblivious that I didn't see Maggie was flirting—in a teasing kind of way. I mean, she wasn't trying to hide it. The fact is some people are so constituted that they cannot actually flirt at all without appearing corny or lame in their own minds, and so they adopt a prickly, defensive attitude to keep themselves from being corny and lame, offering sarcastic one-liners and barbed comebacks to nearly everything you say and

"Alex?[12] She's hot, yeah, but she's strange," Sean said. "There's something I don't know... *disingenuous* there. No one can really be *that* happy. I don't know. I'd almost have to go for it, though."

---

this is what passes for flirting. If you indulge these people long enough and give just a modicum of encouragement, they will move directly from teasing and making fun of you to sighing and saying romantic things like "someday I'll tell you all my secrets", spouting lines straight out of romantic comedies, which are just as lame and corny as flirting anyway. Anna, the girl I was with at Yale, was a case in point: coming into my dorm room at Durfee on Old Campus and making fun of me one minute, and the next night lying on my twin bed with matching comforter and exhaling like she'd just run the 200 meters and whispering in a husky voice, quite sexy actually, "Someday I'll tell you all my secrets," which I didn't even know how to respond to except with my usual noncommittal smile—but, like it or not, I got to hear all about her losing her virginity to some Costa Rican dude named Juan Carlos who rode a motorcycle or moped or some motorized vehicle, a scooter maybe, over the washed-out, boulder-strewn back alleys of the tourist resort at Playa Portrero where Anna was "studying abroad" her junior year of HS, and took Anna one night to some deserted shack with a busted roof and some silhouettes of palm trees and went at her gently, like a pro—apparently he had long hair and beautiful "almond-eyes"—just taking it nice and slow in a way that made Anna perfectly comfortable, until there was an enormous pop (I was cringing at this point) and Anna yelped and Juan Carlos was like "Should I stop?" in Spanish, and Anna was like "No, no," which is the same in Spanish or English, and Juan Carlos kept going, until it was over, and *finito.*

[12] Alex—I.E. "the hot girl"—had red hair that wasn't curly (as per usual with red hair) and as far as I knew neither Sean nor I had ever had a real conversation with her, I.E. a conversation lasting longer than the usual back and forth workplace banter that occurs during a 15 second elevator ride or on the walk

Maggie raised an eyebrow again and laughed, a brittle laugh. "Let me know when that happens."

"You don't think Sean has what it takes?" I said. I also laughed, though not so convincingly as Maggie because I a: didn't think it was funny; b: was distracted; and c: had that itch on my neck. I just touched my fingers against my pocket where I had the phone, searching for a phantom vibration, which your legs—especially the fast twitch muscle fibers—sometimes trick you into believing is your phone going off. No new messages. Then I scratched my neck, fixed the tag that kept itching me.

---

down the block to the Spring Street C/E subway. She was the new personal assistant for the Executive Director of the Fund, but since the Executive Director also had an administrative assistant—who, by this point, could probably do her job and the jobs of five other people in the office (not naming any names)— we couldn't for the life of us figure out why Alex was even there unless like certain tropical plants that only thrive indoors and look pretty, such as, for example, hibiscus, bougainvillea, and coconut-less palms (most of which are on display in your standard Wall Street atriums), her purpose was merely decorative and salutatory. She was tall and extremely slender, and was always happy to the point of being saccharine, according to Sean, who was likewise puzzled by her ambivalently flirtatious habit of leaning over the phone console while he was passing out the mail, with her boobs half falling out of her bra (not that he really minded). Unbeknownst to Maggie, Sean had already invited Alex for a beer after work, but on the agreed-upon day she came down with a horrible case of swine influenza and had to cancel. He took her cancellation in stride—chin up, head held high, no regrets—and didn't even tell anyone about the let-down until a week or so after the fact, by which time Alex had made a speedy recovery and was back at her desk looking gorgeous and bending in Gumby-like provocative ways to reveal the convex density of her large breasts, which were maybe too heavy for her.

"No," Maggie said.

"Thanks, Maggie."

"I'm just being the voice of reason," she said.

"You're saying, she's out of Sean's league?"

"Uh... yeah. That's about it."

Sean was like "Friendly wager?"

"Don't do it, Maggie," I said. "I've seen him operate."

"I'm sure you have. You're equally clueless when it comes to women. From everything I've heard," she said to me, "you[13] tend to go for crazy people."

"Yes," Sean said, "his MO is definitely batshit insane."

"You sure know a lot more about me than I know about you," I said.

"I pay better attention."

Sean was like "That's why they pay you the big bucks."

"Big bucks, my ass," went Maggie. "I had another job offer, but I turned it down once they gave me Program Manager. It looks better on my résumé."

"Congratulations, by the way," Sean said. "For getting that Manager position."

"Go fuck yourself," Maggie said. "You're the one slumming it."[14]

---

[13] This *you* was so unabashedly accusatory, that I had to believe Sean—in an unguarded or voluble moment—had told Maggie a little too much about my relationship status with Olivia Walsh. Even so, I wouldn't go so far as to call Olivia "crazy," as Maggie was about to do, categorically. Eccentric, yes, maybe.

[14] In reality, Sean had the most responsibility of all of us. He was the "office manager", a jack of all trades, the primary receptionist, and—in some respects—the "face" of the organization, operating the main switchboard and routing all incoming and inter-office calls. He was also the first responder for office personnel frustrated by their jammed printers and malfunctioning copy machines. Sean handled these machines

"It is what it is," Sean said.

———————————

the way trainers handle horses; the girl from *Wild Hearts Can't Be Broken*, after losing her eyesight, couldn't possibly have found her way around a horse's body as well as Sean found his around the three main copy machines in our office, damaged or in good condition. At one time, he completely dismantled the copy machine adjacent to my cubicle, laying out all the parts like extracted vertebrae from a Pleistocene tiger in neat array on a tarp, while he puzzled over the exact nature of the dysfunction in the hollow bowels of the machine. Sean taught me the correct way to shake a new toner cartridge as well as how to determine if printer paper was loaded correctly in its tray, the trick being to hold the ream by the corner: if the paper droops with minimal elasticity then the grain is right side up, but if the paper flops or remains stiff without bending at all, you need to turn it over. These tricks of the trade were invaluable in the office, and often overlooked, the way some 6th men on basketball teams, I.E. the 76ers' Kevin Ollie,[14A] are unsung and underappreciated—but try as he might, Sean's lessons failed to catch on. Sean also had the only set of keys to the office supply closet, where post-its, staples, paper clips, push pins, matte paper, mailing labels, laminating sheets, glue, etc., were all stored haphazardly in bins. Once a month, he passed around an office supply magazine for purchase orders, and a week after you'd filled it out, the supplies appeared miraculously in tidy stacks on your desk. "It's like Christmas," Preston had said the morning he caught sight of the Louisville Cardinals decals he'd somehow managed to write off as a justifiable expenditure (probably the admin who monitored these orders had been sick the day he put in his request). In the almost two years I was on the staff, those Louisville decals were the only items Preston ever ordered—and his excited reaction the morning they arrived was about the happiest I ever heard him.

[14A] Later head coach of UConn's men's basketball team, leading them to the championship in 2008.

"You said that already." Maggie fussed with her hair like it had fallen out of place—an impossibility, it was too short. "I'm only a glorified Administrative Assistant."

Sean was like "Aren't we all?"

"We must be rolling in the dough, to have all the admins," I said.

Sean puckered his mouth wryly. "Your department is definitely the poster boy for the whole Fund," he said.[15]

---

[15] It's worth mentioning here that working for The Fund, with Maggie and Sean and Preston and Esther and Velma and George so-and-so and Joyce and Harriet and all the others, comprised one of the most peaceful, most relaxed, easygoing interims in all my professional life—and like so many easy-money jobs where you basically just show up and occupy space in a cubicle and emit CO_2 and are paid a not-measly $34 grand (which is enough to live on, even when you're renting a $750/month coffin-sized room in Soho, sharing a bathroom the size of an airplane john with two not exactly tidy girls), I fell into it by accident because of calamitous, near-disastrous circumstances. The fact is, I'd been out of work, in between jobs, recently let go, waiting for a temp agency to call me back with a placement, chewing off anxiety by walking along the East River by the Baruch Houses, early in the morning, with a sick sort of curiosity about whether or not there really were dead bodies floating in Hefty trash bags out by the shoreline as my former roommate Tamara had claimed on several occasions at Apolo Restaurant over fried rice. It was around this time, Olivia and I went for dinner the very first time, at some run down noodle house—I think called Noodle House—on Walker Street, a couple blocks from the Pagoda in the island between Canal and Walker with its WELCOME TO CHINATOWN information. Of course, I couldn't hold back. I told Olivia all about my bleak prospects and sundry circumstances—painting myself in pretty good colors, nonetheless—and waited, breathless, with a queasy feeling, for Olivia to process the news and start to panic.

"Yeah, we sure are sexy, huh?" Maggie said. She followed the direction of my hand to my pocket, where I'd again been tracing the outline of my phone against my jeans. "For Christ's sake, go answer the friggin' phone," she said. "Stop fondling yourself and call her back."

"My phone's not ringing," I said.

Maggie was like "Oh, OK." She stared at me like she'd caught me in the act of something much worse, the corners of her

---

To my surprise—and probably one of the reasons I liked her so much—she didn't care at all about my employment or lack thereof and actually that was the night we first kissed, that very same night, after eating a mysterious concoction of floating seafood and tender vegetables in a mild noodley broth and walking home through Little Italy, shaking our heads at the maître d's with their menus offering half-price wine bottles and a romantic atmosphere, past the karaoke place on Mulberry which I didn't even know existed yet, past Kenmare or Delancey or whatever, and onto Spring again, stopping, heart-pounding, with that now-or-never-feeling of tight squirmy anxiety that comes right before you attempt to kiss someone you aren't sure will kiss you back, leaning forward, Olivia not resisting, and finally putting my lips to hers right outside the stairs leading down to the 6 Train on Spring Street in that kind of covert train entrance tucked between commercial buildings, under a neon glaze of shoplights and streetlamps in the brackish air, us both in our raincoats on account of the spotty weather, hoods down, Olivia's neck sleek and shimmering against the raincoat's hood, without a thought about anybody else. Within a week, I had a temp assignment at The Fund. Two weeks later, during a gala luncheon to celebrate some old woman's retirement, Esther approached me, asked me a bunch of questions, seemed impressed by my credentials, and offered me an administrative assistant job starting immediately. And that's where I worked for a year and a half.

mouth creased in a disappointed smile. "Whatever," she said. "Where the hell's our waitress?"

Sean was like "Patience." He'd been massaging his eyes with his middle finger and thumb, a technique for stimulating blood around the eyes and reducing under-eye circles, which I'd seen him demonstrate to Alex, the hot girl, as an excuse to make conversation. Earlier in the afternoon, he'd gulped down a 5-Hour Energy when he thought no one was looking. "Insomnia," he'd said, offering a brief grin. The pressure from his fingers now caused the bags under his eyes to darken. "How'd the move go?" he said, blinking away an eyelash. "Sorry, I was out of town for it or I would've helped."

The room was getting nosier; it was suddenly harder to hear. Outside, a song was playing on someone's car—that hit of the summer "Alone Together" by Daryl Throbhart.[16] The car must've just been idling there; I think we'd heard most of the song. A girl in a yellow dress a few tables over stood, smoothed her dress over her backside, sat.[17]

"Yeah right," Maggie said. "Out of town? Why didn't you call me? I'd have gotten my brothers to help. And my brother Andy has a truck too. It's not like you had that much stuff, right?"

"Nope. It all fit in a van."

"You're moving down in the world, aren't you?" Sean said. "Soho to Brooklyn. No. Just kidding. Brooklyn's lovely."[18]

---

[16] That throwback, wannabe soul crooner (riding on Amy Winehouse's coattails), who'd even attracted Preston's attention since he'd included him so prominently on his playlist (note 4).

[17] The ratio of women to men in this place was maybe 1:6.

[18] Nick Amante said something similar about Brooklyn, in a more pivotal moment in our acquaintance (note 123). I'd been meaning to ask Sean for his impressions of *Inferno* but it seemed a bit highbrow of a topic. Plus, I could tell he hadn't read it. Now's as good a time as any to give a synopsis: *Inferno*'s a modern gothic novel, I guess you could call it, hinging

---

on a disappearance, or rather an abduction. This slippery S.O.B.
Ernest Marsh (who Amante seems to have created out of pure
spite) finagles his way into the arms of a wide-eyed Southern
belle, Sybil Auberle, from a prestigious farming family. Her
abduction looks to be inspired by the music video to "Strawberry
Wine" *first taste of love, bittersweet*, we all know the words.
Marsh transplants poor sixteen-year-old Sybil to the outskirts of
a smoggy industrial town up north and, after he's done with her,
sets her up as a kind of *Maggie: A Girl Of The Streets* to fend for
herself, although he's a nice enough guy to give her a house—
with the express purpose of pimping her out. Eventually, Sybil
(the name is a tad symbolic, wouldn't you agree?), now going by
the name Hannah Sparrow, grows up and falls for a
conservative-minded reverend, Robert Udell, who's a sort of
ineffectual, effete do-gooder, a meek and humble guy, and a
major complication for Marsh's whole prostitution thing. The
book's told mainly through the point of view of Marsh's
legitimate daughter June (yes, turns out he has a "real" family
this whole time), about 10 years after Sybil's abduction. Sybil is
now dead from an overdose, and the grief-stricken reverend,
who abandoned Sybil in a moment of spiritual crisis, is
beginning to dig deeper into the whole mystery of who exactly
she was—he doesn't even know her real name. June Marsh
ends up sleeping with the reverend—don't ask how this comes
about—and Marsh makes it his personal vendetta to slit Udell's
throat. All of this melodrama escalates into a frenzy, during
which, yes, flammable items get consumed and Marsh hangs
himself from an abandoned bridge and the reverend renounces
all worldly pleasures and accidentally drives his car into a
swelling river where he has a waterlily-and-nymphet epiphany
(credit Nabokov here, Amante's lodestar, and see note 53) and
resolves to run off with the nubile June just as soon as he can
extricate himself from his flooding vehicle. In the end, most of
the characters are dead and the mystery of Sybil Auberle is
unveiled by Marsh's decrepit wife Annette (racked by lung
cancer and near-death herself) who, along with June, helps

"I'm sure you spend a lot of time there," Maggie said.

Sean was like "I was there just this past weekend."

"Well, compared to Staten Island, I'm sure it's paradise."

"Nothing wrong with the island," Sean said.

Maggie was like "Except the smell."

"You get used to that."

"Some smells you never get used to."

I nodded like this was some deep insight, although I was sure you could pretty much get used to anything—except perhaps those flowering trees or whatever they are that smell like semen (Olivia's landlady had one growing in the courtyard behind her brownstone), the uncollected fish heads and membranes putrefying on Broome Street and Allen, and the periodic discharge from the Owl's Head Sanitation Plant, Bay Ridge.

Sean was like "Don't be so prissy."

Now Maggie was a lot of things,[19] but "prissy" she was not, as Sean well knew, as did pretty much anyone with half a brain who'd engaged Maggie in conversation for less than ten minutes, long enough for her to start tongue-lashing whatever

---

contact the Georgia family so they can bury Sybil at the ol' manse down South. This is a very roughshod summary; I'm afraid I don't do it justice.

[19] Uptight, neurotic, obsessive-compulsive, type-A, overachiever, agnostic, once-Catholic, fanatical groomer, fanatical runner (I.E. to the point of shin splints), now fanatical elliptical trainer at the Tenafly Planet Fitness, mildly dyslexic (e.g. her constant "Foxfire" instead of "Firefox" when she saw my computer updating or was unable to open a certain screen in Internet Explorer and wondered if "Foxfire" would fare better), genetically prone to osteoporosis, though not to heart or renal failure or diabetes I or II, fanatical toothbrusher and Crest Whitestrips applier, etc.

political/fringe/religious group had made news[20] most recently and deserved complete black-venomed derision.[21] She

---

[20] Maggie also had a penchant for *National Inquirer*-caliber stories involving octuplets and genetic abnormalities, like that "poor girl" from India born with eight appendages, who Maggie said was supposed to be a reincarnation of Shiva or whoever (she wasn't familiar with the Indian pantheon; it took enough effort to ridicule the Christian trinity). This girl had undergone a successful operation in November, 2007.

[21] In fact, lack of prissiness and her self-proclaimed desire to be "one of the boys" were two more of the reasons Preston fell for her so hard. From his own admission later, it appeared that Preston's wife Allison was a girly girl to the core, or at least she had been before having kids, at which juncture she rather impressively about-faced and became the responsible parent (as in solely responsible), responsible for things like catering to the needs/whims of babies/toddlers, transporting said babies/toddlers (kicking and screaming) to the doctor's after their noses had been plugged with green boogers anytime longer than three days, arguing with doctors about potentially harmful medications doctors so blithely prescribe for the minutest things, cooking dinner, packing snacks, fixing lunches, showing up to parent-teacher conferences, grilling teachers on young Jill's reading level and younger Zoe's sociability as measured by "informal" assessment, and then—for a change of pace—bending over backward to sanitize and cleanse their living quarters of all bacteria, mold, crumbs, pubic hairs, and plant material, turning off powerstrips and unplugging appliances before any lengthy car trip or (usually Florida-bound) vacation. While Preston and Allison had never been incompatible, they always struck the casual observer as somehow "not-clicking" very well; the impression wasn't they'd grown apart over the years, as is natural even for couples who fall hard for each other; it was like they'd gotten married in a shotgun wedding for maybe the wrong reasons, like to avoid public embarrassment, or—if Allison's dad really was a mobster

belched— albeit in a demure, though not altogether ladylike way, something in between a severe hiccup and an accidental low-level-sodapop-induced burp from a man—to prove her point. Sean shook his head, no comment, and sat back in his chair, taking it easy and savoring the beer. "Would you care to amend that?" Maggie said.

Sean just held up his hands, like *you got me*—he knew enough, plus he was just too darn nice of a guy to engage her on such an insignificant point as whether or not Staten Island smelled like septic waste because of the humungous landfill known as Fresh Kills, which wafted its brown aroma seaward like a disease-ridden crotch.[22]

---

instead of just looking like a blend between Sammy "The Bull" Gravano and the Quaker Oats dude—for Preston to avoid a secret and quite possibly agonizingly slow and painful demise at the hands of Irish-Italian operatives—in despite of which, Allison's dad still treated Preston like a piece of fecal matter, whenever he happened to stop by the office to talk to Esther— our department's boss—about maybe persuading some of his colleagues in the legislature to adopt part of her software for monitoring street conditions in real time.

[22] In terms of overall grossness, and considering Chuck Palahniuk didn't publish anything that year, I'd have to give the palm to Nick Amante for the grossest scene of 2006. His description of oral sex on page 123 of *Inferno* is maybe the most thorough and revolting in the English language. I can't even think about crotches without a residual memory of this little episode from his book—the same way I couldn't think about wizards without remembering the evil dude from *Dragon's Milk* who murders a cute little dragon and then eats the dragon's heart. In Amante's book, it's Ernest Marsh and a lady going by Babsie who get the honor of doing the nasty. You can just imagine the logistics when Babsie, "a round, unbeautiful woman, corpulent as a baby, with blue eyes set in ridges of fat," after more or less blueballing Marsh with an interrupted hand

"Look at that. Silence," Maggie said, taunting but teasing and now smiling wickedly, the wrinkles all gone from her forehead and the beginning of an alcohol-induced flush adding some pink to her face, at the same time revealing spots in her makeup which were darker and more saturated than other spots that had looked smooth and really almost professionally made-up[23] only an hour or two earlier, or whenever I first spotted her at the table there. Meanwhile, the waitress in her tasteful ensemble of forest-green pleated skirt and gossamer

---

job, "[pulls] her thick calves over his shoulders, her negligee hitching up her thighs." Let's just say the words "humid" and "popcorn shrimp" and "coalesce" (as in the "meat of her legs… [coalesced] around his face") are sort of tainted after reading it. So… perhaps, yes, maybe Amante does have some talent (derivative talent), though he buries it like the poor fool in Matthew's Gospel (25:14) and more or less forgets where he left it for whole chapters, making for some snooze-worthy reading. Amante picked a less egregious passage to read at the Abrons Arts Center at that holiday fundraiser Fershleiser helped put on (note 3A).

[23] A credit to Maggie's punctiliousness; again, sometimes a turn off for guys who don't cotton to obsessive grooming and elaborate preparation time, not to mention the overcrowded medicine cabinet and accompanying bathroom drawers which become necessary receptacles for all of a woman like Maggie's cosmetic and beauty supplies—plus there always has to be like one "secret" drawer or compartment or hidden shelf or lock box like Olivia with her "Olivia's box of tricks" as she called it, ordering me "DO NOT EVER OPEN THIS" using the "do not" and not the contraction, I.E. she meant business, since she would've been embarrassed if I saw her collection of vibrators and who knows what else, which is the same directive she gave re: going through her dirty laundry, which isn't something I'd even thought about doing (although she felt no compunction reading her mom's own journal—see note 77A).

peasant blouse with ruffled sleeves materialized, her face looking like it was coated with an egg tempera gloss, and Maggie ordered another sommerbock.

Looking at me, Maggie was like "So do you like it there?" I.E. *in Brooklyn.*

"So far so good," I said. "I mean, things were getting pretty dicey with the roommates."

"What? Did you bone[24] one of them?" Maggie said.

"You know, living situations involve very complicated dynamics," Sean said. "Boning roommates is almost never a good idea."

Maggie was like "Yeah, this coming from the guy who advertises he only wants *female* roommates."

"It's a strategy that's worked well for me," Sean said.[25] "It doesn't work for everyone. It's not like I want to have a

---

[24] See note 21.

[25] Sean learned his lesson the hard way, previously he didn't have a care in the world about his (potential) roommate's gender. But after this guy Keith, who was clearly high on bathsalts, arrived with a suspiciously bulging military-issue knapsack from which he removed and wrapped around his arm a huge metal chain—which he seemed to believe was his pet ferret Morris and which he repeatedly asked Sean to "give a gentle pat, don't be shy"—after Sean idiotically opened the front door to him (he'd noticed a bit of inflammation around the dude's eyes but figured Keith just had bad allergies, it being the season for allergies and all, which Sean could sympathize with), and then had to entertain the guy for like two hours, pouring him a stale bowl of Captain Crunch—his purportedly favorite cereal, and actually the only cereal he remembered after he asked Sean to play a game called "name all the cereals you know" which ended when Keith stalled on Captain Crunch and then made a devious face almost slobbering and snickering over the word "crunch" which he said reminded him, he didn't know why, of "munch" which of course reminded him of "butt munchers"

---

which was hi-la-rious, did Sean get it?—and the poor, delusional, simple-minded, bathsalt-afflicted lunatic didn't even end up eating the Captain Crunch; he and Sean spent the next part of his unwelcome and creepily prolonged stay in Sean's two bedroom apartment singing the "I've Been Everywhere" song on account of Keith's huge obsession with Johnny Cash and Sean again unfortunately admitting that he also was a big fan of J.C., which got them into a circular discussion about just how damn good J.C. was, he was the king of country music, no one came close, *he was the man in black, man, the man who sang that song, man, that song that, I don't remember it but it fucking blew my mind the first time I heard it, and now I remember, it was that, you know, that song that I could probably hum it, you know, you know how a song just goes out of your head, man, and then comes back like when you're taking a shit when you least expect it, you know that damn what the fuck, man, it's like a song and it goes like "Winnepega, bubbapegga, mubbapegga, how's that song go man, you know, I've been everywhere, man, I've been everywhere man?"* which Sean then started humming until Keith said something borderline psychotic—to his credit, he was only trying to give Sean some encouragement, like Bob Knight-style, a little tough love, so to speak—yelling, apropos of nothing, "That's Morris' favorite song, man!" and then uncoiling the chain like medieval weaponry from his arm and dangling it and even waving it like a mace until Sean was really singing, 'cause his life depended on it, meanwhile fingering his cellphone with its little emergency button, which he wasn't exactly sure how he'd talk to the dispatcher, unless he ran into his room and locked the door, and to play it safe, slid his chest of drawers in front of the door and maybe even several other large pieces of furniture since the door itself was pretty fucking flimsy and not even real wood, just composite, not even cut correctly to fit the frame as evidenced by the gaps of light which you could see at night, especially on the upper right quadrant, and he was having visions of Jack Nicholson's head ramming through the splintered wood of his cheap-ass door with that relationship with my roommate. I've had to turn down potential roommates because they're too hot."

"How big of you," Maggie said. "You deserve a medal."

Sean was like "No, I look for just the right balance when it comes to roommates. Not hot, but not like trolls either." He reflected. "It depends on their personality," he said. "If they have a good personality that'll tip the scale if I'm on the fence about somebody being hot or not."

"Wow—are you hearing this?" Maggie said to me.

"The main thing is I don't want to be bothered," Sean said.

"Agree with you there," Maggie said, "except I don't get your thing about women—sure you had a run-in, but women? Really? That's asking for trouble."

"You'd rather live all with men?" I said.

---

crazy look in his eyes, only instead of Jack Nicholson's head, it was Keith's head with his bugged out, shot-to-hell-bloodshot eyes and his screwy teeth, yelling: "Give Morris another pat, man! A gentle pat! Come on, brother!" and so Sean was belting out the song, literally bellowing whatever U.S. cities came to mind so long as he could figure a way to rhyme them by adding Spanglish pronunciations like Tucsona, Denverana, Bostoña (adding the tilde for that one, which was an on-the-spot aesthetic sparkle), etc. God knows how he got through the whole thing; it was one of those experiences where time condensed into this one pinprick of a moment, during which, of course, all the clichés ended up being accurate: he could see his life passing before his eyes, he remembered ex-girlfriends and long ago childhood friends he hadn't remembered in years, he made his peace. Anyway, after the whole Keith episode, Sean started advertising specifically to women, got his bedroom door resized, and even had a padlock installed on his front door, until enough time passed for him to see the whole thing as a fluke and not at all the usual course of affairs, even for Craigslist apartment advertising—though there's always that wee little risk, isn't there?

"Hot men," Sean said.

"You know, I don't really care if they're hot because, unlike you, I never get involved with roommates. There's such a thing as boundaries."

"Exactly," Sean said. "The boundary is: if they're hot, I don't live with them."

"Don't you think that's being a little prejudiced?" Maggie said. "Just because a woman happens to be physically attractive?"

"The thing is, if they're really that attractive, the chances they want to live with a single guy in a pretty small—decent but small—two bedroom apartment in St. George are already pretty slim."

"Yeah, I don't know anyone who'd want to do that."

"There you go."

"But that's because Staten Island's a dump and the people who live there are freaks." Maggie smiled into her glass. "The two of you are hopeless when it comes to women. How you made it this far is beyond me." Maggie's eyes, even when she didn't mean them to be, were sort of glaring. "You still haven't said why your roommates turned on you."

"'Turned'[26] is a little strong," I said.

---

[26] More like an already sour relationship had curdled and gone rancid, I'm guessing from right around the time of that Nick Amante reading (note 3A again) or, rather, the after party, when I put my foot in my mouth in a big way. I'd been ready to leave for hours and jumped at the chance to hitch a ride with Fershleiser who was kind of an old lady when it came to parties. I didn't even mind sharing the back with this creepy dude in a fez and a failure of a Che Guevara beard. Fershleiser and Fake Che were just continuing some highly esoteric conversation about their favorite depressing books, *The Magus*, and *The Glass Bead Game*, and *Under the Volcano*, getting into *Inferno*— which at that point Fershleiser still hadn't read but wanted to, especially after hearing Amante in person and since he was such a hotshot and all. "What'd you think of it?" she asked me.

"Right-o," Maggie said. "That's OK. I'm sure you had your reasons."

"Let's get one thing clear," Sean said, breaking into a smile, "I've never initiated anything with roommates. It's always the other way round."

Maggie scooted back mechanically as the waitress returned with her beer and then sipped it as if she were tasting a wine. The waitress didn't stick around to see if she liked it or not; in the next moment, she'd covered half the room like a Valkyrie, appearing in front of one of the windows where it was already getting dark.

"You read it, didn't you?" Fake Che studied me intently like I was some curio like an inlaid table or a bronze figurine of a horse and I stared back at him a bit more aggressively than usual but the fact is no one likes being stared at—even by a simpleton. Then I shrugged. Fershleiser was like "What? Not a fan?" She already knew I wasn't and I didn't like being put on the spot for Fake Che's amusement. "It's all right," I said. Fershleiser was like "Hear him. It's all right. OK. You don't have to like it. I'm sure *you* can do better." Even this was sort of cruel of Fershleiser. I'd entered that romance novella contest with her last Valentine's Day and was rejected by automated message, though she bought me a case of Tsingtao from the Dollar Grocer underneath our apartment to quote "drown my sorrows". Not only that, a few nights before, I'd complained for an hour about Olivia and her cycle of Russian boyfriends, who kept reappearing on the scene whenever I thought they might be going out of fashion. I was like "Probably. Just give me some time." Fershleiser rolled her eyes. "I'll pull it together," I said. I tried to laugh it off. But Fershleiser pretty much dismissed me out of hand, and her and Fake Che exchanged a knowing look. "Beware the green-eyed monster, jealousy," Fershleiser said, quoting poetry now. That was pretty much the last time we hung out.

"Oh, this is precious," Maggie said. "Your *roommates* come on to you? It's almost like you want me to have a bad opinion of you. This is why you choose ugly roommates? So you can score with them?"

"I don't ask about your personal life," Sean said.

"Three words," Maggie said. "FULL OF SHIT."

I was like "It could've happened."

"It's happened," Sean said. "More than once."

"*Sleaze*—ball," Maggie said. "I never thought I'd say it, but you make Preston look good."

Sean grinned and raised his voice "Hyperbole."

"Yeah, you're right," Maggie said. "Preston's in a league of his own."

Sean was like "I'm offended by that. You make it sound like I take advantage of people. When the reality is sometimes, you know, it's late and you've just shared a bottle of rum and, you know, shit goes down, one thing leads to another."

"Don't get all 'one thing leads to another' now," Maggie said. "You're talking about fucking your roommates."

"God, Maggie, that's blunt."

"I just call it like I see it."

"Anyway, here's the thing. Whatever happens happens. If my roommate, who just happens to be female, and I end up in bed, I'm not going to act awkward. No regrets. We're consenting adults. There's no pity involved."

"Oh, of course not!" Maggie said. For a second, it looked like she was going to appeal to me,[27] but then she clicked her

---

[27] My own housing experiences wouldn't strengthen Maggie's case. My first place in New York was a 6 by 5 foot room on Grand and Columbia, rented by a frisky Haitian lady (the Tamara of note 15). The apartment was nice enough—they even had a doorman—but the living conditions were less than ideal. As part of my "informal" lease agreement I had to walk Tamara's six-year-old son to school each morning while his mother worked

the night shift at Metropolitan Hospital. I even had to sign in like I was the son's guardian. Tamara's dream was to save up enough cash so she could buy a ticket to the Dominican Republic and have breast and butt implants—the entire procedure was cheaper and they asked fewer questions there. In the meantime, she cajoled me into writing her Craigslist personals, telling me all about her figure, dimensions, etc., her love of cooking and generally "being there" for her man, but don't forget also: her resemblance to Tyra Banks, the host of *America's Next Top Model*, her big lips, breasts, and smooth, firm backside (all of which she wanted enlarged). She tried to smooth things over by taking me to Apolo Restaurant, right under the Williamsburg Bridge, where I usually picked up the tab. She even hinted at possible sex, since I seemed to be incompetent in that arena. This went on for a few uncomfortable weeks, until Tamara insisted I co-sign on her breast implants. She explained that it was simply a legal thing, she trusted me, she wouldn't let me down. Most importantly, she stressed, I wasn't financially liable. "I'm not sure," I said. "Fuck! Fuck! Fuck me!" I said to myself later that same day. Luckily, I found Fershleiser's "Roommate Wanted" ad within a week and—after a successful interview—I moved out of Tamara's place on a Saturday afternoon. I left my last month's rent in an envelope on the kitchen table, and wrote a respectful letter, in which I apologized for my sudden departure, offered to let Tamara keep my security deposit, and said how sorry I was for not providing longer notice. She was furious—I knew she would be. The first night she called nearly ten times and left messages until my phone was full and drained of batteries. I didn't listen to it all—the first message was enough, a litany of accusations which devolved into an elaborate Haitian-Creole anathema: "I curse you…" etc. It scared the shit out of me; for a week or so, I really believed I'd been legitimately cursed, by an expert. I only started to feel like myself after my pal Angie Zhuo uncursed me using a Chinese incantation she claimed was just

tongue and panned her eyes over the room, before fixing her attention back on Sean, who was now keeping Maggie in his peripheral vision like two people talking in a pew during church.

"It's got to be a mutual thing," Sean said. "I mean it. When you first meet a roommate, you can just tell right off if there's going to be emotional issues. I don't preclude roommates on the basis of emotional issues. What girl doesn't have them?"

"You're fan-fucking-tastic," Maggie said.

Sean was like "All I'm saying is I give everyone a fair shot. Borderline suicidal, no. Self-centered and whiny, no. Once in a while, a real headcase mindfuck slips through the cracks and I've got to wait for her to want to move out, which usually happens naturally if you're willing to wait long enough and put up with some unpleasant whiny crying in the bathroom and late night calls back to Topeka or wherever."

"Right," Maggie said. "Topeka. I'm sure you know a lot of people from there." She drank, clutching her oversize beer with two hands.[28]

"But—here's the thing," Sean said. "I never even give a remote hint of being sexually interested in any girl with any vestige of weird relationship problems or plain trauma. I was just saying how I do a kind of intake evaluation, at the start. First impressions are usually pretty spot on. But I'm not perfect. I can't always read someone. Plus, sometimes it takes more than a week for someone's true colors to show. General rule of

---

as powerful, if not more powerful, than anything developed anywhere else (having millennia of Chinese culture behind it).

[28] I'll say this for her: she did have quite a tolerance. The only way to tell she'd been drinking at all (apart from the mauve-like red of her cheeks and a couple burst blood vessels in the whites of her eyes—which could as well have been from pre-existing capillary damage, allergies, etc.) was her prolonged staring. Even her staring wasn't out of the ordinary, just an exaggeration of her usual forthright glance.

thumb: never fuck one of your roommates until you've passed a comfortable threshold of four weeks. Give or take. It's not an exact science."

Maggie went "I can't believe I'm hearing this." The tone of her voice was not very surprised at all.

The fact was, Sean virtually never went into this level of detail[29] re: the administrative side of apartment living and, to a certain extent, he sounded like he was parodying some smooth operating braggart he'd run into back in the day when he was more of a player himself. I didn't for a second think Maggie was taking him seriously, despite her wincing facial expression and the exhausted look she threw back at me while Sean went on and on. By her own admission, Mags was immune to shock

---

[29] He could be a bit closed off on the whole. In fact, there were whole areas of his life that he kept walled off from us—not to mention whole periods of his life that were total blanks. He'd share one or two experiences to make us laugh, or for mere shock value, employing a Henry Miller-like style of impressionistic pornography to discuss the most mundane accounts of one night stands and missed connections and embarrassing sexual encounters in night club bathrooms, but these were rare events and always for an audience of at least three, I.E. for entertainment, like a form of bardic poetry. When it was just me and him, however, Sean barely reciprocated, even on those confessional mornings at the coffee and donut shop close to the ferry where I often spilled my guts out about this and that. He'd heard all about Olivia, all about Anna, probably all about Cindy, my high school girlfriend, until I realized how one-sided the conversation had become and—not wanting to be like those egotistical people who talk only about themselves—I'd prod Sean into disclosing something about himself other than how long it took his stomach to digest Indian food, a favorite topic of his. Sean obliged every now and then. Mostly, he just redirected the conversation back to me—that's what made it so easy to talk to him (as note 2 indicated).

anyway—growing up with four older brothers (and three at home for her formative years) had removed most of the mystique from the masculine gender, and she didn't pass up an opportunity to say she'd "heard it all before."[30]

"I never initiate anything either," Sean said. "It's not being creepy. I don't quote 'make myself available.' I don't sit out on the couch so my roommate has to pass me on the way in. I don't volunteer to give back massages. I don't knock on their door. I don't randomly do nice things, other than just picking up my trash and washing my dishes and being an all-around exemplary roommate."

"Congratu-fucking-lations." Maggie let her neck go slack and brought it around in a rapid circle as if she were doing neck stretches. "Exemplary roommate. Good one."

Across the room, the table with the girl in the yellow was making the waitress laugh. She turned, her eyes still crinkled with laughter, our eyes met, then she nodded, glancing back at whoever was talking to her, her nodding becoming short and preoccupied as she caught sight of another group motioning for her to come over. Then she was off and away, her ruffled blouse pivoting, avoiding a corpulent gentleman backing out of his chair. She went out of sight behind another one of those decorative beams, this one containing black and white pictures of chateaus and coniferous trees in a Nordic landscape.

"Mostly nothing happens," Sean said. "It's just the occasional girl—once I've made my evaluation, and four weeks and all that, and she's not a nutcase, then it's fine. Everything's cool. In general, girls who get involved with guy roommates aren't in it for the relationship value."

"You could write the book[31] on this."

---

[30] Maggie had also told us she was mainly friends with guys, a circumstance in her life she shared with Anna, my college girlfriend—make of it what you will.

[31] Now I'm sure Maggie knew that Sean himself was something of a writer. He'd been writing stories and poems off

I raised my beer as if Maggie had meant this as a compliment and sipped nearly half of it. Sean didn't even acknowledge me.[32]

"It's reality," Sean said. "Ian, you need another drink."

"I'll get it," Maggie said. She looked behind Sean for the waitress and waved in an unmistakable 'We're empty and you've been hard to find' wave.

The waitress came over and asked, "Another sommerbock?" and Maggie said, "No. Him," and I said "Sommerbock, sure" and Sean said "Why not?" (even though his current beer was full) and ordered another too.

"Sommerbocks all round," Sean said. "Anyway, I'm pretty good at reading people." For whatever reason he was looking at me when he said this.

"Don't flatter yourself," Maggie said. She looked bored; she'd fallen into that abstracted, zombie gaze that commuters on the six PM D Train sometimes get, as the train stalls under the river for like the fifth time since leaving Grand Street after absorbing a tidal wave of slack-jawed straphangers.

---

and on for the last six years, none of which he showed me or anyone, so far as I knew, except maybe Sajal Amar (see notes 50, 67) who, at lunch once with Sean and myself, all but implored Sean to finish this paranormal romance set in Memphis, which Sean claimed would make his fortune and pay off his student loans.

[32] I'd made a point not to pester Sean about his story. If he wanted to tell me about it, he'd tell me in his own good time. After a few beers at Barrio on 7th Avenue, near Methodist Hospital, he let fall his "working title," either "Aunt Gretta" or "Aunt Gretel," I can't remember. By the way, this whole time Sean hadn't taken a sip of his beer. Just by looking at his beer, which was still normally carbonated, you could tell it had been sitting for a while, unattended, with that lonely look of a forlorn glass of beer, beaded with condensation, without any trace of finger marks to wipe the condensation away.

"I've gotten a lot better," Sean said as if Maggie hadn't even spoken. "It's pretty easy to tell right away if someone's lugging an awful lot of emotional baggage. It's like they got a suitcase with no room for anything else. They're the worst. But, actually, there's even worse: the people who don't have any baggage at all—the ones with like empty suitcases, who at first seem like, wow, they're so open and free and laid back but are actually so inexperienced and immature they're like a bomb waiting to explode since they haven't had their heart broken, or wrecked their car, or gone through hell and back yet, already in their early twenties."[33]

---

[33] I guess Nick Amante, the *Inferno* guy, belongs in this last category. He dropped out of Yale his sophomore year (when I was a freshman) and basically went incommunicado. The word was he was a total basketcase, though it turned out he spent only a month and a half in actual rehab (probably spying on other residents for potential story ideas) and the greater part of the year in his childhood home in Morristown, no doubt waited on hand and foot while he churned out reams of stories, poems, and critical essays, a pajama and slipper wearing invalid like a Proust or Emily Dickinson type, only not quite as good, even if he was capable of a verbal onslaught on par with Thomas Wolfe. All that aside, I never really knew what trouble Amante got mixed up in—pills or alcohol or costly cocaine, or whether like some wannabee junkie too smart for his own good he'd simply mastered the art of consuming pills with no adverse side effects like expired codeines and hospital grade pain relievers that had lost their pizzazz, maybe mixing in a few scary looking green pills containing nothing more than ginseng and seaweed extract, which in high enough doses maybe could give you the same high as one Coca Cola, and which bended his mood just enough to indulge in his ennui in that familiar troubled artist way. More likely, he was just suffering from mental problems, manic depression, stress, anxiety, panic attacks, or just general dissociative disorder—as in he disassociated himself from all

Maggie did a pirouette thing with her nose and mouth "Wrecked their car?"[34]

"It's just a figure of speech," Sean said.

Maggie arched her eyebrows, but right then the waitress came back with our beers. She didn't bother to ask Maggie if she wanted another (she'd worked her latest beer down to about half). "I'll be right back," she said, our empties clattering on her tray as she walked away.

---

academics, maybe buying into the fallacy promulgated by *A Beautiful Mind* that school was "for the birds," or in the words of Russell Crowe playing John Nash "classes will dull your mind," and was thus in danger of failing out. I sort of subscribe to this last theory since Amante was a staple in the Dean's office all through the fall. At first, I thought he might have been a part-time secretary, he was in that office so often. Then again, Amante had a habit of turning up where he wasn't wanted (see note 121 especially; also 117; 119; 183-185).

[34] In *Inferno*, car wrecks are associated with (perverse) beatific visions (note 53!). Also, before I forget, another argument for Amante's dissociative breakdown—his consistent depiction of June Marsh as hallucinating outside herself. E.g.:

What was happening? The walls scaled in nacreous slime, dripping stalactites of quicksilver, a caul. Blinking. No, I'm here. Blinking. I'm here, aren't I? But it wasn't her anymore, no. She'd slipped outside her own body. The girl with the small buttocks, cowering there, was a feral child, whimpering. She, June, observed it all from some place higher up. That's where she was: higher up. She was the spider on the wall. She was inside that spider, the velvet membrane with the eight red eyes, the adhesive spider fingers. That spider. That was her. And yet she was also attached to the girl. She was the spider and she was the girl, connected by a nerve, an umbilical link. Come home, come home, come home. She was the spider girl, pulled in two directions, pressed into two bodies, the substance of her own body dilating outward, coming. (*Inferno*, p. 98)

Sean took a determined sip from the first stein—he now had two to choose from. "Drink up. Drinks are on Mags."

Maggie was like "I'm paying for Ian's, not yours."

"Well, that's disappointing."

Maggie burped without covering her mouth and grimaced at the two of us. She'd taken out her phone while we weren't looking and now she opened her hands like a nest, cradling it. "When's your job starting?" she asked, with a sort of rote, uninterested flick of her eyes.

"The sixteenth."

"And it'll be in Brooklyn?"

"Probably."

"Good for you," Sean said. "I'm a bit jealous to tell you the truth."

"Where do you live now?" Maggie said.

"Sunset Park," I said.

"Is that like Park Slope?"

"It's right below Park Slope."

Maggie was like "I dated a guy[35] who lived in Park Slope."

---

[35] Nearly all of Maggie's friends at The Fund had heard some (abridged) variant of this story, the one about the guy she'd dated for four years, who had let her down somehow in the fourth year and had just not been up to snuff in the general reckoning. Nevertheless, despite the fact that this guy she'd dated for four years was a total dud and would never be capable of orchestrating some kind of comeback to rewin her heart—point blank, she'd told him not to bother calling unless he'd purchased a ring beforehand and was serious "this time around", knowing full well it would never happen—despite his obvious flaws, not the least of which were his arrested development and immaturity and gross splurging binges during which he'd put himself into a food coma eating a combination of Velveeta Mac & Cheese and Nathan's Ballpark Franks and having very little to drink except maybe a splash of generic-brand Kool-Aid, not even real Kool-Aid, which was absolutely

disgusting if you asked Maggie's opinion, she still had gotten to know him quite well and had virtually been living with him for the majority of those four years as if they were husband and wife or common-law married—a situation which her ultra-Catholic mother would have termed "living in sin," and which had contributed to her further alienation from the church and the precepts of her youth—cleaning and cooking for him out of a tender affection which even the most sarcastic among us sometimes feel for those incapable of doing any cleaning or cooking themselves (other than the aforementioned unhealthy binge-worthy items) and are more or less helpless as puppies. So, whenever a coworker or friend was going through a shitty relationship or even just the normal ups and downs in any relationship, Maggie would use this guy she had been dating for four years to provide some anecdote apropos of the coworker or friend's situation; for example, after hearing the friend out, Maggie would say, "You know, Phil reminds me a lot of [that guy I dated for four years] because even though he was a meatball and pretty much inept at anything romantic, he still when I was having a really bad day would do this thing where he'd turn on this really cheesy like smooth jazz Kenny G CD and start running the bath for me, no questions asked, and with no like ulterior (sexual) motives at all, which wasn't normal for him" or—in the opposite case—she might say, "You know, Brandon reminds me a lot of [that guy I basically wasted four years of my life on] pulling the same, 'Oh, sorry, I didn't realize you called, I was just out with the bros you know, like Maverick, and Little Henry, and Tattertot, no I'm not drunk, what makes you say that?" The surprising thing was, despite the fact that the negative anecdotes far outweighed the positive ones, this guy Maggie had dated still came out as a likeable, even fairly decent fellow when all was said and done, and several people in the office felt—or at least implied they felt (Velma, Sean, and Harriet, our computer specialist, for example)—that maybe Maggie should have stayed with the guy, since he really wasn't all that bad. In fact, Harriet once told me that guys like "[the guy

"Really?"[36] Sean said.

Maggie was like "There's a lot you don't know about me."

When no one followed this up, she went "He had an apartment on top of some Chinese fast food restaurant. All the rooms reeked like wontons."

"Try to flag the waitress again," Sean said. "I'm getting hungry."

Maggie was like "Seriously?" She'd run through the gamut of shocked and disappointed expressions—mostly directed at me since I happened to be sitting across from her. She widened her eyes at Sean to let him know the waitress was nearby.

"Yes. Hi. Hello!" Sean said. The waitress came up, pursing her lips. "We'll share an order of wieners—and an order of bratwurst."

"And some Bavarian pretzels," I said.

The waitress smiled at me and scooped a few strands of hair behind her chubby ear.[37] She had to wait a sec for a tall lady in an ostentatious dress—it looked like a print of a 16th century cartographer's map, complete with shaggy, dog-faced leviathans resembling Falkor from *The Neverending Story*—to sidestep out of the way, the waitress' eyes moving from the

---

Maggie dated for four years] just have to be trained··· that's Maggie's mistake··· once you train them they're loyal and obedient and will stay by your side and will even fetch and roll over for you."

[36] Ironically(?).

[37] The waitress reminded me of Anna in a vague way, something about the skin under her eyes, maybe the dark rings in the shape of perfect crescents, which her concealer didn't quite conceal. The crescents themselves looked like they'd been drawn on with violet oil pastels, like you could just rub them away with your fingers. Anna and the waitress also shared a palimpsest of freckles on the roundest part of their cheeks, freckles which might or might not come out in mid-to-late summer (Anna's freckles hardly ever did).

lady's rearing haunches (her dress was unflatteringly tight) to my eyes with an unmistakable "are you seeing this?" which, even for a waitress who's seen a lot, must have been mildly amusing. She left, burying her smile by tucking her chin to her sternum.

"It sounds like you two were doomed from the start," Sean said.

"I could have gotten over the smell," Maggie said. "He would've had to move eventually. And when I was actually there, it wasn't so bad." Her face was all scarlet. "Don't they say that smell is the most primitive of all the senses?" she said, flustered, smoothing down her hair. "You should know that," she said to me.

"Yeah, sure."

"What the hell do they teach you at Yale?"

Sean was like "So what's the real reason you broke up?"[38]

Maggie went quiet for a moment, but it wasn't like she was purposefully delaying like those clowns who bounce a tennis ball like five million times before serving—it actually looked like she was having some last-minute reservations and needed to rehearse her response at least once so she didn't embarrass the memory of this old boyfriend. "OK, what I'm about to say stays between us," she said.[39]

"Got it."

-----

[38] Yes, the office had speculated about this question off and on for quite a while, but true to Sean's nature he had refused to take part in these rampant (hushed, of course, and never in the vicinity of Maggie's cubicle) flights of fancy. Neither of us betrayed any curiosity at the prospect of learning the "real reason" why Maggie and the almost fiancé hadn't made it once and for all, from the horse's mouth. At least, I'm fairly sure we didn't.

[39] See previous. With a teaser like this, it's hard not to betray a smidgen of curiosity. Also, not the last time tonight she'd use these words.

I was like "What, do you want us to pinkie swear?"[40]

"Grow up," Maggie said. "I mean it. Eh, just looking at you, I know you're not going to tell people." She let her voice trail off and become almost wistful. "He had a *fantasy* thing."

"Whatcha mean? Jinx," Sean and I said at the same time.

"He wanted to wear costumes," Maggie said.

Sean was like "Oh. Catholic schoolgirl? French maid? Nurse? Amazon priestess?"[41]

Maggie went "Sure. I'll leave you to fantasize all about that."

"Don't be coy," Sean said.

Maggie was like "What's it matter?" Her voice was a snarl now. "Costumes are costumes. I don't do costumes."

"My philosophy is try anything once," Sean said.

---

[40] Not so far-fetched a suggestion. It was Maggie herself who told us all about this cousin of hers who was missing his pinkie or ring finger—the exact digit didn't matter—and was always able to cheat his way to victory in thumb wars by waggling his stump. Even though you knew exactly what he would do each and every time, something about the way he waggled his stump was so fascinating or hilarious that you'd break concentration and just be mesmerized by his stump and inevitably lose the thumb war. Maggie'd told us the story at Hibernian on some other after-work occasion, when Preston was still in her good graces, and one thing leading to another (I'm not sure if it was Preston's suggestion or not), we'd all had a round robin thumb war. The old thumb war strategy (not Maggie's cousin's strategy but the general male-female thumb war strategy going back to elementary school) is a tried and true method for holding a girl's hand in a competitively sanctioned way, without it seeming like you're just trying to hold her hand, like you "like" her or something.

[41] Astronaut, hula girl, Marie Curie caliber chemist, Venetian prostitute, Tchaikovskian ballet dancer, the list is virtually endless···

"Come on," I said. "In the grand scheme of things, costumes is pretty tame."[42]

"I guess you guys are just *waaay* more sexually liberated than me. It's no surprise with you," Maggie told Sean, "but I'm kind of disappointed in you," she told me.

"OK, Mother Superior," Sean said. "Wait. Was that one of the costumes?"

"You know what else pissed me off about him?" Maggie said. "He used to complain if I missed shaving like one day."

"Well, good for you," Sean said. "Way to stand your ground."

"I told him I wasn't going to be part of anyone's creepsoid fantasy," Maggie said, reverting to the costumes again, her main complaint.

"Just stick with the real thing. Nonfiction," Sean said. "Who needs fantasy? Fantasy bites."

I was going to offer my own comments on fantasy when my phone buzzed three times: new text message, and then on top

---

[42] I didn't always think so. My college girlfriend Anna once purchased a costume at some shady operation near the mall in New Haven—the same place where she got penis-shaped water guns in assorted fun colors for our friend John's birthday. You've probably got to be in the right frame of mind to appreciate a costume, but for me the French maid getup that Anna squeezed into was hardly provocative. Mostly, I just wanted her to remove it—immediately. Anna's penchant for costumes was notorious. She took Halloween very seriously, almost as seriously as Passover or Yom Kippur—knowing there were right-wingers in various Christian churches who cast aspersion on Halloween only made Anna support it more. My freshman year, she dressed up as a bowl of Cheerios by painstakingly stitching actual Cheerios to a white T-shirt, supposed to represent milk. The next year, she was a Tootsie Roll, a less successful project, perhaps. I have no memory of junior year.

of that started ringing.[43] I tamped my hand down on my pocket and just caught the vibration, but I didn't open up the flip phone right away.

"Couldn't agree with you more," Maggie said. "Girls have to put up with too much already."

Sean and I were both like "Yup. Yup."

"Yeah, you two sound real convincing."

"I don't know what to say," Sean said, holding up his hands in an innocent way.

"I'll say I agree," I said.

"Now *you* want a medal?" Maggie said. "You should hear the two of you. The age of chivalry lives on."

"Not inaccurate at all," Sean said.

"The thing with shaving is I have sensitive skin," Maggie said. "I nick myself once every time and the blood gets really dark when it clots. It's genetic. Here, see here. Here's the evidence." She scooted her leg out. I gave it a cursory glance, my eyes sweeping from her leg, to a side angle of the table, to the table's surface and the slick residue from beer steins slid this way and that. "You didn't even look," Maggie said.

"Sorry," I managed.

Sean was like "Maybe you have too much iron in your blood and that's what makes it so dark? I don't know for sure. I'm not a doctor. But I knew a guy who had too much iron and they had to perform bloodletting, to demineralize him."

"Really?"

---

[43] The message read: WANNA HANG OUT LATER? The voice recording was kind of inaudible when I listened to it in the bathroom. I typed back: SURE, but left it at that—no response for a while. Looking back on it, it amazes me how much mileage I could get from one text message. Just one message from Olivia and I was good to ignore her for another hour. Of course, that's not how relationships are supposed to work. Sometimes, you actually respond right away to someone's message. These behaviors have to be learned···

"His name was Bruce," Sean said. "Bruce Heinz. His nickname was Pork Rinds Heinz. Poor guy. High school can be cruel."

"I don't want to know what goes on with teenage boys in high school."[44]

Sean smirked. "He had, how can I put it? Terrible BO. Like the kind that makes you want to vomit. Like human waste. Like if a whale beached itself and then slowly rotted. He was also pretty overweight."

"Fuck was his problem?" Maggie said.

"In part, hormonal," Sean said. "Sheesh. It is true about smells. It really is. Memories involving smells are un-erasable. And scarring."

"Speaking of scarring, there's Preston,"[45] Maggie said. She could see him best from her angle. He'd paused by the entrance

---

[44] Probably a smart move considering the rampant masturbatory/scatological/penile/testicular/perineal/butt obsessions that occupy that demographic's creative resources. Then again, Maggie had probably "heard it all"—like it or not—from her brothers.

[45] Although Preston was strictly speaking our department's technology guru, the chances of him calling any of us via cellphone to say he'd be late were like zero to one. In fact, Preston was one of those rare dudes whose job involves DreamWeaver and InDesign and Photoshop and other Adobe programs, who own like old-ass Nokia phones without Internet—phones that barely function at all, and are usually kept in glove boxes or similarly out-of-sight places for emergency use only and never for like regular calling/texting—who instead prefer to converse via their landlines or, in Preston's case, his work phone, which he used egregiously to place all kinds of personal calls to friends back home in Kentucky—mostly to catch up on sports, or make plans for his next (wifeless) visit. Although neither Maggie nor Sean had said anything to the tune of "Hmm, wonder where Preston is?" I think we all pretty clearly felt that if Preston stayed home tonight, none of us would lose

and was making as if to check his phone, which probably didn't even have texting capacity now that I thought of it.

"Looks like he's scoping the scene," Sean said.

Maggie was like "That's in keeping."

Sean half stood up and made a seesawing motion with his quarter-full stein. "Over here."

"I kind of enjoy watching him," Maggie said. "Maybe he'll stay over there."

"You're a cruel, cruel woman, Mags," Sean said.

"Hey. Let's see how you feel when Preston comes on to you at your place of work."

"Could happen," Sean said. "I've been told I look metrosexual."

"That's so true." Maggie almost sprayed some beer out of her mouth. "I never would have said it myself, but now that you've said it, it's kind of true."

"And why is that exactly? Is it my shirts?" Sean said. "No, I'm really asking."

Maggie caught my eye and we both nodded. "The shirts."

"That's a start at least," Maggie said. "It's the patterns, see? Like here," she indicated the wavy lined pattern on Sean's Charter Club button down. "It's Euro, man. I'm not saying it's bad. It's just sort of a European look. You could be batting for both sides, is all I'm saying."

"Preston's wearing like a luau shirt," I said. He was dressed casually for sure—in fact, it looked like he'd just updated his wardrobe. His pants were almost black and yet very clearly denim, like Fubu or something, wide enough for sky-diving, definitely spacious enough to conceal his trademark flask.[46] I

---

any sleep over it. I was actually kind of hoping he *would* stay home—though, realistically speaking, Preston would be the last person on earth to turn down a chance to get hammered with friends. The Maggie situation was the wild card.

[46] Another wildcard. Mags had teased him about it kind of harshly at Home Sweet Home before the whole CD incident

made a note to compliment him on the ensemble but instantly forgot.

"Preston can pull that off and still be one hundred percent undeniably heterosexual," Maggie said. "It's because he's got that creepy uncle beard."

"So, you're saying if I also grow a creepy uncle beard, I'd look straight?"

"No. And please, don't attempt it."

"You don't think I can grow a beard?"

"No, I have faith, but then you'd look like my Spanish teacher, Mr. Ramirez. Another creepola."

"Preston's checking his phone," I said. Really, he hadn't left off checking it since he arrived. "I bet he can't see us."

"I don't know how much more obvious I can make it," Sean said, standing again and waving his arm slowly like an air traffic controller. "Hello. Hello. Hello."

"Goodbye," Maggie said.

Preston raised his arm and walked toward us, the edges of his lips rising in an uncomfortable smile. I'd never noticed before, but his teeth weren't in that good condition. They were bordering on brown in that sweaty, guffawing smile of his.[47] His

---

went down. The flask was a present from his wife and had his name engraved—no, not his initials, his first name, that was what Maggie had teased him about, the cursive *Preston*, like what you write on a first grader's lunchbox.

[47] He was known sometimes to use chewing tobacco, every now and then, ensconcing himself in one of the bathroom stalls whenever he wanted to pop in another wad of Skoal. He kept a toothbrush somewhere at his desk, too—and the sound of his brushing was powerful enough to reach the corridor between the restroom and a board detailing Children & Youth Initiatives, most commonly between the hour of 4 and 5 PM, when he had to wash out the tobacco shit in preparation for heading home (that his wife didn't allow chewing tobacco was another of his constant gripes on the phone with his buddy Rick).

forehead was shiny, hair waxed instead of gelled tonight, with some of the substance melting anyway in clear ribbons down his temples. He wore a dark green shirt with brown Easter Island statues in repeating diamond formations. His pants were definitely flaring, which probably would have provoked Maggie into another derisive comment, except he closed the distance between us too fast, accelerating with bear-like alacrity and doing a kind of what they call in figure skating a "toe-loop" to avoid a collision with the harried waitress and our tray of food, which she now set down.

"Record time," Maggie mouthed in my direction.

"Don't stand on ceremony," Sean said, pushing the pretzels to the center of the table.

Maggie was like "Fuck that," breaking off a bit of pretzel and dipping it in mustard.

"Gentlemen. Maggie," Preston said. For such a big guy, he had a real simian posture, his arms hanging and his shoulders slumped.[48] He remained standing, as if he was waiting for someone to say something. Then he sidled onto the bench next to me, wrapping his legs—first one, then the other—around to face forward.

"I'm thinking of growing out my beard," Sean said, stroking his chin. "What do you think?"

Preston went "Go for it, man!" His tone was that over-the-top enthusiastic that was pretty transparently masking some real misgivings about seeing Maggie again in a social way. "I just gave this puppy a little trim," he said, meaning his own beard, or (more accurately) goatee.

"Me," I said, "I can't grow a beard."

Preston slung his arm around me good-naturedly, as if he were going to lead me in a traditional German drinking song. "In time, my son."

---

[48] Seeing him standing there like that just made your heart go out to him. But that was just the way he stood—there was no like symbolic meaning to it.

"Isn't puberty a bitch?" Maggie said.

"I'll let you know when it happens," I said, uncomfortable with Preston's close grip.

"Bartender! Bartender!" Preston called with more of the same canned glee. "I'm dry."

The waitress met Preston's eyes with a steely glance and nodded slowly in an unvoiced *I see who I'm dealing with.* "Yes," she said.

Preston was like "I'll take a lager."

"Good choice," I told him when the waitress left. "I had one of those."

"Man of my own heart," Preston said.[49] He planted his freckled elbows on the table, and scanned some people behind us.

"So," Sean said.

"So," Maggie said.

"Help yourself to the grub," Sean said.

Preston was like "No worries. I ate at home."

"There's plenty," Sean said, arranging a piece of very hot bratwurst in his mouth.

"Actually, I'm kind of watching my weight," Preston said. "But I wouldn't be opposed to a pretzel."

Sean was like "That's the spirit."

Preston was sweating like a madman. His forehead was beaded with more condensation than my beer glass and the excess sweat was running into the creases of his neck. The sweat did something to make his Old Spice like doubly strong.

---

[49] Preston's blustery enthusiasm was probably getting on Maggie's nerves, though she was doing a good job not paying attention. This was a classic "vicious-circle" situation, with Maggie's blatant silent-treatment causing Preston to feel anxious and as a result to act the clown, which in turn caused Maggie to give him an even greater dose of silent treatment, which in turn···

It had also activated some pre-existing detergent smell from his luau shirt, which was unidentifiable as any store bought detergent such as Cheer or Tide but not unpleasant.

"Got any summer plans?" Maggie said.

"Me?" Sean said.

Maggie still hadn't looked at Preston, who was fidgeting and squinting over at her and Sean and kept brushing all against me and readjusting his position, creaking and jostling the entire bench, upsetting my knife as I cut into a brat.

"I'm saving money," Sean said.

Preston was like "I hear ya, brother."

"I'm really hoping to get out to Minneapolis," Sean said.

"It's a good time of year for it," Maggie said. "Not friggin' freezing."

Preston was like "What do you got going on out there? Wait."[50]

------

[50] Preston could play the cretin, but that didn't mean he didn't have feelings, and he almost certainly had to remember that Sean's own star-crossed love, maybe the only woman Sean was seriously attached to, the Human Resources Assistant Sajal Amar, had moved out to Minneapolis last fall. Sajal had worked at The Fund forever, before Sean even, long before me; she was kind of depressed with how long it had been. She was a self-styled "letter writer;" she would write letters whenever she could, preferring the feel of pen and paper to email, and "sighing a little inside" whenever she received emailed messages in response to a letter that might have taken her days to compose. She had also been engaged. She was never upfront about this; even the ring she wore—which was silver and left a tattoo of tarnish on her finger—was kind of nondescript and easy to miss except when she took it off and wiped it with restaurant napkins, a peculiar habit she had. Her fiancé was just finishing up his residency when I met her—they were moving for his work. She'd known about this move for a while, for a long time she'd felt like she was just treading water. Still, she had no idea

Maggie glared at him and shook her head—to her credit, her headshaking was very subtle and Preston almost certainly didn't notice this additional sign of her disapproval. Preston wound up with "I've always wanted to check out Minneapolis. You been?" he asked me.

I was like "Naw."

"I need more money first," Sean said.

"What exactly do you spend all your money on?" Maggie said.

Sean was in the middle of chewing another bratwurst piece. "Medical expenses," he said, his mouth all full.

"Ho ho," Maggie said. She had wisely decided to let her bratwurst cool before eating it. "I forgot. You're like the Tin Man."

"Not that bad," I said.

---

what she would do in Minneapolis—at first she only planned to write a lot of letters. I went with her and Sean to Peep a few times, Sajal having a hankering for Thai food, and although she preferred Thai Angel since their food was spicier, she'd compromise with the closer restaurant, which allowed us to have a more leisurely lunch in our one-hour lunch break. The first few times I met them, Sajal and Sean were talking about her wedding; this type of wedding planning stuff was so abstract, and my pad thai was so filling, I zoned out and entirely missed what they were discussing. She finally got married that winter, a big festive affair in Forest Hills, to which Sean was invited, but he never talked about it. I think the fact he never talked about it showed how much he cared about her. After her departure, he was glum for a few weeks, unusually brusque with his telephone operator duties and also brusque with my lame requests to get into the supply closet—he had the only key. Pretty much no one who knew Sean ever brought her up—even Preston, which is almost miraculous given the number of times he's put his foot in his mouth: a situation he avoided at this very moment.

Sean was like "I've been to Beth Israel twice this last month for my knee."

"Don't let it hold you back, though," Preston said, taking a stab at Sean's money problems/physical wear-and-tear. "So far as I see, doctors aren't going hungry. They'll be just fine. Put the medical stuff on credit. Pay it off later. Go to Minneapolis. You can't wait around to live your life."[51]

Sean was like "That's terrible advice, you know."

---

[51] Maybe it was different for Preston, since his Don Mafioso father-in-law apparently financed several of his trips, including an almost open invitation to visit Preston's mother-in-law in Florida—the Don could kill two birds with one stone this way: keep his ex-wife happy, spending time with Allison's kiddos, and also give Allison a break from what her dad had to know was a less than idyllic home life. If Allison's lot in life could be improved by offing Preston and sealing him up in one of those Hefty trash bags which mobsters use to deposit corpses out on the East River before dawn, as I'm assured they do, causing massive back-ups and road rage on the FDR the next morning, due to the common phenomenon of gaper's delay, drivers staring transfixed as teams of plainclothes and regular clothes police officers stand around drinking coffee from those blue "We Are Happy to Serve You" cups while forensics teams that are never as glamorous as they appear on television help to identify the bloated remains of humans invariably resembling Pre-Raphaelite paintings of Ophelia, though with more anguish in their expressions and oftentimes more facial hair (if they were men), the higher-ups chatting amiably about Derek Jeter's late night heroics—and no one has a bad thing to say about Jeter, aging or not—while grunts and underlings act like they're busy doing important stuff, all too conscious of the commuters who are slowing down and giving them popeyed stares, Preston would've been long gone, "swimming with the fishes," etc.

"But he's got a point," I said.[52]

"What's the story anyway?" Maggie said. "You don't take care of yourself."

"That's not true," Sean said. "Conflicting opinions. One doc says this, one says that. You go to a surgeon, of course they want to put you under the knife. That's their calling. It's just a fluid build up. I don't want surgery, if I can avoid it."

"Meanwhile, you're hobbling around like peg-leg," Maggie said.

"Slight exaggeration."

"If it's holding you back," Preston said, without finishing the thought.

I was like "You sure you don't want a sausage or something?" since Preston's glance had kind of fallen on the food and he'd been moving his tongue around and mumbling his lips in a sort of pre-prandial anticipation.

"Naw, brother," Preston said. He patted his waistline, hidden under the fold of his shirt. "I had a what-do-you-call-it. A Lean Cuisine."

I was like "For real?"

"Yeah, I washed it down with a Bud Light. All told: 400 calories. Not bad. It's a start."

"Good for you, Pres," I said.

He was like "Got to start somewhere."

"OK, so maybe sometimes I use it as an excuse," Sean was saying, speaking more or less to Maggie now. "'Oh, Sean, can you get me that box of laminating sheets way up there?' 'No, sorry, Joyce, bum knee.' I'm not the only one. I don't want to name names."

Maggie laughed. "At last. The truth."

"It doesn't mean it doesn't hurt," Sean said.

---

[52] I'd been fishing for something nice to say to Preston since I realized it was partly on my account he'd come out in the first place.

"Why you walk around all gimpy then?" Preston said.

"Because it's a real thing," Sean said. "Do you want to see?"

Preston declined.

Sean was like "Let's drop it. It'll be fine."

Maggie clicked her tongue. "Men," she said. "You treat your own bodies like they're friggin' cars."

Sean was like "Meaning?"

"Meaning until they like fall apart, you don't do shit."

"Either of you have a car?" Preston said.

Sean and I shook our heads.

"Think Maggie's the only one out of us with wheels," Sean said.

Maggie had refrained from answering Preston's question, but now she was drawn into it, like it or not. "You're not some working class hero," she told Sean. "You can afford a car."

"Don't need it," Preston said. "Not in this town."

"Exactly," Sean said. "I had a car, back in Colorado, yeah. But I sold it, last time I was out there."

"What'd you got?"

Sean was like "A Camry."

"Aw, shit," Preston said. "How much you get for it?"

"That's my business," Sean said.

"Jack shit, I bet."

"Let's just say, I almost got more for my Atari."

Preston was like "You had an Atari and you sold it? You know those things are collector's items? How many miles on the Camry?"

"Forget it," Sean said, shaking his hand. He pulled his spare beer up to the edge of the table and siphoned off a draught. "The thing had zero pick up. I drove to San Jose, what? God— like seven years ago now. Oh my gosh. Longer. I was flooring it on the Rockies, on the way, with trucks passing me. A horse-drawn carriage could've passed me."

"Lucky your Camry didn't just blow off the side[53] of the mountain," Preston said.

---

[53] Speaking of cars going off inclines, Amante scores a success with his description of Robert Udell's own (pivotal) car accident, even if his Nabokovian urges bubble up a bit too strong:

The wind hissed, the crone's first warning cry, sibilant and oddly dry. The front slashed toward him, a scrim darkening the parking lot. He paid. He got into the car and now (Eli, eli, lema sabachthani) the rain was thickening and the entire car was bombarded in pearling raindrops that skittered off the edge of the windshield and ran in smeared fingerprints along the side windows, and the second warning cry came, and he heard it— distinct and chilling. He turned on the wipers. He pulled onto the road. He navigated by the line of trees. Beyond the trees— swamp: bleak, gray and molten, sweating like meat on a skillet. The road looking down over that festering ooze of the Mesozoic and whatever hellish Calypso had called him, beckoning, his frail shapeless body in her hands, molding him to insensibility. He was not thinking straight. June. If only he had known her sooner. He drove. The car swayed. The car (good God) where had it gone without him? The car caught wind like a sail. He felt it skidding. Down down down. Swamp bed wetting his face, splayed fingers, and her unapologetic mouth on his again, no, no, no, no, yes—into a blackness that was yet more dense and sluggish, almost like a dream, oh June, (was it offal was it offal?) and he choked on water and clay and his eyes rotated through to the back of his head and the color was blood and (God!) June her wild hair, nipples pendent, his nurse, nursling. He was going to die, yes? Right. At his age, and with his body, the dark shroud of water aligning itself over him. Yes? Right. He was wishing at that crucial moment when he could taste the extinguished agony of his lungs and his beating arms, flailing torso, like a mangled insect, wishing that he had sinned, that he

"Yeah, well it felt like it would."

"You drive?" Maggie asked me.

"Sure," I said.

"Standard?"

"Nope," I said.

Preston was like "What's wrong with you, boy?"

"Don't worry," Maggie said. "I can teach you sometime."[54]

"What kind of car you got, Mags?" Sean said.

Maggie looked at him as if he'd insulted her. "An Audi," she said.

Preston was like "Hey, now."

"It's not my car," Maggie said. She was still staring at Sean and only Sean, annoyed that he'd disclosed this info.[55] "It's my mom's."

"Sure it is," Sean said.

"You think I can purchase an Audi on my salary?—which you know," Maggie said. "Get real."

"Trust fund perhaps?" Sean said.

"I'm going to smack you." Now Maggie really laughed, her eyes straining, and her face in an overall contortion that made her cheeks and forehead look like elastic stretched to the breaking point, a gleam of not-quite-perspiration reflecting off the curvature of her jawbones, and that imparted a slight

---

hadn't waited so late in his life to sin, and it was June, June, June pink June until it wasn't. (Inferno, p. 201-2)

[54] I haven't yet taken Maggie up on this offer; by now, I'm thinking the time is past.

[55] If it made any difference, Maggie never actually drove her car into Manhattan, unlike some idiots wedded to their vehicles. She took a bus in from Tenafly over the George Washington Bridge and then usually took the A/C/E train down from Port Authority, transferring if need be at West 4th Street, arriving nearly one hour before anyone else and on her third cup of espresso-laced coffee by the time I'd arrive.

tangerine glow to the normally shell-pink, lanugo surface of her cheeks. "Trust fund. That's the first thing my parents said when I graduated from college. *There's no trust fund. Good luck.*"

"Well, you're moving up in the ranks."

"I've got a friggin' MBA and I'm working with people who can't operate Excel," Maggie said. "Excel. Excel? Forget Excel. People who can't operate Word. How's that? How's that for moving up in the ranks?"

"Should make it easier for you to advance," Sean said. "No competish. Anyway, we got the tech whiz with us tonight, eh Pres?"

"No work after five," Preston said, kind of burying his mouth in his beer.

"I forgot," Sean said. "Preston doesn't like talking shop."

"It's not that I don't like it," Preston said. "It's all good. It's just I compartmentalize. The last few days have got me burned out. Esther wants an entire new interface for the web site and Joyce's been up my ass with those bilingual brochures."[56]

---

[56] Preston had been working on those brochures since the beginning of May, roughly four weeks ago, to give you an idea of his pace. But (in all fairness) Joyce wasn't an easy person to work with either, sort of a micromanager type. Joyce maintained a gray beehive hairstyle, and an aroma of incense candles and exotic spices emanated with the potency of a clergyman's censer from her collection of Chinatown scarves, sort of her trademark, which she wore at all times to complement her ROYGBIV assortment of cardigans and oversize cableknit sweaters. The tricky thing with Joyce was she was liable to change her mind in bold, drastic ways, come up with a "really great plan" and then nix it the next morning. To be honest, she might have had ADHD or something, undiagnosed all these years (she must have been at least forty-five or thereabouts). Nevertheless, I always thought Joyce was an ideal partner for Preston: if he did no work at all, he'd be in exactly the same position as otherwise whenever Joyce came to him the next

Sean was like "All told, how many work hours, estimated time of completion?"

"I don't know. Two weeks."

Maggie cleared her throat with an excessive grinding noise.

"Two weeks, you do it right," Preston said with an effort to sound convincing.

Maggie was like "Let's just be happy we don't have any oversight."

"What?" Preston said. "You think two weeks is too slow?"

"You said it, not me," Maggie said.

Preston slid his beer stein from hand to hand reflexively, and slouched farther back on the bench, wobbling the two of us like we were on a rowboat.[57] I'd pretty much finished with my beer by now, the last few sips flat and tasteless. I reached for another pretzel.

"What's next on the old docket for you, Maggie?" Sean said.

"There's no work unless I make it," Maggie said.

"Especially now there's two admins."

Preston was like "Too many. I can't keep them straight."

"One of the admins[58] is a family friend," Sean said. "I get that. Nepotism. Totally cool. I don't even think Esther wanted to hire her. I think she was pressured."

Maggie didn't even cover her yawning. She was like "The other one—Eileen—comes over to my desk like ten times a day, asking dumb questions. It must be her first job to be so gung-ho."

"You're her mentor," Sean said. "You should feel flattered."

---

morning cradling a spearmint tea and said "You know what? Scrap what you're doing. Let's try this instead."

[57] He was going to take both of us down with him, if he toppled.

[58] Janine Roth. She was hired to replace me while I was still there. In about a week, she'd learned how to appear busy without having anything to do. She was a natural at it.

"Yeah, well, she's driving me friggin' insane," Maggie said. "She couldn't even use Expedia because she kept picking some day in the past. She kept getting some error message. Dumbass."

"Booking flights, eh?" Sean said.

"Yeah. San Diego. That technology conference Esther's going to. This Eileen girl's telling me the flight'll be eighteen hundred dollars. I was like 'What the fuck are you talking about?' She was booking Esther for Santiago de Chile."

"They kind of sound the same," I said.

Sean was like "Esther deserves a little R&R. I bet she'd really enjoy Chile."

"She'd be clueless enough to get on that plane," Maggie said. "That's what she'd do."

"It wouldn't be nonstop," I said. "They'd probably stop in Houston or something."

"Esther always requests nonstop," Maggie said. "At least for continental U.S."

"Otherwise, hands down, she wouldn't notice," Sean said. "I love Esther to death, but she's like Mr. Magoo."

"She probably uses her passport too, since she doesn't drive," I said.

Maggie was like "Somehow I don't think she'd be amused."

"Why not?" Sean said. "Make a weekend of it. Take her husband. They have great wine in Chile."

"Come on," Maggie said. "You think Esther does vacation? Florida, maybe. Even then I bet she doesn't enjoy it."

"Man," Preston said. "Life's too short for the rat race. The way I see it, vacation's for recharging the old batteries. Stress kills."

Maggie was like "Some people are wired differently."

Preston didn't even acknowledge that Maggie had spoken. "I'd be in Florida a week ago, if Allison's brother wasn't in the hospital getting his face put back together."

"What happened to him?" I said.

Preston shook his head. "Bike accident," he said. "He was in a competitive bike race in Eugene and just lost control coming off a turn. He spun out, at like thirty miles an hour. He fractured his eye socket—looked like Jean Claude Van Damme, Cyborg. At first, the docs were like, 'This is the best we can do,' with his eyesocket all sunk in like that so it was not, what's the word... "

"Symmetrical," I offered.

"Symmetrical—no, not at all—it was like one eye was exposed. The way Allison described it his face was flat on one side, a little like a Coke can when it's smashed in."

"Unlucky," Sean said.[59]

---

[59] Preston's brother-in-law Damon had had a string of mishaps, which had become office fodder, mainly because Preston rehashed all of them so loud on the phone with his buddy Rick. First and foremost, Damon had probably married "the wrong girl"—some high-flying freelance photographer, Lisa Chen, who had told Damon repeatedly on their first dates that she never wanted to settle down, get married, have kids, etc. so it wasn't like she didn't warn him. All the same, Damon must have charmed her enough to get through her initial barrier to the whole marriage thing, and they ended up getting hitched— though not before Damon's dad (Preston's father-in-law) flew out first-class to California, where they were living at the time, and told Damon in no uncertain terms that marrying "that woman" was a grave miscalculation and that he'd regret it the rest of his life, especially if they had kids, and that take it from him a divorce wasn't as easy or inexpensive as he might think and that if the best divorce lawyers were charging X amount in New York, just imagine what they'd charge in San Francisco, where the prices are like ¾ higher (the dad took it as a given, Damon would be married in the church, but here again he miscalculated—they were married in the courthouse and their celebration was so left-wing and nutty the dad up and left before the toasts and would not be reasoned with, flying back to New York for a Mafioso get-together the very next day). Preston

and Allison got their first taste of Lisa's eccentricities when the newlyweds flew into NYC for a week, ostensibly to spend time together, bond as a family, always a noble intention. At an opening at the International Photography Gallery in Midtown, Lisa got drunk on white wine and had to be escorted out of the building by an armed security guard because she had tried to smuggle a Dasani water bottle into the downstairs gallery despite repeated warnings. The guard was high class about the whole thing; he saw the tottering Lisa almost fall down the last three stairs and instantly spotted the Dasani she was attempting to mask behind her purse, like an inept shoplifter at a 7-11. "Ma'am. Ma'am. No beverages in the galleries," was his ineffective cry. Preston and Allison also reasoned with her as she stumbled forward, not heeding any of them—this whole time Damon, her spouse, was nowhere in sight. Maybe he'd had a premonition of what was about to go down and had decided to eat his fill of appetizers while the going was good. While the guard escorted Lisa out of the building, her face red with anger, she writhed and screamed profanities, and made ineffectual, purely theatrical attempts to bite and kick the guard, enough for the other patrons to stop what they were doing and stare at her open-mouthed and with the typical snide comments New Yorkers make whenever their attention is forcibly captured by someone acting like an imbecile in public. "Allison had never been so embarrassed her whole life," Preston claimed. Over the past year or so, things had thankfully cooled off—enough so that Damon's latest problems had absolutely nothing to do with his wife. Around Christmas, he'd eaten some kind of contaminated pork or something and developed this weird parasitic worm, which took up residence in his gut, the whole time Damon getting skinnier and looking worn out and frazzled, until finally, one night at Café Bruxelles in Greenwich Village, he'd enlisted Preston's help to go to the bathroom, and then after straining on the john, asked if Preston wouldn't mind having a look at something. Sure enough, there was unmistakable worm-like evidence lying inert in the toilet bowl,

"Tell me about it. I'd be on the beach if it wasn't for him," Preston laughed—no one joining him. "Naw, man. I hope he gets better. They've taken him to another doctor, some specialist in Seattle. They're going to repair his face structurally so he won't look like the Terminator anymore. Allison's there with the kids and everything and all I got to do is just make sure our pets don't die."[60] Preston flagged down the waitress. "Another lager. Thank ya, ma'am," he said. "You?"

"Me, too," I said. "Lager."

The waitress spot-checked the other side of the table and went away.

"Why don't you get that admin to book me a flight to Santiago de Chile?" Sean whispered to Maggie. "Fringe benefits or something. We're in the black this year, right?"

Maggie was like "Wrong business model. It's a 501(c)3 or whatever. So no. I think we're always *not* in the black. That's kind of the point."

Preston was like "What's amazing about this whole thing with Damon's accident—Allison's brother Damon—is how his wife has risen to the occasion. Everyone, and I mean everyone, myself included, all thought she was worthless. I mean, I don't have to tell you. I've probably told you about her before, all the weird shit she does."

"Sure," I said.

---

and after vomiting and turning white, Damon said he'd lost his appetite, could Preston please drive him to the nearest hospital ASAP. He ended up having to take some medication, which allowed him to push out the worm, segment by segment, in a matter of weeks. Lisa's calm and steady hand during this whole ordeal was the first sign that maybe she was coming around and actually going to be a support to Damon rather than a scourge.

[60] By "pets," Preston meant "chinchilla." Apparently the chinchilla had developed the rodent version of conjunctivitis and had to be eyedropped every night—a chore Preston found intolerable.

"Right," Sean said.

"Anyway," Preston said, "she still is pretty worthless, but after this recent fiasco with his face, she stepped it up in a big way. I don't know if she's back into him, or what, or maybe she just felt sorry for him, or maybe she just doesn't want to live and, like, be associated with some guy with a fucked-up face, but she really went the extra mile. When the first doctor, in Eugene, was like, 'This is the best we can do,' she was like, 'I want the name and number of every cranio-surgical specialist on the West Coast, and then I'll make my fucking decision, thank you so much for your help.' And that's how they found this dude in Seattle. He's, like, apparently some renowned surgeon who's dealt with, you know, dudes who've been in ten car pileups and Evel Knievel car wrecks and far worse shape than Damon. So they're pretty optimistic he'll come out looking like a person again."

"I'll be right back," Maggie said, cutting into Preston's little family update.

I was like "I got to go, too."

Preston eyed me like I'd seriously inconvenienced him or maybe he thought I was taking sides, going with Maggie to the bathroom at the same time. Anyway, he pulled himself up and stood aside.

He was still talking as we left "I mean—I don't blame the wife—that's Lisa, you know—if I was her, I'd be calling up all the surgeons in the Pacific Northwest to see if they could repair my husband."

The bathrooms were on either side of a closet-like structure, with pine wainscot panels and a bleached white wall, reminiscent of a New England kitchen. They were single stalls, and right then, both were occupied. Maggie hadn't turned around while I followed her over and I had a chance to observe—or rather re-observe—how small she was; barely five-four, I think, but also just a slim, muscular woman, not at all curvy, with what you might call a boyish figure (she wouldn't call it that probably)—the fleshiest part of her, I guess, were her

61

legs, though I'm not sure she'd feel flattered by that observation either. While we were waiting, she took out her phone and started in on a message.

"I'm babysitting for my brother Andy tomorrow," she said, without looking at me, "so they can go to the Met."

"The museum?" I said.

"The opera."[61]

---

[61] Until college, I'd never known anyone who went to operas; even the best of them are kind of long—some even clocking in at three plus hours, so that if you have a tendency for your mind to wander and the screen displaying the translation of the libretto is in anyway malfunctioning you might actually stop "paying close attention" and instead go on all kinds of tangential daydreams and garden paths. But it's worth listening to, and I can really say this now, if only so you don't pass over the hints and resonances and echoes—forward and backward—which any work of art can't help but contain. For example, if I hadn't snapped to and concentrated on at least some consecutive minutes of *The Magic Flute*, I might have missed the rather subdued, and on the whole quite ephemeral, choral number, something like "O Isis unt Osiris"—just a transition piece between the principal singers, practically a throwaway number when matched against the rest of the opera, a quiet almost Gregorian chanty-thing—the melody of which furnished Calixa Lavallée with the score for "O Canada." And this little connection in and of itself is noteworthy since it shows how people (musicians, yes, but also painters, writers, sales staff) get their inspiration from others and—not to be too blunt about it—*steal* part, parcel and often whole cloth the melodies, techniques, styles, and salespitches of those who've come before, which are likewise stolen or modified from even older sources. The arrangement is the only novelty in art. (I admit this is getting philosophical, and I'm out of my depth in all matters remotely connected to what people call "metaphysics" which I still can't adequately define). Still, again, the arrangement is the

"Nice of you," I said.

"Yeah, well. I waited till my nephew was potty trained. I don't do diapers."

"Smart."

"Eh, not like they would've let me babysit then anyway. I mean, when Thomas was a baby. They're both serious control freaks."

"No."

"Shut up." Maggie rapped my arm. "I don't think I'm that bad. They're like germ *fanatics*. When my brother Chris flew in from California last Christmas, they made him strip and put all his clothes in a trash bag—they were worried he'd contaminate the baby. From the plane."

My phone started ringing, and I opened it without thinking, holding it waist-high and nodding to Maggie. "Hullo," I said.

"It's me," Olivia said.[62]

"Hey Liv," I said.

Maggie was like (whispering) "Liv?" Even though my entire relationship with Olivia had overlapped my time at The Fund, I don't think I'd ever mentioned my ex-girlfriend by name to Maggie.

I was like "Where you at?"

---

only novelty in art, it's how these artists avoid the charge of plagiarism, the fact that they are fitting all these old designs into a new pattern, Ariadne-style, rendering them in their own way, transmuting them in a new composition, sure—though the links are still visible if you go hunting hard enough or, like Sister Wendy, you've got an eye for detail—and all the "artwork" is just bringing the past to bear on the present, the dead to the living, and everything quote "artistic" to itself, a closed circuit, a self-sustaining system.

[62] Her usual salutation. Cellphones have made announcing yourself obsolete, is her explanation.

"I'm about to go underground. To Manhattan. But I'm only going to be there for about an hour [indistinguishable]."

"What? Whereabouts?"

The phone was going all staticy. "Then I'll be in Brooklyn again," Olivia said as if there'd been no interruption.

I was like "You're not underground now, are you?" The men's door opened, and I scooted closer to save my place. "Hello?" I said. "Hello?"

"Ian?" Olivia said.

"Yeah? Yeah?"

"I've got to go. Call you when I'm there."

"OK," I said. Of course I was thinking: why didn't you just call when you *were* there?

"About thirty minutes," Olivia said, sounding farther away, or in a crowd, or going down an escalator, her voice muffled and crackling and lost in the noise from the beer garden too. "F train's broke. Got to take the A. Jay Street."

"Fucking F train," I said. But I don't think she heard me.

"Dude, are you in line?" some guy behind me asked.

"Yup, sorry," I said. I stepped inside and latched the door. Olivia had hung up or gotten disconnected; anyhow she was gone. I re-opened her message and stared at it, wondering how she managed to sound urgent and unconcerned at the same time, or if she even knew how she sounded. I don't think she did it intentionally.

Maggie was taking her time in the bathroom when I got out, so I waited; I wanted to laugh off the phone call I'd just had, which had pretty much cut off our talk, but the exact words for how to excuse myself weren't coming to mind. Olivia had said "Jay Street. About thirty minutes." I was almost positive I was going to see her now—but on the off-chance I didn't, I wanted to keep cool, you know, play it off.[63]

---

[63] Already I was devolving into that clammy anticipation I'd often experienced on days past when Olivia would call me out of

"What are you, stalking me?" Maggie said, catching me by surprise (I'd stepped away from the makeshift line of women waiting for the bathroom).

"No-o," I said.

"Why're you acting all weird?"

I was sort of put off by the question and I think I even flushed. "Me?"

"No. Yes, you."

"Nothing," I said. "Should we go back?"[64]

"As opposed to standing here like a couple of pervs? Sure." But before we'd gone all the way back, skirting the tables which were clearing, Maggie turned toward me. I almost stepped into her and I didn't have any excuse, I'd been staring at her the whole way, my center of gravity just a bit off-balance, the edges of my vision starting to flicker and make me more self-conscious and protective of my own radius of space. She smiled. "You're going to miss this, aren't you?"

"What?" I said.

"The office," she said. "Us. I'm not going to say the job."[65]

"Sure I will," I said.

Maggie was like "Just don't believe anything Preston says. Ever."

I was surprised Maggie felt the need to even say it, like I was really that gullible or naïve. I was like "I know better."

They were clearing a table next to us. A waiter lifted up the plastic placard with the beer and appetizer specials, and slid a dishrag underneath, looking up with a snarky glance as our eyes locked accidentally.

---

the blue—I.E. note 201—and I'd respond with kneejerk obedience to her summons, never realizing how ludicrous or moronic I was behaving until after the fact.

[64] This question, I realize later, was maybe slightly more flirtatious than I meant it to be.

[65] One can only stretch the truth so far, I suppose.

"You won't miss any of us," Maggie said.

"Shut up," I said. I stumbled a bit, literally, and hoped she didn't notice. "Of course I will."

Back at the table, Sean and Preston were sipping their beers like they didn't even know each other, like two strangers at the communal table at Le Pain Quotidian. Preston had gone and ordered four more beers, his effort at smoothing things over—but only three had arrived so far, Preston's own beer (he'd gone with a dark this round) required mysterious preparations or a goblet style glass, who knows. Sean hadn't really made a dent in his other drink and he was still pulling it up to his mouth and then stopping with a vacant expression, the way he sometimes looked at 4:50 on a Friday afternoon when I'd come into the office from mailing a letter: his eyes turned down as if he were reading, yet with a total absence of recognition, like he'd lost all familiarity with language and signs, and was viewing whatever crap he had on his desk with the uninformed gaze of a newborn (but without a newborn's interest). He managed a tired smile as Maggie sat next to him, then relapsed into staring at nothing. Preston had to stand again for me to squeeze into my spot.

"What's up?" Maggie said. "Who's this for?" meaning the new beer—clearly the P-man's doing.

"You," Preston said. "Drink up."

"Here's your Dunkel," the waitress said, depositing Preston's beer on the end of the table, her attitude toward Preston—you could see it in her overall look of resignation—only slightly improved since the time he'd placed his first order, all blustery and ready to carouse, like a sailor on holiday in Port Royal in the time of Henry Morgan. "Anything else?"

We just shook our heads.

"No thanks for me," Maggie said, pushing her beer toward the center.

Preston pretended like he didn't see what she did.

For the first time that night, it really seemed like we'd been there a while, like other people had come and gone and we were still at the same table, taking up space. But the place was less crowded now and outside was even darker than it had been when Maggie and I had gotten up, the streetlights at full strength, their light competing with the unnatural pink haze[66] in the sky which—on its own—would be enough to illuminate most of the boulevardy type streets in the city with about the same power as a lava lamp in an undergrad's dorm room.

Sean was like "How do you feel about mobilizing?"

Preston went "Beer's still fresh."

"After that," Sean said. "No rush."

Preston held out his palms in a Eucharistic pose. "I'm down with whatever, man. I don't got to go home early. I've eyedropped that damn chinchilla—he can shit all over his pen for all I care. One more week. One more week, and then me and Allison are going to have to settle this whole Furbie biz."

Sean took out his phone and was temporarily occupied.

"What's the plan then?" I asked Preston.

He shrugged. "You're asking the wrong guy."

"We were thinking Brooklyn," Sean said, without looking up. "Grand Street and Roebling. Up for it?"

"What's over there?" Maggie said, yawning.

"Music place," Sean said. "Trash Bar. You'll like it."

I reopened Olivia's first message: HEY. I started typing: OFF TO BKLYN, but erased it and put my phone back. I'd call her later, when we were there; that's what she should've done, that's what I'd do. I had a tendency to get overexcited whenever Olivia contacted me and it was an unfortunate tendency, on the whole.

Sean looked like he was hitting the same key over and over on his beat-up phone.

Maggie was like "Easy, bud."

---

[66] An effect, so I'm told, of all the factories along the Jersey side of the river, discharging who knows how many pollutants into the air, I.E. a chem trail.

"Message sent," Sean said. "Sajal."[67] Sean slid his phone into his pocket and cradled his beer, the one he hadn't finished, not the one Preston had ordered. "Preston and I were reminiscing about our college days," he said—though without much enthusiasm.

"That's right," Preston said, taking him up. "I was telling him about this old pal of mine, Kyle Weir. That's his name: Kyle Weir, but everyone called him Danny Deckjumper, on account of him falling off this two story deck in the back of some dude's house at like a Phi Delta something-er-other party. He was an accident prone motherfucker."

"Danny Deckjumper,"[68] Sean repeated.

Maggie got my attention and tapped the table with her index finger, as if to say "You can tell a lot from a person's friends, eh?"

"Yeah, he was a real nice guy, just a bit... ." Preston scratched his chin. "Kind of an idiot. Daredevil, maybe. I don't know. We were all out back around the keg and stuff, hanging out, and all of a sudden, someone sees him falling, his arms flailing and shit, I mean he kind of flipped over in midair like a cat, that's the thing. He landed right on the freaking patio. I didn't see exactly how he fell—but it wasn't like he softened the landing. It sounded bad. Like broken bones bad. I mean, we were afraid to touch the bastard, like he might've exploded[69] or something. At the very least: broken ribs. He just lay there about thirty seconds, and meanwhile we were all like 'Should we move him?' 'Is he breathing?' 'Call an ambulance!' His girlfriend was hysterical. It was a bad scene. And then—I can still see that

---

[67] Again, no one followed up on this, not even an "oh, how's she doing?" or "you guys still talk?" or "how's that husband of hers, Frank or whatever his name is?" (his name wasn't Frank). Sajal Amar was the one area of Sean's life which was totally private (see notes 31, 50).

[68] A play on *Danny Deckchair*, the movie.

[69] Rather: imploded.

crazy bastard—he just gets up like *what's the big deal*, dusts himself off, and's like, 'What?' Fucking Danny Deckjumper."

I was like "So—he didn't break anything?"

"Nope," Preston said. "Nothing." He brushed down his goatee. "That wasn't the first time he'd fallen. Apparently in high school, he fell off some guy's roof, getting drunk. He was fine then too. He was just a faller. It was kind of like his thing."

"Falling?" Sean said.

"Yeah. Treehouses, trees. He fell off the bleachers in marching band. The guy just didn't learn. He was also kind of a klutz."

Maggie was like "You don't say."[70]

"Anyway, the reason I was thinking of him," Preston said, "is we just got a notice a week ago. The dude freaking died—for real this time."

"Seriously?" I said.

Sean was nodding; I guess he already knew about it.

"A freak accident," Preston said. "He was riding a motorcycle somewhere like the Black Sea—he was doing one of those cross-Siberia tours, God knows why. What the hell is there to look at in Siberia? He just sped off the fucking road and died."

"That's awful," I said.

"His luck finally caught up with him," Preston said. "He'd kind of escaped death one too many times, you know."

"Nine lives, eh?" Sean said.

"Yup." Preston took another long sip of beer. "The worst part about it is he left behind that same girlfriend from college—no one thought she'd actually stay with him. I don't remember her name. She was smoking hot. Man, they were an odd pair. And they had a kid, too."

"She was *pregnant*?" I said.

"Naw, like a three-year-old," Preston said. "The kid and her were over there too, wherever the fuck the Black Sea is, when it

---

[70] Her first almost nice response to Preston that night.

69

happened. I sure hope they didn't see—you know—the actual wreckage or whatever. It couldn't've been pretty."

"Jesus," Sean said.

"It could be worse," Maggie said.[71] "You could be on your honeymoon, and you're just-married husband could gut himself in the bathroom, with the bath running."[72]

"Jesus Christ, Maggie," Sean said.

Maggie's cheeks had gone yellow. "Too much?"

"Look," Preston said. "It's like I said, you've got to live life your way. But after you have kids, things change."

---

[71] As mentioned in note 20, Maggie liked to indulge in morbid, sensational stories, every once in a while, as a way to break up the tedium of office life—though in the current circumstances, it seemed a bit gratuitous.

[72] This particular husband, an alumnus of Maggie's Catholic high school, had taken a turn for the worse while studying philosophy up at some Maine school like Bowdoin. Maggie's conclusion: weather had been a factor. With all the snow, and the New England cold, and the generally skeletal New England atmosphere, exacerbated by a small student body, and a tendency for all the students to batten down the hatches and remain in hermetically close quarters, basically drinking whiskey and completing homework assignments in rooms that have been sunk and snowdrifted in an endless accumulation of snow, sleet, and freezing rain, like the animal abodes in *The Wind in the Willows*, this guy had just plunged into depression. How he'd managed to date a girl long enough to propose and eventually get married, without her suspecting something was wrong, I.E. that he was depressed out of his freaking skull and not taking any medication for it, was anyone's guess. The fact that he killed himself while abroad on some Caribbean island, only pointed to how messed up he must have been. The family had some small trouble getting the body transported back to the U.S. and the whole story had appeared as a blurb in the *St. Ignatius Quarterly*, Maggie's alumni newsletter.

"It's not just you anymore," I said.

"Exactamundo, brother."

"I really don't think I'm going to drink this beer," Maggie said like no one had heard her before. She glanced at Preston and he glanced at me.

"Give it to Ian," Sean said. "It's his night."

Preston was like "It's all about you, kid."[73] He put his arm around me again and shook my shoulder.

"You take it," I said. "You're still catching up."

"I'm already there," Preston said.

Maggie arched her eyebrows but was distracted by the waitress. "I think we're ready," she said to her.

"The check? Should I... are you splitting this evenly?" the waitress said.

"No. Here," Maggie said. "How many drinks did he[74] have?" she asked Sean.

"Four. Right, Pres?"

"Correct," Preston said.

"Four for him, and then everything else is me and him."

"Separate checks then?" the waitress said.

"Yeah. Three."

I was like "Thanks, guys."

"Don't mention it," Sean said, reaching for his wallet.

Preston leaned over the table to address me and Sean. "You guys seen that Japanese movie?"

Sean was like "Which one was that?"

"*Fade Out*," Preston said. "Check it out. It's pretty in line with all this depressing shit."

"I saw it," I said.

"What'd you think?" Sean said.

---

[73] Attempting a Humphrey Bogart impression.

[74] Preston.

"It was some fucking movie," Preston said, before I could respond.[75]

---

[75] *Fade Out* (released late-May 2008). The plot's indeed depressing: Taka is a brooding marine biologist studying jellyfish along a remote island off Shikoku, Japan. He's played by the late Riichi Hasegawa, and part of the movie's notoriety, according to *Time Out New York*, is the fact that the suicide plot in the movie has some parallels to Hasegawa's own sad end, although the exact circumstances of the great Japanese actor's death remain clouded in mystery. As a young man, Taka is impressed by an irascible loner scientist Dr. Kihara, played by the legendary Victor Matsumoto, who has made it his personal quest to study a reclusive hydrozoan, *Solus peregrinus*, which so far as Kihara knows is the only animal on earth which can spontaneously regenerate and thus live forever. Dr. Kihara is convinced that in two more years he will distill an elixir of immortality from his slimy captives—he is shown repeatedly pulling *peregrinus'* cells apart by means of tiny forceps and a microscope and watching with a subdued grin as the separated cells (here shown in accelerated timelapse video) regrow and branch into polyps—Dr. Kihara's strict devotion to science makes his quest for immortality more conceivable than the slapdash approach of Ponce de León scouring the Florida panhandle for the Fountain of Youth. Here's where young Taka comes on the scene. He's fresh out of the University of Tokyo, his own preference for invertebrates dovetailing nicely with the old man's. After a few short bonding scenes, Taka makes the not-very-hard decision to join the elder scientist in his remote laboratory located in the aforementioned island in Tokushima Prefecture where the two work diligently for many years. Then— a change starts to disrupt the somewhat staid routine: Taka begins to suffer from debilitating headaches. At first, he attributes the headaches to stress and lack of physical conditioning. After obtaining a gym membership, and taking some personal time, during which he gets high once or twice and ventures off to a karaoke bar on Shikoku Island, Taka meets

a young punk girl Airi, played by the Japanese version of Audrey Tautou or Zooey Deschanel, Eme Yoshikawa, a brilliantly facile actress whose eyebrows contort into a variety of Tetris-like shapes, and who is clearly—again, this is pretty obvious—just the antidote poor floundering Taka needs to get out of his rut and start being productive. Here's where the movie makes an even more interesting turn, kind of spiral actually: just when it seems Taka has it all—the girl, the old mentor, a fulfilling job, a small but cozy cabin by the sea—his headaches return. And now, he realizes, that the strange otherworldly noises— something like a glass harmonica or an infinitely extended track by Enya—that are needling the squishy folds of his brain, and are agonizingly resistant to the migraine pills he's started to pop indiscriminately, are the voices of whales migrating, pod by excruciating pod, just off the harbor. Somehow, Taka has the unwanted ability to hear whales in like surround-sound, and not only that, he can parse through individual voices and almost *understand* what they are saying, which is off the fucking wall. He still goes to work, but now his jellyfish collecting is dreadfully shoddy; instead, he spends most of his time on the beach suffering through ear piercing oratorios (which are thankfully rendered in smooth, easy-listening Humpbackese for us, the ones watching this offbeat comedy), memorizing the voice parts and later transcribing them by means of a Casio keyboard on a loose set of composition paper which he's bought on one of his days off, learning to read music in the process— necessity being the mother of invention, etc. So now, more or less withdrawn into his own painful interior, Taka rejects Airi and even chews out his mentor in a harrowing scene in which the old man is standing in a Speedo, raising what looks like a Medussa's head out of a tidepool and pointing at some whirly white blobs. The camera zooms in for a close-up of Dr. Kihara's weatherbeaten Martin Laundauish face as he receives these harsh words from his mentee, his eyes folding down and his mouth sinking into his gums, where he's lost a few teeth. Now Taka holes himself up, with only his Casio, headphones, pencil and paper, and starts wildly transcribing whale songs first as actual music and then in a very rough translation, eventually developing a sophisticated shorthand that allows him to decode 7-8 sentence paragraphs of whale material per sitting. By the end of a delirious month, he's lost the girl, pretty much gone AWOL from his job, and has what amounts to a novella of transcribed whale, most of which is incoherent though it's a bit more ambitious—given the fact that cetaceans aren't known for their literary prowess—than *See Spot Run*. It's stream of consciousness stuff, real Garcia Marquez, but when we get our first glimpse of the mystical writing, the message is clear: whales and all natural life are dying as a result of human selfishness and greed—forget the dire predictions of that cheesy song "In The Year 2525," at this rate we'll all be extinct in 100 years and good riddance. Not exactly an original thought, but rendered more tragic because of the whales' Faulkneresque delivery. Taka is now ready to tell his mentor. In a scene rendered in sepia tones, the two men meet and share a tea on a promenade overlooking the graying ocean. Dr. K shushes the Tak-man when clearly Taka wants to unburden himself, telling his prodigy not to feel bad, that he's decided to retire, that it's time, and that there is something, a secret, that he has been withholding all these years. Taka, although intrigued by the secret, now can't help interrupting his mentor to tell him "That's all well and good, but I also must tell you something," (this of course is what the subtitles say, since I don't speak Japanese) at which point he pulls out his dog-eared, handwritten manuscript of whale utterances and starts giving like a tree-hugging stump speech on the inhumanities human beings have inflicted on nature through the ages, from the extinction of the last great South American sloths, saber tooth tigers, wooly mammoths, auks etc. etc. Dr. K's face is grandfatherly and mellow as he patiently listens to all this vitriol and then assumes a genuinely curious expression as Taka reads the most comprehensible parts of his manuscript. It is clear that whatever Dr. Kihara wanted to say will be trumped by a deluge of whale jabber. The scene ends with the old man patting his young squire on the back and telling him that he will check in again tomorrow, but it looks like Taka could use a long nap. Taka, in despair, believing his mentor is dismissing him, and acutely aware now of almost every human-derived extinction event in the history of Planet Earth, trudges home, resolved to off himself that very night. Unfamiliarity with weapons and knots makes it difficult for him to zero in on an effective means of suicide, but eventually he decides the most fitting thing will be to drown himself in the ocean, as a sort of expiation for marine desecration and unsanctioned whaling. He therefore puts on his best clothes and then takes out an old camping backpack, which he loads with scientific instruments and cases of Airi's Singha beer which she left in his refrigerator whenever she stormed off. He walks down to the ocean and attempts what will be suicide attempt # 1. It turns out, however, that unbeknownst to him, Dr. Kihara was finally able to isolate some kind of immortality enzyme, and has laced Taka's tea on the sly. Taka's first suicide (which is presented in an uncomfortable two minute clip consisting of gurgling, gargling, choking, and mild vomiting into the choppy burnt sienna-tinted water) fails. Taka just assumes he's not doing it properly, he doesn't have the will to die, etc. He tries again, this time with what he feels will be a relatively painless overdose of his entire medicine cabinet, but this just lands him with some dietary disorder and a case of the runs. He's wracking his brains now, wondering what he should do. He tries jumping off a bridge: also a failure, not even a scratch. Then he studies up on *Knots for Dummies* and goes ahead and hangs himself, but even though he's fairly sure he's snapped his neck, he's still alive and ticking, and what's worse he has to hang there for a good four days until Airi comes back to pick up the last of her shit, figuring Taka won't be gentleman enough to drop it off as she's already requested on numerous answering machine messages which Taka had to listen to while he was dangling off one of the beams in the living room, each message becoming more and more acerbic and derogatory. As

---

the movie proceeds, Taka's driven to wilder and wilder suicide attempts—confronting bears, lions, bull sharks, anacondas, and each time maybe losing a pound of flesh here or there, but never dying. He has a permanent crick in his neck and he's starting to look more like one of the aging punk rockers Airi turned tricks for prior to meeting him, but he's not giving up. He realizes, somewhat late in the game, that Dr. Kihara indeed has given him the immortality enzyme, and he flies back to Japan (from the Amazon, where he was ingested by a python and pooped out of the python's butt in a scene no one really needed to see) to have it out with his old pal. After a brutal confrontation with Dr. Kihara, Taka boards a plane for Siberia. There, he convinces a gang of sadistic unemployed Muscovite interrogators to assist him in his planned demise. They meet on the tracks of the Trans-Siberian railroad, one of the Muscovites, a spindly, hook-nosed fellow, assuring Taka that the next train will pass through momentarily. At the distant whirr of train wheels, Taka spurs the crew into action; the first douses him in lighter fluid and the second lights him on fire, while the hook-nosed fellow, who has been busy fiddling with what looks like a case for a trombone, removes a chainsaw and chops off Taka's head and then his arms but can't quite get the legs before the train is so close the first Muscovite (who has taken a hatchet to Taka's buttocks) has no choice but to push him in front, and then the flailing, flambéd Taka is ground like a meat patty, deposited half a kilometer farther along the tracks before the train can disengage from his smoldering hide. But even then, Taka isn't dead. He's brought, moaning and singing what sounds like a 1940s Louis Armstrong scat tune, to the station, and there to a local doctor, who eventually has him transported to a hospital, where a stooped Dr. Kihara is already waiting. Over the meat patty's bedside, Dr. Kihara confesses his love for him and kneels down and promises to remain by his side until the end, a touching moment—rendered creepy by the odd camera angle which prevents the viewer from seeing what old man Kihara is doing with his gnarled hands under the covers of

Taka's cot. Several scenes follow in succession—showing Airi going down on one of her old friends and shedding a small tear for Taka, who she is convinced was a fucking genius and has actually left her pregnant. Then we see another scene of Dr. Kihara burning the whale manuscript that Taka so painstakingly wrote. Finally, we see a scene of some of Airi's punk rock roommates rehearsing a song that sounds surprisingly like a Ramones version of one of those earlier Humpbackese songs Taka was listening to when he first became aware of his powers—which means that somehow Taka's musical transcriptions have made it out in the world—perhaps Airi mistakenly snatched a few of Taka's music sheets when she was grabbing the rest of her crap that last time in Taka's cabin? This constitutes the only upbeat moment in the entire last third of the film. We close with a shot of Airi giving a Courtney Love-like interview for Ryan Seacrest before the Grammy's, where Taka is slated to win (posthumously) a Best New Artist Award for a collection of whale songs as interpreted by the Jelly Hed Sisters, Airi demonstrating remarkable restraint with her spastic eyebrows; in fact, the actress Eme Yoshikawa here modulates her entire performance so that instead of resembling the Audrey Tautou of *Amelie* she now resembles the far more conventional, dare we say boring, Audrey Tautou of *The Da Vinci Code* as she chainsmokes Pall Malls and says things like "yeah I [bleep] loved him⋯ he had a [bleep] spirit [bleep-a-dee-bleep] than you ever dreamed of⋯ I wish [bleepy-a-dee-bleepy-a-dee-bleep bleep] here for this [bleep] meaningless [bleep]." And then the credits start to roll.

Book Two

With Preston jabbering like he was on talk radio and Sean and Maggie in good spirits too, I only thought to check my phone after we got inside Trash Bar. I opened it, saw Olivia had sent a new text: AT A THING AT THE LES. DONE SOON and wrote back: GREAT! AT TRASH BAR... CLOSE BY. CALL YA! I didn't even wait to get a drink—that's how excited I was to hear from her. I was even mapping out train routes and figuring which car was best to sit in if I wanted to get off at the correct side of Classon Station, summoning up a fairly accurate schematic of NYC transit before I had to laugh at myself and these half-baked schemes, assuming X, Y and Z, all the pieces falling into place, etc. Besides, I wasn't in any hurry to leave—unless Olivia asked, which was looking more and more like a near-certainty based on our history.[76] I just excused myself and went into the lobby and dialed her up.[77] The phone rang and beeped

---

[76] And we all know how history "repeats itself." I think it's the first thing we learn about history in school, right before the American Revolution.

[77] In my head, you know, I pictured her sitting there, bored at some function she'd been cajoled into attending, probably a meet'n'greet for students in the School of Public Health, or else maybe she'd accompanied those forty-year-old women she'd been known to hang out with, who she introduced to me as her closest friends, ladies who'd taken her in and befriended her when she didn't know anyone at all in the city, and who may or may not have been sexually active with her bohemian professor dad who was some sort of underappreciated adjunct at The New School and dabbled in the fine arts, creating Styrofoam sculpture and little figurines out of soap, that sort of thing, but who was otherwise a man about town, always busy, going to clubs and hooking up with young women who saw something charismatic and fiery in the way he spoke about Claus

Oldenberg and Jeff Koons and Keith Haring. Her dad, according to Olivia, had truly and passionately loved her mom when they were both in their early twenties, but couldn't get over her mom's past sexual indiscretions which Olivia's mom had kind of hoped would diminish with the passage of time, which forgiveth all things, but which, on the contrary, continued to haunt her in the shape of obtrusive pre-dawn phone calls from irate ex-boyfriends and former lovers turning up at her door. Olivia's mom had inherited a house, which sweetened the deal for her dad, who was dead broke and kind of a mooch. But the journal ended it—that was the quote "nail in the coffin," the day Olivia's dad came home to make amends, let bygones be bygones, and instead found his wife's journal lying in plain sight on the lower shelf of the bookshelf like it had been left just for him.[77A] Olivia's dad had come to work things out but ended up curled on the recliner for over an hour, his entire fist stuffed in his mouth, as he read about his wife's casual blowjobs and full-on prostitution-level behavior, including trading anal sex for a jean jacket (it was the 1980s and denim was in; a decade later leather might have been preferable, such are the vagaries of fashion), which she'd recorded in big, bubbly cursive like a 4th grader, with full circles (but no smileys) over her "i's" and "j's"— indeed, the penmanship added to Olivia's dad's horror, since not only was the writing completely legible, it looked almost *innocent*, flying in the face of everything it was describing, which was very bleak (and graphic) indeed. When he finally finished, Olivia's dad launched into a mad rage, tearing down a bookshelf which contained the complete works of Tony Hillerman stacked in herring bone formation similar to the Roman brickwork emulated by Brunelleschi in the dome of Santa Maria del Fiore. Then he left for New York. Olivia's mom took on a succession of boyfriends, each no better nor worse than the last, but all equally insolvent and parasitic, such that Olivia's mom eventually had to sell her own house, which even if it was a little clapboard thing had been in the family for two generations. Her mom moved into a trailer with her own mom

suspiciously like I was about to hear a storm warning and then disconnected, so I wandered toward the front hoping for reception, and tried again: same thing. I skirted around a few girls in heels and puffy skirts who were getting ID'd at the door and went out on the sidewalk to make one last attempt. This time I connected, but the phone just went to voicemail, and Olivia's message came on, "Hi, this is Olivia's phone. I'd love to hear from you. Leave me a message!" in that faultless pronunciation with a heavy emphasis on the fricative consonants, and no clear regional influence, difficult to peg.[78] I closed my phone before the beep so I didn't get recorded and walked back to the door. The bouncer was like "ID."

"I was just inside," I said, showing my hand where he'd stamped a faint purple outline of what looked like a dancing carrot.[79]

"ID," the bouncer said, same as before, holding out his hand. He didn't even look at me. He was this big, Samoan-looking guy in a black T-shirt, sitting on his stool, with his legs stretched out and the bulk of his stomach forming a solid rectangle under his shirt. He didn't say anything else, or turn, just waited there with his hand out.

I took out my wallet and had to massage the driver's license out of the plastic sheath. "There."

"Thank you," the bouncer said, in a bland tone of voice indicating he had no feelings about it either way. Unlike before,

---

sometime while Olivia was in school at Hunter. Even now, her parents weren't technically divorced.

[77A] Olivia would later read the journal herself, which her old lady friends called "sacrilege··· reading someone's private journal."

[78] I'd never asked her why she didn't have an accent, being from Savannah and all, but then again she said she travelled too much for anything to stick.

[79] Or turnip, or rutabaga, some species of root vegetable, with an expression of unbounded glee.

when he'd shepherded us in so he could chat up some girls in fishnet stockings and S&M leather doublets who'd perfumed the sidewalk behind us with a scent like decaying wisteria, he spent a while studying my card, turning it, and watching the hologram of all the various counties in Pennsylvania shimmer iridescently. "Five bucks," he eventually said.

"I paid," I said. "I was in there already."

"Five bucks."

"You already stamped my hand," I said. I showed my hand again.

"It's five bucks," he said. He raised his eyes for the first time. "There's no all-night pass. You leave, that's it."

I was like "You kidding me?"

He laughed and shook his head. "No man, you're all right. I just was playing with you. You're the one on the phone there."

Maggie had come up to the door now, like she knew I was outside. "He giving you trouble?" she said, meaning me.

The bouncer was like "This your friend?"

"I've never seen him before in my life," Maggie said.

I opened my mouth like a doofus. "Oh funny."

"Sorry, I can't let you in," the bouncer said. "Only if *she* says it's OK."

"Fake ID?" Maggie said.

"You know he's from Pennsylvania?" the bouncer said. "How many people you know from Pennsylvania? What the fuck you doing from Pennsylvania? We're cool. We're cool."

"He's a New Yorker now," Maggie said. "He lives in Park Slope."[80]

"Almost," I said.

"We're cool," the bouncer said. "I was just messing with you. Come on. Even though you look like a kid. Man, how old are you?"

"Twenty-four," I said.

---

[80] Sunset Park, but whatever.

"He looks fifteen, if that," the bouncer went to Maggie. "That's why I was double checking. I thought, 'hmm twenty-one maybe, but twenty-four—no way.'"

"He's got good genes," Maggie said.

"And hair like a motherfucker," the bouncer said, rubbing his own bald scalp. "Twenty-four, *sheeit*," he said. "I looked twenty-five since I was in diapers. My face did. I've been the same size since I was twelve. They had me snapping footballs for the high school team back in junior high. I ate like five servings of Ragú every night. Damn near ate them out of house and home. Eat a whole Thanksgiving turkey like it was nothing. I was a big boy. But I had to grow into my face. My face was an old man's face from before I could talk. Imagine having this face, only you're in sixth grade. I must've looked like Gary Coleman. The way he looks now all pissed off, hang-dog like. That's OK. I look about right now."

Maggie was like "I'm Maggie." She shook the bouncer's hand.

"Quarter Ray," he said. "Ha ha. See. My name's Ray, but everyone calls me Quarter."

"Twenty-five, quarter?" Maggie said.

"No. But that's a good one." The bouncer looked pleased. His face did sort of look like Gary Coleman's, but bigger and more Samoan-like. "I'll have to remember that. That makes it even better. Wow. All this time, I never thought of that. You're blowing my mind. No—it's because my dad, he's Ray. Big Ray. I didn't want to be Ray Junior or Little Ray, so I made everyone call me Quarter Ray. Now I'm even bigger than my dad, but it doesn't matter. He'll always be Big Ray."

"You can never be Big Ray," Maggie said. "Your dad's got priority."

"Got that right."

"What about Sugar Ray?" I said.[81]

---

[81] Sometimes you shouldn't blurt out the first thing that comes into your head.

"Quarter Ray's all right," the bouncer said, ignoring me.[82] "I don't have to explain. People just get it, 'oh, Quarter Ray.' Say it fast it sounds like *corduroy*. It's all right. It's all I've ever known. I'll also answer to Bill." The bouncer lowered his voice. A few more dudes were coming up. "Don't ask."

"Bill? Is that right?"

"Yeah. Not William. Not Billy. Not Billy Bob. Not Willy. Unless you want to get flipped. Bill. I'll respond to Bill. Everyone in my family's name is Bill—Bill Ray. We aren't famous for our names. You got a girl: that's Bill too. Billie Holiday. We don't have many girls in our family, one named Ray Ann—that's my cousin. We just call her Ray, not even Ann. Too feminine, I guess. Who'd want to date a girl named Ray Ann? 'Sup fellas," he said to the dudes.

"Nice to meet you Bill," I said.

"Or should we say Ray?" Maggie said.

The bouncer nodded, scanning an ID.

I was like "If you want to stay and talk. Don't mind me." But Maggie pulled a face.[83]

I followed her inside the lobby and over to the side where they had all these glass cabinets with playbills from past performances and black and white pictures of Patti Smith lookalikes and other CBGB acts in the spirit of this bar's particular raison d'être.[84] I could see Maggie wanted to detain me for a sec before we went back through the double doors with the blacked out windows, which every half minute or so emitted all the noise of that punk band they had playing in there, as well as the crowd noise and one or two hooligans yelping and catcalling.

---

[82] Thank God.

[83] She'd been giving me the stink eye ever since the cab ride over, when I mentioned her knees were kind of knobby (see note 81).

[84] Based on the CBGB rip off, I was pretty sure Olivia wouldn't like this place (see next note).

Maggie stopped pretending to look at the décor.[85] "Are you OK?" she said. "You're jumpy."

---

[85] It was tacky, for sure, and definitely inauthentic, though what is authentic anymore? On our second date, Olivia had gotten all high and mighty, on a soapbox, on this very same theme, only her focus had been the entire Lower East Side. She went on and on about how the place was so shabby chic, intentionally grungy, overrun with hipsters and yuppies and gentrifying scoundrels, who'd all but run out the bad element and reduced the genuine working-class population to a nexus of housing projects scattered along the banks of the East River, and don't for God's sake walk down Orchard Street without being bombarded by overcharging coat sellers with their honeycombed racks of leather and suede jackets[85A] and fashionista garments. Because only a tourist or an ignorant bumpkin wouldn't already know that the real deals were elsewhere, and all these so-called clothing stores were a front for middle class hacks posing as Puerto Ricans and Dominicans and perhaps one or two lone Yiddish speaking Jews, speaking of which the only good thing left was the pickles—*Crossing Delancey* had saved that industry no doubt—and the bialys at Kocer's Bialys, and perhaps the seasonal donuts available for purchase at Donut Plant, but even those gourmet donuts (a distant cousin of NYC's famous gourmet cupcakes which were all the rage throughout the early zeds) were losing their appeal as the beret wearing, David Byrne imitating, CBGB wannabe, butterfly and Chinese zodiac symbol-tattooed, just out of Yale mama's boys and squash-playing sorority girls, waving their trust fund money in the air like Barnum & Bailey clowns, making the rounds and whistling like so many Fred Astaire's out for a jaunt on these mean streets, *were* in effect raising the prices for everyone and more importantly annoying the shit out of Olivia and anyone who could tell what from what. We were more or less trekking aimlessly along Houston while Olivia ranted, passing Allen and the smoothie stand and that Thai place and One and One and Sugar's Cafe (also a sham, Olivia pointed

"What makes you say that?"

We edged out of the way, so the next wave of attendees could pass. Maggie stared at me, with a tough unflinching look, something she must have perfected on her daily commute into Manhattan: a look that said *I'm not to be fucked with* and is kind of your first, best defense against crazy people and religious fanatics and overzealous Rolex salesmen.

"Sorry," I said. "I don't want to hold you up. Were you looking for me?"

Maggie was like "I wasn't looking for you. I needed to rest my ears."

"What?"

---

out—very pricey) with their specials displayed on cellophane-wrapped plates and Katz's Deli like a beacon farther east. And so we'd gone up Avenue A in search of a dingy bar. I mentioned Holiday Cocktail Lounge on St. Mark's, which is a real pit, and definitely authentic in that its clientele are all certified drunks, but Olivia was too tired to walk that far.[85B]

[85A] She was still sore about her mom's jean jacket, which she'd inherited and slept in during cold weather for the nostalgia and her mother's scent.

[85B] We ended up at Doc Holliday's, maybe the most cartoonish establishment on the entire corridor, but at this point Olivia had concluded her proletarian rant (she mentioned the redeeming figure of Vladimir Lenin on top of some building on Essex).The night was getting cold; the special was a Genesee Cream Ale and a shot of Jim Beam. Olivia said she missed Savannah and how open and friendly everyone was, and I told her how my sister went to Savannah and came back with a huge clump of Spanish moss plastered to the ski rack on her car and some biologist or botanist working at Penn had said, "Pardon me, ma'am, but if you don't mind, I'm a botanist, and I would love to have a look at that specimen you seem to have acquired on your travels."

"Ha ha," she said, relaxing her eyes and brushing back the short part in her hair. "I'm not so young as you. If I'm going to sacrifice my hearing, it's not going to be for this kind of music."

"Whatever," I said, but she was smiling now. "Not a fan, then?"

"There was a time maybe. Now not so much."

"For real?"

"Maybe not so much punk rock,"[86] Maggie said. She sighed. She stepped in, and I realized again how short she was. "I dated a musician, though."

"In a band?" I had to yell now with the open door.

"Sort of," she said. She was smiling with that shy, embarrassed smile you'd expect of someone about to offer an intimate secret. "He played accordion or melodeon. We call it accordion. Yeah. He played in an Irish folk band. You might of heard of them.[87] Do you know Irish music?"

"Not particularly," I said. I was standing uncomfortably close to the cabinet windows; more people passed by. Maggie still looked unsure, like she hadn't made up her mind to trust me— though it was clear something was weighing on her—and then and there (call it tipsy insight) I realized that we could just walk back inside. If I said a few words along the lines of "hey, let me buy you a beer," in a firm enough voice or even like I was drunk and couldn't help being a boor, we'd just walk back inside the concert and lose ourselves in the crowd and the noise. Then whatever Maggie wanted to get off her chest would sink back, give way, and go dormant again, and in the end she'd even forget about it, and would it really matter? But I didn't want

---

[86] People who use the term "punk rock" generally aren't its biggest fans.

[87] The Rakes of Mellow, responsible for renditions of such classics as: "Ballyholey," "Killaloo," "The Old Settoo," "The Young May Moon," "Believe Me, Of All Those Endearing Young Charms," "Lovely Mary of the Shannon Side," "Kathleen Mauvourneen," etc.—I later learned.

that to happen. I shifted into a better position against the actual wall, on the corner of the glass display windows, and gave Maggie my attention. "Where'd you meet him?" I said.

Maggie was like "I don't want you judging me."

"What are you talking about?"

"Relax. We're friends," she said. "But, don't tell anyone. When I was eighteen, I dropped out of college. It's not something a lot of people know about me." She looked up as if expecting me to say something, then dropped her eyes and adjusted her purse and then just took the purse off her shoulder and held it like a clutch. "See, my suitemate Kimmy was boy crazy. I'd come home at night and she'd be sitting there in a cami, doing her sexy voice on the phone, and I could tell she just wanted me to clear out, she was ready to get down to business. Yeah, that kind of girl. During the day, she was all smiles and acted like a ditz, but I knew what she was really about. No Care Bears t-shirts or Lily Pultzer pants with macaws was going to cover that sleaziness. She wasn't even discreet—back in the dorm. I don't want to totally throw her under the bus."

I was like "No." I had a bad habit of predicting the ends of stories before I'd heard them, so I tried to keep an open mind and not jump to any conclusions, even if the whole Kimmy thing was an open door to all sorts of speculation.

Maggie was like "Whatever, you get the picture. She had some loser boyfriend going to UC Santa Barbara, who she was obsessed with. I mean, she acted like she was married to this kid. She wasn't interested in anyone we knew, not in the guys who'd call at all hours and ask me to take a message, which I'd never take. She only laughed at those guys anyway, sympathetically, like 'oh, too bad I'm married.' But I wanted to be like—'hey, aren't you interested in getting some now? I mean, sure, masturbation's fine and everything, but don't you miss the real thing?' Eh, who am I to give her advice? She was tiring herself out all night as it was, falling asleep on the couch, all wrapped up in a quilt her mom or aunt had made for her, which I never sat on by the way, who knows how often her naked ass[88] had been on there—it's absolutely fucking disgusting, but well college is college. A different world. I always wondered about girls who come into college in like a serious relationship—from what, high school? It's like, *really?* Do you really think you're old enough to be in a committed relationship? Isn't that what college is for? Finding out about yourself?"

"I'd agree with that," I said. If I'd taken my relationship experience from high school as a rough guide to male-female interaction, I'd be in pretty poor shape.[89]

Maggie's eyebrows were pinched together. She was like "Not my style at all. But Kimmy was one of *those* girls. I didn't really care for her, to tell you the truth. She was moody and depressing and, you know, all moaning about how much she missed her boyfriend (to deaf ears), unless Bryan—that's her boyfriend—called and then she'd be on the phone for like three hours, just sitting there, hanging on his every word, then dropping into the sex-a-thons again, with her blanket wrapped around her like a friggin' cocoon—and that was curtains for me. God knows no one else was using that phone—the landline in

---

[88] See note 7, e.g. the "large yellow couch."

[89] Though my memories of Cindy, my HS girlfriend, are fond and growing fonder all the time since people in the distant past, even the worst sorts of people, obvious manipulators, kleptomaniacs who would steal your parents' cutlery right from under their noses, liars, burgeoning psychopaths, all seem less malicious and more good-spirited, more salt of the earth, more stand-up, and more wholesome too—like the extended cast of some benign past generation's sitcom like *Taxi* or *Cheers* or *Welcome Back, Kotter*—the retrospection acting like a tonic on all of these past acquaintances, who might really have been detestable, arrogant, self-centered, egomaniacs, thus giving way to the common clichés "in my day, the people were just better, you knew where you stood" (though in these cases the clichés aren't even true and probably never were).

the dorm. Anyway, a couple months in, Kimmy started getting even more annoying. She'd linger. As in: linger at my door. Like a fixture. She was a chronic lingerer. I'd look up from my desk or something and she'd be standing there at my door, lingering, who knows how long. It was weird."

"We had a kid like that in school," I said. "I think his name was Charles."[90]

---

[90] In college, Anna and I used to get in fights about this same Charles—an acne-scarred blonde kid with a handle bar moustache of flaxen, translucent hair. I thought the moustache was unintentional (a result of not being able to cut close to the grain on his scabrous face) or, alternatively, a misguided attempt to cover up his pustulant skin. But Anna wasn't buying any of it. She wouldn't give this Charles guy any benefit of any doubt. She claimed he was a first class creep, probably one of those psychos who'd one day blow up Morse College (if he did it when no one was there, it wouldn't be a total loss), a wackjob school shooter type, a walking caricature of the ugly nerds one associates with Yale and the Ivy League in general. As far as the moustache went, Anna saw it as a weird attempt to channel like the Dukes of Hazard or Duane Allman. Putting all that aside, even if that was the extent of it, Charles eyed her provocatively whenever she was at the salad bar getting chickpeas—Anna hadn't wanted to tell me, but as her boyfriend I was duty-bound to put him in his place. In conclusion, as much as she felt sorry for him, some people dig their own pit and let them lie in it; they have no one but themselves to blame—and Anna would know— she herself had antisocial tendencies as a teenager; she'd recognized this fault in herself, gotten help and done something about it, problem solved, she hadn't clung to a corner, or buried her head in the sand, or retreated underground like a vole or a naked mole rat. I was like "But don't you think he could be shy?" "How should I know?" Anna said. "All I know is I don't want to sit with him." "Aw, come on," I told her. I'd made a point of joining Charles for a few meals, mostly just lunch and the

Maggie went "Yeah, well, I'm not saying it's unheard of, but this was my friggin' roommate so you can see the dilemma. She'd sneak up and not say anything, and totally startle me whenever I noticed her. Yeah, her eyes were looking like she hadn't slept in years. She thinned out too: no freshman fifteen for her. She was depressed. She needed fresh air. Despite all that, despite her personal problems, and her insomnia and whatever, she always thought she was better than me. She was always pitying me, to the degree it made me want to slap her. She was forever wanting to set me up. She'd be like 'I can totally set you up with Bryan's friend Cam. You'd be perfect.'[91] I'd be

---

occasional dinner, and the first few times, Anna sat with us too. But that didn't last. Eventually Anna drew the line—"him or me." After a week or so of watching all my friends join Anna and leave me at the table with Charles (who only responded to yes or no questions and even then had about the same grasp of social cues as the hapless primate in *Dunston Checks In*), I stopped eating with him too.

[91] Sure, I could see why this was annoying. The whole "lunch with Charles" fiasco reinforced the platitudinous truth that "you can't force friendship," you can't even force acquaintanceship, let alone romance. I learned later that Charles—at the same time I would sit with him, with the same attitude of smug self-satisfaction as the narrator in "Bartleby, the Scrivener"—was actively trying to befriend another circle of friends (whom I later housed with). According to one of them, one day Charles kept going on and on about an upcoming basketball game—Yale versus Dartmouth or Quinnipiac or something. They told him they weren't going, figuring Charles wouldn't be bold enough to attend the game on his own. So they went without him. About five minutes into the first half, Charles appeared by the side of their row of seats and went "Fancy seeing you here!" and walked off in a huff. I've always wondered why they thought Charles wouldn't go to the game alone. He went everywhere alone.

like, 'Thanks, but no thanks, dear.' It's like, I've got better things to do than date Bryan's friend Cam. And why is everything all about Bryan? I couldn't give two shits about Bryan. If you had any sense, you'd dump his ass and just move on. Fine, you're happy. Don't dump his ass. You're totally addicted to phone sex. I get it. Fine. Get your rocks off. Just don't wake me up, and don't leave a stain on the friggin' couch. Leave me the fuck alone. But, no, she'd be there, in her stupid Care Bears t-shirt, like she'd never grown up, just standing there, basking in connubial bliss, and like spilling over with that stupid happy grin, like the world is my oyster, la di da di da, and she just couldn't help but spread the love."

"Sorry, Mags," I said.

"I was a silent sufferer, through all of her little innuendoes and hints," Maggie said. "'Bryan's friend Willis. Bryan's friend Marshall. Bryan's friend Mitch. Bryan's friend Abe, who lives outside Boston.' No, thanks! A friend of Bryan is not a friend of mine. Let's just say it's my personal rule never to date anyone who knows Bryan—any Bryan. Fuck Bryan—no that's what she did on the phone. I was sick of Bryans. I felt like screaming, 'Fuck you and double Fuck Bryan!!' She wasn't getting it—I mean, each time the same dopey smile, the same stupid setting me up like I'm the one with problems because I don't have a sex addiction."

A real cute girl with a button nose just passed, presumably searching for the bathroom. She wore a sky blue track suit like an Argentinian soccer player on the sidelines—I had her pegged for an Argentinian for sure—but right then a clearly all-too-American loafer dude in hammer pants and the upper part of a tuxedo, including the vest, snuck up on her and grabbed her round the waist, and she was like "Rodney!" or something equally bizarre, I stopped paying attention (this whole episode was a blip, really, not above 20 seconds max) and now Maggie was scrutinizing me.

"Like what you see?" she said.

I dropped my eyes.

"Men," Maggie half-whispered. "What I was saying was one day, as a friggin' joke, I was just like 'Kimmy, I'm a lesbian.' I only wanted her to leave me alone. It wasn't even true. I'd gone to a Catholic high school, where the message was pretty much what you'd expect, but it was coed, I mean it wasn't single sex, and I had boyfriends and stuff. I never did anything, but that wasn't anyone's business. It wasn't like I was saving myself or something. I just found high school boys to be very... very immature and conceited and I wasn't going to waste my time. When I went to college—this was back in the dark ages compared to you—I thought all-girls would be better. I figured, to hell with all those boy crazy sluts from high school. I'm just going to work and focus and enjoy myself without all the pressure. I didn't need it. Plus, I needed to be somewhere away from my brothers, who were always looking out for me, and treating me like a baby. I mean, what boy was going to approach me with them around? I was like under lock and key, and college was where I was going to be free. Free on my terms. You know?"

I was like "Sure." I would've never dated a girl with four older brothers in high school.

"So when Kimmy started pestering me, appearing at my door anytime Bryan wasn't available for a quickie, I just had to think on my feet. 'Yes, I'm a lesbian,' I told her. So just leave me alone. I even made up some shit, like I hadn't come out yet, don't tell my parents, I was kind of embarrassed, but no, I wasn't interested in men, so let's drop all this boyfriend business."

"Maggie," I said. "You know... I don't know."

"It was a fucked up thing to say?" Maggie said. "Yeah. I know. I could tell I'd upset her, too. She got all quiet, and just stood there like someone having a hard time swallowing, and then she nodded and left. I mean, she was one of those girls who'd probably never met a real lesbian, and I think I scared her, since people like her think lesbians are boogeymen."

"What school was this again?" I said. But I knew what school it was, she'd mentioned it before.[92]

"Go fuck a tailpipe," Maggie said, loud enough for a couple others near us to look over. Maggie glared at them.[93] "It worked; at least she stopped bothering me, until sometime in November or so, when she knocked on my door—she wasn't being so sneaky anymore, which was a good thing—she came in all disheveled and then I found out she was stoned or drunk. She'd drunk like half a bottle of Southern Comfort which some idiot had left in our common room a few weeks ago, and we'd just forgotten about. It had turned into sort of a decoration on the mantel, and another of our suitemates had hung like a Freddy Kruger mask over it, for Halloween, so whatever. She'd drank it. It turned out this idiot Bryan had fucked someone else. It was bound to happen. I mean, the guy was three-thousand miles away, what did she expect? Was she really holding out hope for that tool? What made him different than any other guy in a similar situation? Wouldn't you have done the same thing?"

"Eeeeee-no," I said.[94]

Maggie wasn't buying it. She was like "Don't get all righteous on me. Of course you would've. And she should've known better, I would think. Anyone as horny as this Bryan guy—from the number of times he called for phone sex *alone*—was clearly not a celibate monk, and it's not like Kimmy was a stunner.

---

[92] If it wasn't Smith, my second guess was Wellesley. Third: Mt. Holyoke. Basically it just had to fulfill two factors: a) women's school, b) in Massachusetts.

[93] Confirmed. This blatantly hostile staring was definitely an effect of the booze.

[94] We always paint ourselves in a better light, of course. I went out with this girl Tammy Gao in college (and by "went out" I mean "slept with," see notes 97 and 185) just to get over Anna—not a very elegant motive. How much better is that than cheating on someone, anyway?

Don't get me wrong, she was pretty enough for Bryan,[95] but not like a knock out. So anyway, the inevitable had happened. Bryan had cheated on her, and they'd had a huge fight, and now she was like belligerently drunk ready to get out of control. I sat there, and reasoned, and tried to calm her down as best I could, but she was out of control. So I just figured the night was shot at this point—I wasn't going to get any of my own work done. I had a bottle of, like, cognac my brother had given me for a joke, since when would we ever drink that stuff, and I pulled it down and drank right from the bottle."

"How's that taste?" I said.

"Like shit," Maggie said. "But you had to be drunk to listen to Kimmy. I just wanted to keep her company, show some compassion, maybe teach her a little lesson about the Bryans of this world. So, I definitely drank too fast, and she had a few sips too, though her tolerance was low as shit, and I made sure she chased each of hers with a good cup of water, since I didn't want her puking in my room or passing out—and she was like crying it out, really bawling, like 'What am I telling you for? You don't even like guys! Did you ever like guys? No. You don't know. Can you? Or maybe you do know. I'm sorry. I'm being such a bitch. I'm jealous of you in a way. I wish I could survive without men.' That kind of thing."

I was distracted, sensing movement, a menacing but restrained presence like a snaggletooth shark swimming by in an aquarium while your back is turned, and right then the huge Samoan bouncer guy passed. He wasn't as tall as I'd expected from his slouched position on the stool, maybe five-eight tops. He acted like he didn't see us, all nonchalant, but I knew he saw me. I guess he'd been relieved from his post—he was headed for the bathroom.

---

[95] Kimmy had enough snapshots of Bryan adorning her walls (I'm assuming) for Maggie to see he wasn't exactly Robert Redford in his prime. Not even Shane West. Certainly no Brad Pitt or Colin Farrell.

Maggie didn't notice. She was like "Then she started hugging me, and we were both really drunk. I'll admit I had more than I should. I wasn't having water either, so I had an excuse at least; she was just a lightweight and probably she'd gotten dehydrated from all her crying. I just remember her hugging me and me saying it will be all right like her friggin' mom, which is what I was to her, pretty much. And then I blanked out. One of the only times that's ever happened to me—also embarrassing. The rest I don't remember so well."

Without realizing it, Maggie had moved so close that the tips of her shoes were touching mine.

"I really don't," she said, "and it pisses the shit out of me. Only, the next morning, we were waking up, and I realized we'd both stripped naked and somehow ended up in my bed. Now, I can assure you: nothing happened. I mean, yeah, the night was a blank, but I would've known if something had really happened. And it hadn't."

"I believe you."

Maggie didn't even acknowledge me—the force of her own convictions just steamrolled right over everything. "Some things you just know, even if you've passed out," she said, the heat back up in her voice. "So I just got up as fast as possible and showered and dressed, and by the time I got back Kimmy was just waking up, and that was that. I thought I'd just been a good friend, helping her out and everything, and I told her again, Bryan was a moron and she was better off. I don't remember her saying anything. So imagine my surprise, when the next week or so I started hearing stories about how I'd like seduced her or something to that effect, like I had taken advantage of poor Kimmy in her drunken state to put the moves on." Maggie's eyes were super-wide now like she still couldn't believe it. She was like "I confronted her—she was evasive, she wouldn't tell me one way or the other about who'd started the rumors. I asked her point blank if she thought something happened and she was like just shrugging, 'I don't know. All I know is I passed out, and the next thing, I'm in your bed without any clothes.' The way she said that just flat out killed me. I was like 'I'm not even a friggin' lesbian' and she was like 'Could've fooled me.'"

I was about to say something to the effect of 'see what comes from lying' but Maggie must've had that same thought because she went "I guess, looking back on it, it served me right. I didn't even talk to her after that. If that was how she was going to take it after listening to her unending complaints about long distance relationships and how hard it was to be away from Bryan for so long, and cry me a river. I totally had the wind knocked out of me. I couldn't friggin' believe it. I tried to ride it out, concentrate on school, but that wasn't a good strategy either because it made it seem like I really was guilty, like I'd really gotten her drunk on purpose or something—as if she wasn't drunk already off like a Dixie cup! While I was minding my own business and just concentrating on school, all my roommates and my circle of friends just concluded that I really was a lesbian and I really had taken advantage of Kimmy. It was so stupid, in retrospect, but it hurt me, getting all blown out of proportion. It got so around April I couldn't stand it. So I left. I finished the term and told them all I was leaving. I took off. I was glad too. It was one of the happiest days of my life, getting my shit out of there and not looking back. I was kind of disillusioned with the whole college thing anyway, even if I'd never met Kimmy."

I balanced my weight from one leg to the other.[96] Maggie's college story was causing a whole heap of memories and

---

[96] I (like the younger Maggie forced to listen to Kimmy's babble) was kind of craving a beer. The dude inside the double doors was selling the stock-in-trade PBRs at two bucks a pop out of a cooler, placed strategically at the back of the room— he'd been shaking this emptying cooler last time I saw him, maybe in an attempt to generate demand, you know, act like the supplies were dwindling, scarcity, simple economics, etc. Anyway, his strategy worked insofar as I was now pretty

fragments of memories to resurface in no discernible order: like the time we went to see our pal Desmond play Pontius Pilate in *Jesus Christ Superstar* and Anna, ignoring me, asked some evangelical dude named Peter to give her a condensed summary of the Gospels; the nights we spent on the gravelly top of the Art and Architecture building, looking down on the Jonathan Edwards courtyard, because one of our friends had a key; the mystique surrounding Jordana Brewster, who brought Derek Jeter to Toad's Place one Saturday night and stayed for a couple hours, just talking casually to people and not minding the attention of moony undergraduates; the life sized dinosaur I constructed for Professor Reed's Basic Drawing Class, which Desmond and Nick and some others outfitted with a disproportionately large penis, complete with Lifestyles condom; Tammy Gao as The Queen of the Night in *The Magic Flute*.[97]

Maggie was like "I don't include it on my résumé. Employers don't need to know about it. Although I'd have to say I'm better for it. Taking time off, that is."

---

concerned there wasn't going to be any PBR left by the time I got in there. I really believed he'd run out.

[97] Somehow, I'd always known, had a premonition, a foreknowledge, that I would sleep with Tammy. She'd been on the periphery of my group of friends for a while, ever since she went to the "Freshman Screw" with our pal Nick McClean and I went with him to pick her up at Bingham Hall on Old Campus, diagonally across from Durfee where we all lived. All the weird stories surrounding her only made her (Tammy) more intriguing the night I legitimately met her in Neat Lounge, sitting by herself—in and of itself a warning sign—since her other Trumbull friends had deserted her, though to be fair her friends were sort of sticks-in-the-mud and were probably already in bed, after having hung up their Ann Taylor cardigans with great care.

"I should've taken some time off," I said.[98]

"Why didn't you?"

"Forward momentum," I said. "Inertia. Who knows?"

Maggie was like "I had to do it. It was for my mental health. That's how I look at it, anyway. I moved to upstate New York, this little town, Wye. I got a job waitressing and later managing a little family restaurant, a good place. I wasn't making a lot, just enough to live on and pay for a loft above a garage, but it was quiet and clean and I started coming into my own, shedding some old personality traits and moving past some old grudges—I even forgave that idiot Kimmy."

I smiled, biting my lips. Inside, the band had paused and the lead singer/guitarist was mouthing some sort of spoken word poem that barely anyone could hear, and the crowd had started chanting that Die Antwoorp refrain "Your mom's suppus in a

---

[98] At the very least, I should have developed some maturity before I started dating Anna, my college girlfriend. Even now, I'll never forget how we argued, the fights we had, our stubborn resistance to each other's point of view—just like children. It almost seemed unreal how one night Anna and I debated for hours the nature of the resurrection and whether or not it would be a corporeal resurrection or a spiritual resurrection or whether, as Anna believed, there would be no resurrection at all, zilch, but rather a complete cessation of thought and feeling and a subsequent eternal darkness, which I couldn't accept and tried my best to refute, citing the rabbinical work of Elijah Ben Abuyah, the prophet Daniel and also Malachi, or whoever predicts the second-coming of Elijah, "Behold, I will send Elijah," etc., and offering as evidence the thorny reasoning that if God or Yahweh or the Un-nameable would deign to raise Elijah from the dead, wasn't it reasonable to assume that he might decide to raise other patriarchs and matriarchs of the Jewish line, and even perhaps, just maybe, ourselves? Arguing for the sake of arguing, is how I see it now.

fishpaste jah,"[99] or it sounded that way to me, and then the bassist played a bar or two and the guitar came in all splintery and in general the music had that silvery ambient quality epitomized by R.E.M.'s *Out of Time*.

"I met this guy James at one of the local bars there," Maggie was saying.

I was just foggy-brained enough to miss how she'd made the transition to whoever James was. So I refocused, leaning closer to her, and she leaned closer to me.

"Yo, Pennsylvania!" the bouncer shouted, strolling back down the hall.

I shook my head and he pumped his fist in the air. I was like "James?"

Maggie sighed. She was close enough for me to feel her breath, and she hadn't let the bouncer throw her off track (he'd sauntered back to the outer door). She was like "Yeah, he was playing one night. I'd gone in there a couple times—the Pig Blind or no—that's on 14th Street. The name's not important. They had live music every Friday, but I didn't think much of it. It's nice to just sit at a bar and not worry about getting hit on, just enjoy yourself and sit. You know? I didn't even see him right away, but then I heard him sing this song, this air, I guess, an Irish air[100]—he'd been playing accordion up till then, but he sang the song just singing, and I looked over and saw him, this older man, actually quite a bit older, but his voice was young and strong."

"Irish music is so sad,"[101] I said. "But pretty too."

---

[99] The rough translation "your mom's [unmentionables] in a fish paste jar."

[100] "By the Rising of the Moon," perhaps?

[101] As attested by the Rakes' B-sides: "Erin's Lost Hopes," "Has Sorrow Thy Young Days Shaded?," "You'll Soon Forget Kathleen," "When Cold in the Earth," "The Times I've Lost in Wooing," "O! Dear What Can The Matter Be?," "Sweet and Sad", "Mary's Lament," "Mrs. Holden's Lament," "The Sorrowful

Maggie was like "We got to talking, just in a friendly way, and he told me he was playing at another place the next night, would I be interested in seeing the show, since he was going to have a full band for this one. I couldn't make it up to see him—I was working. We exchanged numbers and he called me a week later. He was fifty-five—I know, you're thinking that's gross. No judging."

"I'm not." The music was muffled again. It was almost like we were by ourselves in the lobby.

"It's OK," Maggie said. "I'd be judging too. I can't believe I'm telling you this. You're sworn to secrecy. Hey. It's not like we just started sleeping together. We spent time together. He[102]

Lamentation of Thomas Hayes," "Billy O'Sullivan's Lament," "Nora Nolan's Lament," and so on.

[102] This Irish accordionist guy—by all accounts an affable fellow—had a house right near Poughkeepsie, which he rented out most of the year except summer, the only season where you don't have to wear a bison-hair parka lined with foxskin to retrieve the morning paper from the end of the driveway. But now that James was reaching a mellower time of life, he was ready to settle down and just stay in one place. No more rolling stone, here today gone tomorrow, traveling band, hang my weary head lifestyle. Just a quiet nook by an old growth forest, with moose and bears for company, and Maggie curled up beside him, on the couch, warming their hands on shared mugs of black tea cut with lemon. Simple pleasures: like thick toast and an old worn paperback copy of *Tropic of Cancer*. No more of the rat race, the young bucks were welcome to it. Not only that, a music friend of James' had already mentioned the possibility of teaching part time at a music school for developmentally disabled kids. As the years went by James was leaning more and more toward taking that job, reclaiming his house, and just living there like any old guy. So Maggie and him moved there, in the spring, the year after they met, and that's where she lived for around two years during her whole hiatus from college—a

was staying in the next town over, and played gigs that hardly paid, to be close by, and we got to know each other."

"And your parents... " I said.

Maggie was like "They sent my brother Andy up to check things out. I was able to account for myself well enough, I guess. Either way, I didn't hear much from them. They were freaking out the whole time, I'm sure—at least, my mom was—and I'm sure Father Thad had to hear the same weeping shit every Wednesday at confession about 'where did I go wrong with that child, oh please I hope she hasn't made an irreparable mistake and on and on and on'—but I guess they reconciled themselves to the idea that I just needed a little time, and that everyone goes through these 'phases' where you just have to sort things out and come to grips with your life, and that maybe it was better I was doing this now, while I was young and resilient, and they shouldn't force me to return to school—it didn't have to be the same school, my mom made that perfectly clear—since that kid from my high school had only recently killed himself apparently for no reason at all, except depression exacerbated by gloomy-ass New England weather."[103]

Maggie crossed her right leg in front of her left and put her purse back on. She was like "Once they saw I wasn't going to kill myself, they gave me a little slack, just enough freedom to sort things out. They sent my brother up like three times that whole period. I guess they thought Andy was the hardass of the family since he'd married that psychiatrist, and was a broker himself, who'd basically memorized whole sections of the friggin' tax code—plus when we were little Andy was always first to complain if anyone cheated or broke the rules in any game. No one was going to rob the banker in Monopoly under Andy's watch. But they didn't know Andy anymore. He'd grown out of that hardass stuff—he was out there getting drunk with us the

---

hiatus which her parents more or less took in stride, though without loving it.

[103] See note 72.

first night. He was like 'Maggie. James is a hell of a guy.' Though too, James was Catholic, on the right side. That might have sweetened things for my mom, if we had gotten serious. Though I can't imagine her being too thrilled about the age difference: Andy left that out."

"But you didn't stay together?" I said.

Maggie shook her head. She was facing the glass cabinets behind me and I was staring at the door and the edge of the stool with the bouncer and some tall guys who'd just stepped in and were arguing.

"What happened?"

"I grew up," Maggie said. "No, it's not like that. I don't mean to come across so condescending. It's not like I have anything against that lifestyle. I was pretty much a hippie.[104] As much a hippie as I'll ever be since some phases of your life just aren't coming back. I was basically eating, drinking, and screwing.[105] Oh yes, I worked. I made jack shit. I wouldn't have been able to support myself. I didn't mind. It was good while it lasted, even though it couldn't have lasted. I just needed to be centered. To feel centered. You don't have to travel to friggin' Nepal to have

---

[104] Since my impression of hippies was invariably compounded with dirndls, peasant shirts (modern hippies have moved on from the tie-dyed apparel of yesteryear), a profusion of body hair, preference for homebaked wholegrain bread, coffee grinders, yak milk, along with a pseudo-zen-like-cofabulation-of-Chinese-mystical-culture-as-manifested-most-prominently-by-the-anti-Confucian-Zhuangzi, and a sort of perpetually stoned appearance behind aviator glasses or large store-bought frames with the lenses removed, and don't forget untreated woolen thermal underwear, Maggie's recollection of hippie life was a welcome surprise.

[105] I had to take this as Maggie's most aggressive flirtation yet, though it's hard to imagine how the image of her screwing another man (older or not) would be a total turn-on.

a transcendental experience. I sound like a friggin' dipshit. Do you understand? Please tell me I'm not rambling."

I told her she wasn't rambling.

"You're such a fucking liar," Maggie said, still nostalgic. "You wouldn't have recognized me back then," she said. "Maybe I even did sing once or twice, but not for an audience—no friggin' way." Maggie, suddenly carried back, went "We'd sit out on the porch, and he'd play and he'd always try and get me to sing. I'd be like 'Have you heard a dying cat? That's what I sound like.' He was persistent, I'll give him that much, but that's one of my golden rules: never sing. People with bad voices should just reconcile themselves to silence. I cooked. I learned how to cook, I should say. I met some cool people. It was like we were operating a bed and breakfast. Everyone James knew from back home was always welcome and then there'd be various musicians and band friends passing through and everyone'd get drunk and we'd wake up all tight-eyed and stunned and yet those were the best hangovers of my whole friggin' life. I actually miss those hangovers. I don't remember ever being physically incapacitated. And I had my hair down to here," Maggie indicated below her waist. "You've seen my driver's license—I had long hair then too, but not long like it was back then."

She'd shown me her driver's license on I don't know how many occasions since bartenders still carded her every now and again (especially in my company), and anyway she kept it in the front pouch of her wallet where it was visible at all times. She was about due for a new ID, hers was approaching ten years, and the woman in the photo looked like a different person, though it was hard to pinpoint exactly how she'd changed. She was so proud of that picture. Yes, everyone has their vanities.

I was like "Sounds idyllic enough. The town you were at."

"Idyllic, not realistic," Maggie said. "I mean, not realistic for me. The thing was: James had already lived his life. I'm not saying he was on death's door. But he'd lived thirty more years than me. He'd gone out and achieved something, on his own, without help. He was already comfortable, pretty much retired. He could've retired if he wanted. I think that's what I took and admired most about him. The scope of his life. He'd already lived it, and if I stayed with him, I'd have experienced the best parts of him, none of the drama, none of the 'I hate my job.' So then, knowing me, I started comparing myself to him and that's when I realized I needed more out of life. I mean, I'd dropped out of college, I was only nineteen. I hadn't even lived at all, really. I was a kid. In the back of my mind, I always thought I'd do something more than just be someone's wife. I never wanted to define myself that way, like that was my end goal. That's not what I wanted for myself and that's why it had to end."

"Do you talk to him still?" I said.

Maggie nodded but it was that strange sort of nod that actually means the opposite of yes. "I used to, but not anymore. We'd be like strangers now. That was over ten years ago—a long time. Am I really boring you and you're just being polite?"

I'd been flipping the pin on this button a girl in the lobby had given us that said: "i was recorded live at trash bar" and which instead of wearing, I'd put (safety pin side outward) in my pocket, without thinking much of it.[106]

"Not at all," I said.

"Pushover," Maggie said. "You'd say anything I want to hear."

"Not true," I said. "How're your ears now? Ready to damage them again?"

Maggie folded her arms. "Do we have to go in there?" she said. She slouched her hip and unfolded her arms in a dramatic

---

[106] I too have my nervous tics, keeping my hands busy drawing invisible shapes with my index finger. With Olivia, I'd always draw a star on her leg, over and over, when we were sitting side by side on the subway, or I'd mix it up and draw the letter "O" for her name, or "I" for mine. I'd asked her if it bothered her and she was like "No. Only if it's marking me. I don't want to be marked."

gesture like she was shooing chickens. "Go. I'm boring the pants off you. I hope they'll have another band next."

"I kind of like this one," I said, pushing off from the wall where I'd been leaning.

Maggie was like "*You* would. There's no accounting for taste."

Back inside, our voices got swallowed up and each breath was an amalgamation of sweat and spilled alcohol. I couldn't see Sean and Preston right away. The crowd had redistributed toward the back of the room—all except for a group of Swedish or Norwegian or Danish kids who smiled and radiated a banya-like freshness, their cheeks dimpled, their cowlicks set so exactly, it was like they'd been computer generated by Pixar. Toward the middle of the floor this Rastafarian dude had dropped to a squat and was performing a combination of Riverdance and breakdancing moves. The crowd closed around him and the guys started clapping and hooting, while a few girls looked anxiously at an olive-skinned chick in hot pants and an oversized batik tanktop with a tie-dyed replica of Belinda Carlisle who appeared on the verge of joining this rollicking performance, until the music slowed. The band was soloing—I don't know how impressively from a technical standpoint—but the net effect was an exodus toward the beer cooler. My man, the beer dude, was still in position with a renewed supply of hipster beer and a slapdash line had formed around his table, which was set up beside the full bar that occupied the left-hand-side of the room—that's where Preston had picked up the Long Island iced tea he'd been hankering after.

"You want anything?" I said to Maggie. I had to repeat myself.

"No," her mouth said. "What are you getting?" She said something else—it might have been "yes" but the "no" had been clearer. I found a place in line and felt for my wallet.

I was like "You see them?" Only now Maggie was out of range; I had to find them on my own.

I got my beer and stuffed my change in my pocket and then sipped and scanned the room, stepping out of people's way, until I could spot wherever they'd gone. A bottleneck had formed by the cooler, and standing there was uncomfortable, like I was being strip-searched so I squeezed back toward the door, holding my hands in a beer-cradling triangle in front of me, edging out of the crowd. I took a short breather at the door, checked my phone. No messages, no missed calls, and it was nearing eleven. I'd wait ten more minutes and then call Olivia—that was a comfortable amount of time. The only thing was, my self-control was at an all-time low, and Maggie's story had triggered all kinds of soft feelings for the early days of me and Olivia, for the Olivia who'd encouraged me to draw those Max Beckmann inspired crayon drawings, the Olivia who'd tied an orange bandana around my head and burst out laughing, showing her stained front teeth, saying "You look like a German boy scout."[107]

---

[107] At Doc Holliday's (note 85B), she passed me all her Jim Beam shots, and—with the likes of "I Love the Rainy Nights" and "A Thousand Miles From Somewhere" playing on the jukebox—we took possession of an empty booth where I immediately set the mood by sitting on an empty condom wrapper, which just added to the ambience. Before long, I had my hand on Olivia's thigh and we were kissing, our faces pressed together, mouths working frantically, on the same side of the booth now, and after a while Olivia got her breath and went "You almost make me shy." She got up and started dancing to a Patsy Cline song, but I held my ground and only joined her when this Texas cowboy ambled over and performed a two-step behind her back, leering forward as if to twirl her. Then I was up and leading Olivia away, and she was giggling, and we kissed like giddy seventh graders by the restroom, both of us laughing for no reason, the laughter dispelling in kissing, and I was like "Come on." We didn't even know it was raining until we were all the way down Avenue A to Nice Guy Eddie's and then a busted gutter sent water tumbling down my shirt, which was damp enough already, and I grabbed Olivia by the hand and said "Come on!" above the noise of many cars' wheels

zipping across the sodden road. We walked all the way down Houston, passing 1st Avenue and Forsyth and 2nd Avenue and Whole Foods, leaving the tree cover to cross the Bowery, down past the garishly lit Italian place on the corner, to the remains of CBGB and the unlit brick building where the homeless had all been turned away, onto Spring, then the two blocks to my shared apartment—the place with Rebecca and Lizzie—up the six flights of stairs and into the always warm kitchen and my own room and my bed which barely fit inside. Only then did I inform Olivia that I had no condoms. "That's all right," she said. "You don't look like the kind who'd give me a disease." The next morning, we both tasted like onions—nothing stale or rotten, just onions, like sautéed onions that had cooled overnight, maybe not the most appetizing flavor in the world but compared to what our mouths and tongues could taste like not so bad. "You taste like onions," I said. "You taste like onions," Olivia said. "Kiss me then," I said. "We both taste like onions." "I wonder why," I said a minute later. "I don't remember having any onions." "Shh," Olivia said. "Stop talking." And after hooking up again, Olivia noticed my window faced another building's window, and she went "We gave them quite a show," and I went "Pfft—no one's looking" and kissed her some more until she pulled away, sitting lotus position, her breasts totally disappearing as she pulled herself up, the skin on her back still indented with crenulations from the bedsheets. "Yuck," Olivia said, examining her socks. "Second day socks. They're the worst." I walked her out. By the door, we passed Rebecca's full length mirror which gave us back our warped reflections overlaid on a sheen of dust: tired eyes, cracked lips, Olivia's staticy hair, a goodbye smile. I kissed her as she stepped out. "Call me," she said, pulling the neckline of my shirt into a ball and holding on, reaching up to me. And for two weeks—maybe three—we lived in total domestic tranquility, not leaving our rooms, my brain at all times buzzing with the limbic equivalent of "she's so lovely⋯ she's so lovely⋯ she's so lovely."

I backed up to an unoccupied part of the wall and called her—telling myself not to be so second-guessing, it would all work out. Olivia answered on the third ring. She was distant, but she was there.

"Hey, Liv," I said, putting too much space between the words.

"Ian? Where are you?"

I realized she couldn't hear me, and I was shouting, straining my voice against an overpowering vector of sound. I was like "Out. Did you finish?"

"I told you I'd call," she said.

I was like "Did you? Anyway, I'm calling you." I meant it to be cute, but "cute" was never a quality I'd pulled off. I immediately regretted the impulse to be cute. She was too far away to hear any cuteness anyway. "Hello? Liv?"

"Are you drunk?" Olivia said, and now it was as if her voice was magnified, like it was emanating from my own head rather than the phone, or like I had a speaker embedded in my ear for Olivia to talk through, a conduit to Olivia, two or three Olivias at the same time. I couldn't make out any background noise on her end.

"Where are you?" I said.

She went "I do want to talk to you, Ian." At least, that's what I thought she said. "Call me back in an hour. OK?"

"Yeah, OK," I said. I didn't know if she heard me, I wasn't screaming anymore. I was about ready to shotgun a beer and to hell with everything. One thing for sure: I wasn't going to call her back in an hour—that was out of the question now.[108]

"OK," Olivia said. "Goodbye."

I didn't even close the phone. She was already gone.

I found Sean and Preston without any trouble. I actually found Maggie first, standing with her back in my direction, off in a darker section of the room, behind the crowd. She was

---

[108] It was better to chant some kind of Olivia-obliterating mantra.

making a tentative effort to dance, though not with Sean and definitely not with Preston.

"Howdy," Preston said when I got close. I gripped him by the shoulder, way more familiarly than usual, and he grinned.

Sean was opening another beer. "Sorry," he said. "This was supposed to be for you, Ian, but hey. You disappeared."

"No worries," I said.

He must have already given Maggie a beer. She was holding it to her stomach, like she was afraid of spilling. "I'm not going to drink this," she whispered to me.

Preston was now flanking me. "How's the iced tea?" I said.

"You mean the horse tranquilizer?" he said. "It's good, man. Goes down smooth." He leaned backward in a stance almost as flamboyant as a matador. He still had more than half the stuff left, and it didn't look all that diluted either, the brown rum swooshing around in there.

Now the keyboardist (tucked away on stage left, beside one of the colossal coffin-sized amplifiers, and behind a triple-deck table with a bunch of flashing lights like a humungous switchboard) went in for a major solo, playing some funky riff with a stop-start halting syncopation that sounded either unrehearsed, or like a bad parody of Thelonious Monk, not at all in keeping with the rest of the band's high octane punk sensibilities, though the lead singer bobbed her head in fierce encouragement.

"Did you know Preston's a certified diver?" Sean said.

"Not quite certified," Preston corrected.

"He's going to be a dive master," Sean said.

"That's right," Preston said. "I just need to log about twenty more dives."

I was like "Wow. That's great Preston."

"That is great," Sean said. "Wouldn't it be great to be a master of something?"

Preston was like "It's just what it's called. It's not like I get superpowers or nothing."

"But you could if you wanted?" Sean said.

"Hell yeah," Preston said.

"It's like you're a sensei."

"Exactly," Preston said.

"Have you ever gone diving in the East River?" I said.[109]

Preston was like "Hell, no. Florida. Man, I wish I was there, they've been working me like a pack mule, no lie, but that's all right. The way it works," Preston said, "you can log dives at any location so long as they've got the certification and all. What I'd really love is to get back to Belize." He shook his head. He must've been taking some enormous sips because his drink was down to the ice from about three-quarter level not five minutes before. "One of these days." He exchanged a significant look with Sean.[110] "Yessir," he said. "I'll get back just as soon as I've saved my money."

---

[109] In my present state-of-mind, I'd "misremembed" (as Roger Clemens says) that the NYC Triathlon routed swimmers through the Hudson River, way up on the West Side. Either way, swim at your own peril. In Philadelphia, you needed like Black Death vaccination if you fell in the Schuylkill River, and I'd heard about some foolhardy American who'd contracted diseases scientists thought had died out or were only preserved in maximum security research facilities by people in Hazmat suits, all because he "fell" into the Grand Canal in Venice.

[110] Preston had been telling Sean some wild story about his pre-marriage years in Belize—where he'd ended up in the course of some rite-of-passage, south-of-Mexico-tour, with his good buddy Rick, who was more or less Preston's sidekick when it came to making bad decisions—and the story had just gotten "interesting," to use Sean's word, when Maggie had come back, and he'd been forced to cut it short. Ironically, or at least oddly, Preston had also gone to Belize on his honeymoon—reliving bachelor days?—though without Rick in attendance on that occasion.

"They got good diving in Belize?"[111] I asked.

"Yup, you bet." And Preston went on to enumerate all the key features of the Belizean coast. Features such as: Spanish

---

[111] Preston's Belize infatuation was in line with the well-worn path pioneered by Jimmy Buffett, Kenny Chesney, Alan Jackson et al.—that is, a sort of midlife retirement into tropical terrain, where flip flops, board shorts, and Hawaiian shirts are standard attire (or not), and there's always need for an extra bassist or drummer or cymbal or bongo/conga player in some ragtag expat band crooning R&B oldies and classic country at a beachfront bar catering to American tourists.[111A] Truth be told, Preston had already incorporated a tropical style into his wardrobe. He'd worn a Hawaiian shirt (similar to the one he had on tonight) at our last annual Xmas party; this was the night Preston stashed about seven Amstel Lights in a bucket under our table, which was a totally unnecessary maneuver since hardly anyone else was drinking. Our conversation—at the Xmas party—didn't touch on diving. Instead, Preston recounted a hunting trip he'd taken in his younger years, where unfortunately his parents ran over a full-grown bull deer, which scraped and got flayed underneath their van, so that the entire vehicle stunk like rotting deer carcass for the next month despite repeated attempts to wash it and even have the van raised and pressure-washed.

[111A] Like it or not, American tourists have set the standard for what music gets played at such resort-style places, and since Americans typically have rather sentimental (some might say cheesy) tastes when it comes to music, most of us Americans associate vacation with an easy-listening soundtrack somewhat along the lines of the CD Preston made for Maggie (though maybe with even less overt mentions of "love" or "long-term relationships" and more of an emphasis on "casual sex" or mutually fulfilling "one night stands" which is a message most Americans are happy to hear both in and out of their workaday lives. "Sloppy Seconds" or "Let's Do It Like Medieval Times" would fit the bill).

galleons just ripe for the picking, booty and treasure galore, optimal diving conditions off a shoreline girdled by masses of seaweed which had deterred some of the most intrepid dive masters and hid who knows what undiscovered gems, not to mention the obvious perk: the absence or near absence of man-eating sharks and barracudas, which according to Preston are known to "play nice" and then bite you in the rear end out of spite, though an occasional lion fish might emerge from some rocky cove, and jellyfish sometimes hitch a ride on your calves—you have to be careful when you remove the tentacles—and, yes, well, there's sea snakes, but they're totally harmless and even rather shy at heart, not everyone knows that. Preston had clearly done his research and he'd drank his share of Belizean beer, both Belikin and Lighthouse, the former of which he claimed was a "light" black and tan, and came in a glass built to withstand the sultry coastal winds, a typical twelve ouncer weighing as much as an American wine bottle, with a concentration of tempered glass along the base of the bottle about two centimeters thick. "It's been built up a lot since I been there," Preston said. "That's what I hear anyway."

"People," Sean said. "They screw up everything."

"Can't stop progress," Preston said, holding up his glass and clinking the ice. "My my my... "

He would have said more but Maggie was pressing on my other side, and we just watched the band. Despite what Maggie had said, they weren't half bad. The lead singer/guitarist/spokesperson was a slender brunette chick with slanty, apathetic kind of dazed eyes. She played her guitar all cool and distorted, pumping a wah-wah pedal, and sang in a bluesy growl not unlike Judy Garland[112] after she'd wrecked her

---

[112] The only time I distinctly remember hearing Judy Garland (excluding *The Wizard of Oz*) was at the after party for Nick Amante's reading. As I said before, I hadn't really wanted to go, the reading gave me more than my fill of Amante, enough for a lifetime really. But my roommate Rebecca said she didn't have

anyone to go with, and I should be more social, I shouldn't just hang around our cramped apartment feeling blue and watching the WB. If that wasn't enough, she'd keep me company. She neglected to mention that she knew half the crowd. She was whisked away into one of the private bedrooms not three minutes into the event, and it was only half an hour later when the door to this bedroom opened, letting out an odor of cloves and cinnamon and chocolate covered espresso beans, as well as Judy Garland's sultry voice. "Who's this, Tony Bennett?" I said to the short-haired pixie-faced girl who was splayed out on the bed hitting on a doobie and simultaneously eating a piece of pumpkin pie bare-handed. She was like "Come over here so I can punch you," not even joking. "Katie, that's Ian," Rebecca said, in her typically offhand way, without looking up from a stack of Polaroids on the floor, every now and then commenting "Get rid of this one. Are my teeth that yellow? What's going on with my ass in this picture?" The night wasn't a total waste, though. I wandered over to the living room couches—they had arranged them in an "L" shape, enough space for four people to sleep comfortably toe-to-head—and plopped down next to some Gothic theater girl with dark eyes and a pinched nose. We got to talking, and I discovered she was originally from Iowa City, had come to NYC like every "poser and pretender" to make a name for herself as an actor, hanging around NYU and auditioning for minor parts she looked up in *Theatre Space*, and for the time being was making ends meet by working at a pharmacy on Thompson Street. I was still torn up over Olivia, and in a way, I considered this girl a kind of oracle, especially since she'd voluntarily removed herself from the crowd and was sitting enthroned, as it were, on several couch cushions in the dark half of the room, near the fire escape, where a couple knuckleheads had thrown open the windows so they could take their smoke breaks unimpeded; this girl's oracle-ness also gained some traction because of her sleek black dress and the oddity of her not wearing any shoes (this in spite of the fact that she apparently had Raynaud's syndrome, which turned her hands

voice on booze and cigarettes. The rest of the band didn't interest me in the least, and they didn't seem quite up to par, coming off as stiff and disjointed whenever their front woman leaned down and flirted with this tall unshaven dude in the front row, totally neglecting the music and bending at an angle

---

and feet to icicles even in milder weather), and wore no makeup or jewelry at all except for an extravagant Cleopatra-style necklace with topaz balls as gaudy as the gems adorning Miss Cleo, late-night psychic. Considering my own state of mind, and the almost ambivalent way this girl responded to all my initial observations, I made a point not to flirt with her, in fact to write her off, and, in a brotherly way or rather like a supplicant addressing an oracle, I bunglingly asked her if she wouldn't mind telling me what exactly it was—deep down—that women wanted from men. She must have been impressed by my honesty, or maybe found me endearing, or pathetic in the most positive sense of the word, because she didn't make a joke of it, as many people—Mags, Rebecca Fershleiser, even Anna— would've done, living as we do in an age of cynicism and ennui, but instead said, after a moment's reflection, which was in keeping with her oracular dignity, "All women want a Prince Charming. Someone who'll worship the ground they walk on." She said some other stuff too, but that's what stuck with me. Of course, I can see now that her answer is an oversimplification, maybe even an out-and-out lie, certainly not the type of thing a feminist would say, or even an academic for that matter, or practically anyone who is in their right senses, but on that night, at that weird time of my life, I took her answer to heart and seriously wondered if everything really could be that simple. I should add that the next thing this girl, whose name I think was Charmaine but don't quote me on that, said was "But when I see my friends kissing the ground for men who don't give a shit, I want to castrate them." Sort of dashes the romantic mood a tad.

that displayed a ladybug or maybe a Beetlejuice tattoo over her right breast.

I could tell where Preston's eyes had zeroed in, because pretty soon he whispered "Ain't she sweet?"

Maggie leaned into my other ear and was like "Tattoos always make a person look sleazy."

I sort of nodded to both these comments, not wanting to get pulled into any aesthetic debate over body art, and we went on standing there, while the bassist fumbled around and the drummer lapsed into repetitive thumping in march-time.

Maggie was pressing all against me, a little closer each time. Every time I edged away, I felt the fabric of her blouse brushing my arm with a static-cling effect, like the way a balloon feels when you hold it a half-inch away from your skin. The band went right into "Your Face In My Mirror" without any commentary or anything.

"I like this a lot better," Maggie said.

I nodded. The crowd was really swaying now; this was maybe the most danceable song they'd played. At the end of it, as the singer's voice broke up in the echo, they transitioned into Bryan Adams's "Heaven."[113]

I was like "I always like when these punk bands play this stuff."

"You mean when they sell out?" Sean said.

"Hey," Preston said. "Everyone's got to eat."

"You think these people really support themselves playing music?" Maggie said. "No friggin' way."

She'd started dancing for real now, side to side, her hand without the beer open and raised (it kind of looked like she was testifying). Sean waved at me, as if encouraging me to dance with her, and I shook my head. Preston's face had gone weirdly vacant but in a second he turned toward us and went "Dude, is that your brother?" He tilted his chin at the tall barely shaven,

---

[113] By any measure, the Talking Heads' "Heaven" would've made a better choice.

Calvin Klein v-neck undershirt and tight jean wearing guy chatting with the guitarist.

"No," I said. "You know, that looks a lot like the dude I was telling you about."

Sean was like "You're going to have to be more specific."

"Nick Amante,"[114] I said.

"He looks just like you," Preston said.

I was like "Give me a little credit."

"He doesn't look like you," Maggie said, her hand sweeping against my elbow.[115]

"Thanks, Mags."

Sean was like "Him? That's what's his name? Ama... amaretti?"

"Amante."

"Amante," Sean said. "For real?"

I was like "Positive."

Preston scrutinized Amante's general direction and brushed his forehead with the condensation from his glass. "Refill time," he said.

"Get me one!" I called. I wasn't even halfway done my can.

Sean was like "Make it two."

Preston didn't even break stride.

"Hey, I'll pay you back! You hear?"

"Yeah, yeah," Preston said, waving his hand as perfunctorily as Queen Elizabeth II or I.

"Do you think he's doing an article on the band?" Sean said.

"How should I know?"

"He'll probably be doing the guitarist, later."

---

[114] Yes, it had to be him (though the light wasn't all that great): the writer of *Inferno*, in the flesh.

[115] Regrettably, Nick Amante is only the latest in a long line of shadow-versions of myself, who've haunted me and popped out of the woodwork for much of my life, from my early teens. See the beginning of note 3A.

The mere thought of that pissed me off. For the last few minutes the band had meandered through some really shaky Mazzy Star rip-off, while the lead singer—who we all knew as Jenna[116]—laughed *sotto voce* with Nick Amante and two of his friends.

Maggie touched my arm again. "Why are we whispering?"

I was like "Me? I'm not."

"What is that guy?"

Sean was like "Him? He's a writer."

Maggie's view was somewhat obscured by Jenna, who'd hopped off the stage and was now sloppy kissing Amante, her hands laced behind his head, pulling him toward her, her hair swooping around them, swaying to some song way slower than the band's.

"Get a room," Maggie said.

"He can't afford it. He's a *real* writer,"[117] Sean said. "Tell me the name of his book, again? I know you mentioned it."

---

[116] She'd introduced herself during one of her soliloquies while the band was jamming.

[117] No, it's not just defensiveness or me being jealous of his book (which is out of print by the way, if I didn't say so before, though Amazon.com is selling them for 1 cent). No. I disliked him because of his ubiquitous presence in those bleak years of my life. See, Amante was always popping up in unforeseen locations, at weird hours, in the dead of night, etc., which was part of the reason I couldn't get him out of my head, notwithstanding *Inferno* and the shorter pieces I'd read by him. I mean, it wouldn't be unfair to say that he was *following* me, or at least appeared to be dogging my heels like some hobgoblin or sprite or wraith. He was originally from New Jersey, but he'd moved to New York around the same time as me—another unfortunate coincidence—and thereafter I'd spot him now and again, while I was just going about my business without a care in the world for Amante or any of his literary efforts. I'd usually see him first, loitering across the street, or hurrying to make it to

---

a bar in Midtown or failing to catch a cab and hiding his disappointment in a flurry of hand gestures and muffled cursing. Sometimes, I'd catch a glimpse of him behind me, in a window, or maybe I'd just feel him there, the way we're evolutionarily equipped to sense danger or predatory animals, and I'd deliberately cross the street, or enter some behemoth office building's foyer where the security guard would give me the evil eye and wonder what someone with a shirt as unpressed as mine could possibly be up to anyway, and I'd watch Amante walk past: sure, he'd play it off like he *wasn't* following me. The whole thing was deeply upsetting, and hard to talk about. It's not like I wanted to think about him. It's not like I didn't have my own concerns and life to live, apart from Amante sightings. Didn't he have a job anyway? I'd grow accustomed to not seeing him; a whole week would pass and I'd be free of him. I'd say to myself: "What are the chances I'll run into *him* again, eh?" only to have him appear, as if on cue, sometimes three times a day, on the other side of Canal Street, or buying a cannoli at Ferrarra in Little Italy, or wearing a beret and reading Baudelaire at Café Citron across from Old St. Patrick's Cathedral on Mott Street when 5 o'clock mass let out, or paying for a colorful sweater from Uniqlo (his clothes were unusually tight). He kept appearing; I kept running into him; and as the coincidences mounted, I started believing he was somehow heaven-sent, or providential, or more than mere man. There had to be some grand design to the whole thing; and that's what pissed me off. Some people see visions of beautiful women—Laura, Beatrice, The Woman in White, etc.—I saw Amante. Naturally, this is somewhat of an exaggeration, I didn't like see the guy all the time, that would be ridiculous and (if true) frightening and perhaps psychotic, evidence of some sort of mental instability on my part; no, it's just that when I did spot him lounging here or there it was like he was rubbing something in my face. He was rubbing something in my face every time—unintentionally or not—like we had unfinished business or accounts to settle. And, you know, I never really knew him.

"*Inferno*," I said. "Didn't I loan you it?"

"I'm sorry, boss," Sean said. "I've got a stack of books I'm behind on, yay high."

"I think you can read it in a single sitting," I said.

"Wow. That's some hard core kissing," Maggie said. "I can feel my dinner coming back up."

Sean was like "From where I'm standing, I'm a little jealous."

"Oh please," Maggie said. "Is this junior high?"

"The book," Sean said. "I'm jealous of the book. The guitarist? Eh."

"Shouldn't quit her day job," Maggie said. "And when were your standards so high?"

"Since never," Sean said. "But I have a rule: no musicians."

I busied myself finishing my beer to avoid Maggie's eyes.

"Can I ask why?" she said.

"No money in it."

Maggie almost snorted. "You're friggin' nuts."

"Haven't I told you my plan?" Sean said. "Marry rich."

"That's some plan. Very detailed. Did you come up with it just now?"

The house lights went on, illuminating the velourish red curtains gathered along the right-side wall, closest to us, where sets of audio visual equipment were stacked in niches formed by the wall's beams, the wall-panels plastered with skateboarding stickers: smiley faces, peace signs, deadheads, roses, Sonic the Hedgehogs, and the wistful anime-style blonde girl recognizable (in graffiti form) from the side of the former factory building[118] on Lafayette and Prince Street and more iconographically from placards and the Signet or Bantam Classics paperback editions of *Les Miserables*. The band was finally packing up, the bassist doing the gentlemanly thing and

---

[118] The triangle shirtwaist fire occurred in Soho too as Olivia informed me, probably in the midst of that proletarian rant I mentioned in notes 85 and 85B.

helping to pack up Jenna's instrument as well, since right now she had her hands down Amante's pants almost, and was oblivious to the rest of her fellow bandmates, who hadn't left the stage yet and were drinking from cans of warm PBR and Nalgeen bottles filled with an unidentifiable substance. Amante had removed his glasses, I noticed, which gave him a debonair look, especially with his five o'clock shadow or whatever he had going on, and his short, spiky hair, which he wore gelled into fine points like some Rico Suave.[119]

"A week ago," Sean said. "Around the time I paid rent—late as usual, but my landlady's cool."

---

[119] I can assure you, Amante was no ladies' man in college. Back then, I'd often bump into him, while eating dinner with Anna or catching up with the old crew at Hot Tomatoes[119A]—a popular spot known for their reduced price martinis on the odd Thursday night. My first week at school, I'd gone to Atticus with Julia, a girl from my Major English Poets class, and while drinking chai teas, I'd spotted Amante's baleful mug in the window. I didn't know Amante from Asante at that point; I just wondered who he was and what he was looking at—until it struck me, a few hours later, after I'd dropped Julia off at Lanman-Wright, and made my way back to Durfee, that Amante must have been looking at me.

[119A] I avoided Hot Tomatoes after Anna and I broke up, since she would ostentatiously post on her AOL Instant Messenger: "Apple Martinis!" every Thursday, like clockwork. It's amazing how much of our routine we alter just to avoid these little run-ins with our exes, how every decision we make—right down to making out with someone in the wee hours of the morning listening to *John Wesley Harding*'s only two love songs on repeat—negates some other decision and sets in motion a chain of events that carries us forward to the present time: food for thought.

"A lot of musicians make more money than us,"[120] Maggie said.

"What? Maybe like an oboe player, Maggie. Musicians are the poorest of the poor. OK, fine. If I meet an *oboist*—I'll consider it."

"Who knows?" I said. "Maybe there's one here."

"Doubt it," Sean said.

"Let's not make hasty judgments," I said.

Maggie was like "Or maybe you can advertise your apartment to the Philharmonic."

"Not a chance. My current roommate is worth her weight in gold."

"I'm sure she is," Maggie said. "Notice how he never talks about his *current* roommate."

"A gentleman never tells," Sean said.

Maggie was like "A gentleman you aren't."

"Nothing to say anyway," Sean said. "We have different schedules."

"What does she work nights?"

Sean was like "No. She's spending a lot of time with her boyfriend in the city."

"Sounds ideal," I said.

"It is pretty clutch," Sean said.

Preston was coming back with three beers, stopping and sipping and eyeing us as if he didn't want to intrude. He squared his chin and moved around a couple girls. "Gentlemen. Spoils of war." He handed me and Sean a bottle each.

"What the hell is that?" Maggie said. She read "El Presidente?"

"Yeah," Preston said. "Just fifty extra cents and you can get Dominican beer. Why not?"

"Every country has its own beer," Sean said, slurping from the top of the bottle.

---

[120] Yes, a contradiction of her earlier remarks (see page 115).

Preston was like "So far as I know."

"Romania?" I said.

"I'm sure they do. I'm sure it's good. It's probably dark and thick as shit."

"I got the nastiest gut rot from some Ukrainian beer I had at this restaurant in Chelsea," Sean said. "It lingered in there for I want to say three days before I could process it."

"Sounds lovely," Maggie said. To me she was like "Your pal's[121] come up for air."

---

[121] The one other time I followed Amante occurred my sophomore year in college, while I was staying in Anna's room in what used to be Entryway B in pre-renovated Morse College, with her window overlooking the courtyard between Morse, Stiles, and the Off Broadway theater buildings. Anna, among other peculiar habits which set us apart from our brothers and sisters, could only make love while listening to one of the following CDs: Enrique Iglesias, Sarah McLaughlin, or the Indigo Girls. (Later, she expanded to include the Gipsy Kings, and Dave Brubeck, though not Shakira for reasons of tempo and pitch). So things were proceeding nicely enough, with McLaughlin crooning "we are born innocent," etc. which I've got memorized by now, when Anna tensed and clenched and turned toward the wall. I was like "What?" She didn't say anything for a while, then was like "I just had a heart palpitation." Naturally, this seemed a little suspicious, but in a certain mood Anna truly believed she was suffering from heart problems. So I scooted up and sat there, massaging her back, and she rubbed her chest a while and then settled down and pulled up the covers. I was like "Aren't you a little young?" She was like "I don't know. I just felt like a fluttering. In my chest." I considered the reasons for this: muscle spasm, cramp, gas, indigestion(?). They weren't worth mentioning. We sat there, discussing ailments (Anna had an emergency inhaler for asthma but she never used it, she claimed to have outgrown it; she was also lactose intolerant, until junior year of college). Then Anna yawned an enormous

yawn and said, "OK. Bedtime." I was like "What do you mean bedtime?" "I mean I'm tired," Anna said. "What about ten minutes ago?" "I told you, I had a heart palpitation." "I'm pretty sure that wasn't what that was." "Well, I feel *very comforted* by you." "I'm sorry, I didn't mean to make light of it." "You just think with your penis. You don't even care. What if I had a heart attack while we were you know··· doing it?" "Are you serious?" "I am." "I've heard of that happening to eighty year old men, but not teenagers. Maybe Strom Thurmond." "Again. Real comforting." "Can we turn this off, at least?" "Sure, fine." "You're not an eighty year old man," I said, silencing McLaughlin mid-croon. "You don't have to worry about that. Yet," I muttered. "You're missing the point," Anna said. "This is a bunch of what do you call it··· hyperchon... hyperchondria··· hippochondria··· " "Hypochondriac? You think I'm a hypochondriac? Heart disease runs in my family," Anna said. "But you're not an overweight man." "Like my dad. Is that who you mean? Thank you, that's good to know." "That's not what I said at all." "I think it is." "You're the one who told me he's taking Lipitor." "Well, that doesn't mean you have license to ridicule him, behind his back." "Now that's ridiculous. You think I'd ridicule him to his face?" "Conversation over." "Come on, Anna." "Go to sleep." "Come on." "I'm not in the mood." "This is ridiculous." "You can either stay here and shhhh, or go back to your own room." "Anna." I was pacing the room now, super annoyed. I walked over to the window and looked out and there he was: Amante, sitting on the low wall by the gate to Stiles. "Oh ho," I thought. I wasn't about to let some hoochie coochie voodoo chile dark magus Amante cast his evil influence over me. I got dressed and hurried out, pretty sure if I picked up the pace, I'd at least verify if that really was Amante sitting there, basically staring at Anna's window like some lonesome troubadour. I didn't intend to chat with him, or even approach him—the truth was, I'd had a few too many to drink. So I made it outside, and of course I couldn't see him from the angle of the gate, so I had to open the gate—and then I just caught a

"My pal?" I said.

"That guy sure looks a hell of a lot like you," Preston said.

Maggie was like "You really know him?"

"Yup," I said, sipping the tall beer. "Do you want me to set you up?"

"Get real. No. I want to know how you know him."

"He's stealing your lady,"[122] Preston said.

---

passing glimpse of him as he strode up the stairs that led behind the colleges, toward Payne Whitney gymnasium. "What the hell," I thought, kind of intrigued, and feeling a lot braver than normal. I whistled in a mute way, and skipped along after him, keeping about twenty feet behind. He was in the shadows now, moving steadily down Tower Parkway to Grove Street, crossing over onto the other side, by Grove Street Cemetery. I kept at a distance, wondering what in blazes he was up to. I mean, Amante was always a loner, always at the periphery of things, absent from all the usual college hang outs. I wasn't even sure if he attended class (because of his breakdown he was now in our year), and for the life of me I had no idea where his dorm room was or who he roomed with—kids like Amante tend to get shucked in with a bunch of outcasts (e.g. Charles, see notes 90-1) who don't associate with anyone else and eat dinner by themselves and are generally shunned, sad to say. I made it partway down Grove, almost to Commons when I figuratively threw up my hands and turned around. What was the point anyway? I'd rushed out in a blaze of indignation, which was entirely misplaced, only to speculate on what I'd actually say to Amante if I caught up with him, which I had no intention of doing—the fact that I followed him that far was bad enough, and I was starting to feel, if not weirded out, at least confused and embarrassed about my own behavior. Amante was kind of a riddle, a cipher really, and I felt better off leaving him be, which was where I left him.

[122] How Preston figured that I was interested in the guitarist was beyond me. It just proves that some people, when they

"She's gone, dude," Sean said.

Yes, the guitarist was gone, and Nick Amante was still there, laughing with those two friends, who for the life of me resembled the same person—in fact, they resembled Amante himself in some weird way (and by extension, must have resembled *me* though Sean and Maggie were kind enough to keep that observation to themselves), something about their unshaven ruffled appearance, their v-neck shirts, and their designer jeans perhaps contributing to their *Amante*-ness. It was like looking through a prism or a funhouse mirror and seeing the same image multiplied over and over again, ad nauseum, to a dizzying degree, especially when they all took a pull from their Dominican beers in unison, like the whole thing was choreographed, and then resumed their inexplicably cerebral laughter. I was wondering, truly, whether or not Amante picked up these dudes on purpose, like he wanted a decoy or something or if his choice of friends had been accidental—along the lines of pet owners who for whatever reason come to resemble their dogs in some pronounced feature, or harelip, or perhaps dental condition. Amante[123] was

---

drink, can't make sense of anything. God help anyone who needed Preston as an eyewitness.

[123] I should add, here, that there was one moment in my life where I triumphed over Amante, proved once and for all that I wasn't in thrall to his egregious influence, and that (if I wished, and with a little luck) I could outmaneuver him. This was the night I met Olivia. We'd just gotten out of a volunteer project at the Upper East Veterinary Center and we were walking three abreast—Olivia in between Amante and me. We were just chatting, what we actually said didn't matter much. Amante was quiet, absorbed, playing the role of deep thinker, solitary artist, loner, so the burden of conversation fell on me. Somehow we got on the subject of schools. Olivia said she went to Hunter College, and Amante chipped in: "Oh, that's a great school. That's a great school." Of course, he meant what he said, I'm

really furnishing enough to keep me wondering for hours—but that in and of itself wasn't unusual. I mean, the guy was cryptic and not exactly an open book.

"How do you know each other?" Maggie said, directing the question to the three of us in general, annoyed that I hadn't answered her right away.

Sean was like "College chums. Ran in the same crowd."

"He was in my actual college," I said.

——————————

not saying Amante was condescending or vacuous, but his words cast a shadow—a very slight shadow—of disingenuousness, not to say douche-iness (I hate to put it like that), the empty words you might expect from someone who probably doesn't know a whole lot about Hunter College or the CUNY system in general. Olivia picked up on this slight shadow of disingenuousness too when she asked us where we went to school. "Yale," Amante said. "Same," I said, pleased that Amante had spoken first because it sounded less like bragging the second time round. "Oh, really. Well. Ivy league, and Jesus, you two must be smart." "Ha ha no no," I said, indicating the two of us. Amante asked Olivia where she lived and when she said Brooklyn, he went "That's great. Brooklyn's great." You could pretty much see the let-down in her face after that comment. We said good night to Olivia at the stairs to the subway, and then Amante and I shook hands. "Maybe I'll see you at the next one of these," I said, joking since Amante had been clawed and even bitten, and would most likely not be repeating this volunteer experience. "Maybe," he said. "Next time we should choose dogs," I said. "Those cats were vicious." Amante smiled sheepishly. The night would have ended there, and everything would have been OK, except when I went down the stairs and made it to the train platform, the train hadn't come yet. Olivia was still standing there, and that's when I really talked to her.

126

"You mean your *Harry Potter*[124] college?"

I went "Yes, that's right."

"And you've just conceived like an irrational hatred for this guy, why?" Maggie said.

"Well, not hatred... "[125]

"I'm totally on board with you hating whoever," Maggie said. "It'd be nice for you to show some emotion once in a while."

Sean was like "Now, now."

"Kidding!" Maggie said. "You're so friggin' earnest. I have to walk on eggshells with you."

"Thank you, Maggie," I said.

"I really was kidding," Maggie said. "That came out kind of harsh."

"He knows you by now," Sean said.

"Don't think I'm going to apologize to *you*," Maggie said to Sean. "You don't deserve it."

Sean was like "I wouldn't expect anything less."

"I really didn't mean that," Maggie said. She touched my arm. "Anyway," she said as if to clear the air. "I'm going to go to the little girl's room. You all enjoy your piss-water beer."

"This is great, what you talking about?" Sean said.

Preston was like "Refreshing." But he spoke in a low voice, not really to Maggie.

Maggie was like "Why the fuck do they have these anyway?"

"Dominican Day Parade?" Sean said. "I'm guessing."

"Weird," Maggie said. She left me her beer.

---

[124] The school system in *Harry Potter* is modeled on Oxford. Yale is also modeled on Oxford. Hence, Harry Potter College = Yale.

[125] Yes, it's true, that sometimes I've intentionally gone to see Amante, as in *on purpose*, for a specific reason—like that reading—but in the long run, it's always been lopsided, the amount of times he's crept up on me far outweighing any times I've sought him out.

"Double fisting," Preston said after she was out the door. "I like it."

Sean was like "I don't think Maggie likes the music."

"Can't please everyone," I said.

Preston, in a spasm of awkwardness, stared at the floor.

"Who's next?" I said.

"Ball in the Raspberry," Sean said. "The flyer said."

"I am so looking forward to that," I said.

"Man, I wish they had some bluegrass here," Preston said. "Don't get me wrong, this stuff's fine, especially a few beers in, but jeez... can't get a lot of the real rootsy stuff up here."

Sean was like "Weren't you telling me about a bar?"

"Harley's? Yeah, that place is all right. Good brisket too."

I sipped my beer fast and kept my eyes on Amante.

"Think you'll ever get to Florida this summer?" Sean said to Preston.

Preston was like "Man, I hope so. Either way, I need to get Furbie off my hands. I mean, it's freaking ridiculous, right. You would know," he said to me, "you've dealt with rodents."

"Annoying, yes," I said.[126]

"A healthy chinchilla's annoying enough—what with the prodigious amount of shit. But an invalid. Give me a freaking break. I don't care if it means the end of innocence or whatever—it's like having a third child, it really is."

---

[126] Toward the tail-end of our relationship, Olivia (right out of the blue, I should mention) decided to adopt a pet rabbit which she named Josephine after a character in one of her French realist novels. She let the rabbit loose in the apartment to deposit her pellets wherever she took a liking including inside my tennis shoes, and then later this same oversize female rabbit would hop into bed with us and bite my toe at like three in the morning—a sign of affection, Olivia claimed, although the needle sharp quality of a rabbit's teeth is hardly conducive to becoming good pals.

"You can at least leave it overnight," Sean said.

"Sort of. But damned if that thing'll be planning an escape from Alcatraz and then it'll probably wedge its fat ass behind the appliances and stink up the place. I better take it easy. I'm too old for hangovers anymore."

"Hangovers and chinchillas," Sean said. "A lethal combination."

"You're telling me. That son of a bitch had its eye on me ever since we brought it home. Like I've never done enough for it, never combed its fur, never taken it out now and again. It's already bitten me twice, and the third time that's it. My dad was a farmer. If some vermin ever bit him or started acting weird—anything less than a dog, even if we'd had it forever—whatever, that was that—bang. He'd've shot it dead. End of story. Even a dog, he wouldn't tolerate them slipping into senility and all that. It's a tough life, but you got to have priorities."

Sean was like "Well. Hopefully, it won't come to that."

"Yeah. Hope not. But Allison's got to back me on this. I don't want to be like the evil mean parent who won't let them keep their Furbie."

"Just get them one of those fake Furbies," I said. "Would that solve it?"

Preston was like "I don't know, brother."

"Kids don't forget, either," Sean said. "Not for a while."

"Not ever. Yeah, my girls, who knows if they'll ever forget. They still ask me how Nemo—our old goldfish—died and why I didn't just tell them the truth." Preston let his eyes fall on the two blonde girls who were still standing nearby. "Shucks," he said. He was like "It would really be better just to do it now. Maybe let it free in Red Hook, or something. These chinchilla things aren't meant to be caged anyway. They're meant to be eaten by bigger animals, I think."

"Would your wife let you release it?"

"Not yet," Preston tipped back his beer. "I'd need at least a week to outline all my concerns. I don't want it to seem like it was just the heat of the moment. It really would be good if we went on vacation. That would be ideal: an ideal time to just," Preston drew his finger across his throat. "Fix it. I could even have maybe... well, I don't know—I was thinking maybe my sister-in-law might be willing to actually do the deed. Get it over with. Or maybe she could farm it out. You know you can make sweaters and shit from its hair."

"A sweater for a very little person," Sean said.

"Chinchilla onesie," Preston said.

"Or booties," Sean said.

"What—don't you need like a spinning jenny?" Preston said.

"Spinning wheel?" I said.

"Like Rumpelstiltskin," Sean said. "That'll be you."

Preston was almost done his beer at this rate. "Don't count on it, brother."

A large space had opened in front of us; more than half the crowd was gone. The Scandinavians were gone, most of the posse that had come to watch Jenna's band was gone. The two blonde girls who'd caught Preston's eye had moved closer (they'd been standing by the back wall), but they looked like they were having some deep conversation and I couldn't really make them out. I was kind of surprised that Amante was sticking around—after all, his usual style was to disappear when you least expected it. But there he was, in the same place, nodding and looking contemplative, talking to one of the dudes he'd come in with (his other friend had vanished). He had his hands clasped over his beer like the monk depicted on the label of Franziskaner, and the unbearded portions of his face glimmered pale and sickly in the blue lights from the floorlamps.[127] Unlike some of the other guys in the vicinity[128] (and what bar is without one or two weirdoes on the prowl), Amante didn't appear to be scoping the scene—he was probably still working off his high from that ten-minute kiss with the guitarist, and his entire posture—head down, arms folded prayerfully—seemed at least partly a defense against anyone who had witnessed his makeout session coming up and slapping him on the back and calling him "superman" or "the man" or "boss" or "master" and trying to "learn his secrets" which they'd be disappointed to know he probably couldn't even articulate himself.

"Hey. Did I tell you guys about my movie?" Preston said.

I was like "No. What's that?"

"I'll tell you," Preston said, finishing his beer and chucking it with a clang into the trash behind us. "So long as you don't go and steal my idea."

"Depends what it is," Sean said.

"Go on and tell us," I said.

"It's called... Well, the tentative name I got going is *The Underdwellers*. Are you laughing?"

Sean hiccupped. "No. No. Go on."

"Hey, Daryl Throbhart," I said. "Alone Together" was playing on the speakers now.

---

[127] I'd never noticed how sickly Amante looked until now, though, to be fair, I'm not sure how great anyone looks at midnight four or five drinks into the evening, after rubbing shoulders with a sizeable crowd, absorbing the collective frowziness of malt, sweat, vinegary perfume and b.o., to name some of the more prevailing scents, without even getting into the pronounced smells of cigarettes and pot and the musty earthen basement smell of the venue itself, with its cinder-block walls and the humungous tapestry-like curtains with their nap like the hair of an opossum or chinchilla (Preston would know), gray with dust and little lint pellets.

[128] Ahem, Preston.

When you leave, you tell me
There's so much on your mind
You want to leave it all behind
Pack a suitcase, go
To some distant place
Where you can be alone...
"What?"

"The song."

"S'all right brother," Preston said, not even flustered that they were playing the first song from the CD he'd given Maggie.[129] "Titles aren't my thing. The movie's pure gold, though—and if you're good at titles, I'm all ears." Preston nodded and rerouted a burp through his nose—or stifled a sneeze, one or the other. "I just got to write it all down," he said. "Pure gold."

"I wasn't laughing," Sean said. "It's allergies. Give me a sec."

"*The Underdwellers*," I said. "Say it like a movie announcer and it's not so bad."

"Is it?" Sean said, suddenly having a swallowing problem, and covering his mouth.

Preston was like "Just wait till you... There's these people— this is future times. They live in trees. They got this whole society living up in trees. In whatever future world, they have big trees. Like rainforest trees. Trees with big branches. Structurally capable of holding up houses, platforms, you know. Tree schools. Tree warehouses. Storerooms."

"I'm getting a Star Wars vibe," Sean said. "You mean like Ewoks?"

Preston stood with his legs spread out like he really was envisioning the scene right up there on the stage. "Yeah, it's kind of like that, only this is people. People living in trees."

---

[129] Why would he be? That song was so overplayed that spring and summer, it was probably on everybody's "mixed" CD. See notes 4 and 16.

132

"Sort of like Gummy Bears? Gummy Bears live in trees," I said, "or one big tree. I don't remember."

"Forget Gummy Bears," Preston said. "Are you even listening?"

"It's kind of hard to hear you, man."

"People... ... in... ... trees," Preston said, real slow. "Not animatronics. Not creatures. People. It's kind of hopping on the whole dystopian bandwagon, but hey I mean that's where the money's at, right?"

"No doubt," I said.

Sean was like "That's the trend."

"There's a situation going on," Preston said. "The people can come down during the day and farm and shit, but as soon as night falls, they've got to climb back up the trees, or else there's these trolls and the trolls'll kill them. Trolls come out at night. Everyone knows that."

"Daytime they turn to stone or something?" I said.

Preston was like "Haven't worked that out yet."

"Trolls," Sean said. "Really? You had me up till then."

"When I say troll," Preston said, "I'm kind of using that meaning humungous nasty big-tooth guys like *Where The Wild Things Grow*."

"Those are definitely trolls. Wild Things Are."

Sean was like "You mean like the hairy dudes on the Zicam commercials?"

"Is that who puts out those commercials?" I said.

"Look, forget the Wild Things," Preston had swallowed down the wrong pipe and had to clear his throat. "I'm saying 'troll' but you can picture any gremlin demon monster you want, about the size of a linebacker, OK?[130] It's just to help you get the proportions."

---

[130] Size is important here since, Preston would later tell us, the trolls were all former humans who'd mutated. The trolls abduct women so they can have troll babies with them (female

"Got it."

The speakers were going: *It's a feeling for forever. It'll be there when you go. But, baby, when we're together... you'll know...*

"Anyhoot. The people are coexisting with the trolls. They're scared shitless: yes. But they're managing, making it work as best they can. They got a curfew. That's what's going on. It's been like this for years and years, so no one questions it. It's just a fact of life."

"You know, there's a movie like this already," Sean said. "*Green Mansions*. Check it out. Ix-nay on the trolls."

"What about *Blue Lagoon*?" I said.

Sean was like "Is that the one with Brooke Shields?"

I coughed. "No. Leonardo DeCaprio, I think."

"That's *The Beach*," Preston said. "You're way off-track, brother. Trust me. There's no movie like this. Never has been. And that's just the background shit. That's not the actual movie. I'm just telling you this stuff so you understand the context. Comprende? The real movie gets going when this princess has an affair with a—what do you say—common commoner guy."

"Uh oh," Sean said. "Royals."

"Yeah. I've done my research, you know, unofficially, and this has all the ingredients of box office success. I'm going to blow Siskel's[131] freaking mind. Dystopian society: check, fantasy: check, trolls: check, suspense: check, a hot princess fooling around with the help: check, kings and shit, adventure, action, you got it all."

"Intriguing," Sean said.

---

trolls are sterile, like mules or worker bees), but they kill men outright—a plot point that gets fuzzy when they spare the lead actor's life, presumably under the impression that he *is* a woman ("Orlando Bloom maybe?" Preston had suggested for the part.) Trolls have fabulously low IQs.

[131] We didn't have the heart to tell him Siskel was dead.

"*Fern Gully* was kind of exactly like this movie,"[132] I said.

Sean was like "Didn't see it. But you shouldn't rule out animation—it's too early."

"It's more than a dumb movie with folks getting it on in their tree houses," Preston said. "It's a celebration of democracy, the freedom to marry whoever you choose. No arranged marriages. The affair adds a whole new dimension. Critical, you know, analysis of the trappings of, you know... I'm just yanking your chain," Preston said, hanging onto a smile. "I don't give a shit about analyzing crap. Leave that to the critics. OK. So. Tentative, tentative—I'm thinking of the names Nour or Maia or Gaia or something with 'ia' at the end of it, for the princess."

"I'm cool with those names," I said.

Sean was like "Maia's nice."

"Yup. Maia's a solid choice, and Nour has kind of the sexy seductress ring. I mean, Angelina Jolie[133] would be pretty dynamite for the part—just saying."

"Would you consider Jessica Biel?"

"I'm pretty open as far as casting," Preston said. "You got to be cool with nudity. That's my only rule. Graphic nudity. Not over the top. Just enough to keep things spicy. Jessica Biel might not be cool with that. Heard she's kind of a snob."

"Is this a porno?" Sean asked.

"No," Preston said. "I got a family, dude. What do you take me for? Porn's low rent. As far as nudity goes—tasteful, that's the bottom line. I mean, not full frontal. Though I wouldn't be opposed to a quick pan; fly over. You know, like one of those, if

---

[132] Not really.

[133] Preston's preference for brunettes (I.E. Maggie, Angelina Jolie, Jenna the guitarist) was kind of notorious seeing his wife was blonde.

you want to rewind on your own time, and pause, you can. The option's there.[134] Tastefully done, my man. Nothing NC-17."

"Sounds like you've made a good start," I said.

"It's not much," Preston said. "We'll see where it goes." He leaned in toward us. "I'm thinking trilogy," he said.

Sean was like "All the best ones are."

Up on stage, the stagehands were dismantling the keyboard accessories, moving back and forth, waving their glowsticks, their voices lost in the crowd noise and the speakers now playing the likes of "Surrender" and "Time After Time" and "99 Luftballons."[135] Maggie was taking her time, but the line for beer had swelled in front of the door, and I couldn't see where she'd gone.

"Those girls are totally checking you out," Sean said.

Those blonde girls really might have been looking at us; right then, they were half-turned, the taller one wearing a seafoam cami which exposed large shoulders cratered with chicken pox scars and what looked like a big welt or two; the other girl in a dark draw-string t-shirt and jeans.[136]

I was like "Are you trying to tell me something?"

"He's telling you to man up," Preston said. "Strap on a pair and introduce yourself."

"How 'bout some whiskey?" I said.

---

[134] Our 7th grade English teacher took advantage of this option, when showing us the Zefferilli version of *Romeo and Juliet*, the bedroom scene. Over and over and over···

[135] It felt like we'd moved back into some '80s-fest, which I suppose was also retro and cool, but so far as music goes, provided the perfect accompaniment for people who weren't really listening.

[136] Her jeans accentuated what my college pal Angie Zhou called a "pear shaped" body.

"That's the spirit," Preston said. He pulled out his iconographic flask from the back pocket of his oversize jeans.[137] "You're in luck, my man. Never go without. You all right with bourbon?"

"I kind of wanted scotch,"[138] I said.

"Don't be a snob."

"Bourbon," Sean said. "American for whiskey."

Preston was like "Put some hair on your chest."

"And you can chase it with this tropical brew," Sean said.

Preston was like "I like it," meaning El Presidente.[139] "I think I'll try another, make sure it stacks up."

"In a blind taste test," Sean said, "El Presidente tastes the same as every other Latin American beer... " I didn't catch the tail end of whatever it was he said.

I sipped from Preston's flask way too fast, probably, you know, trying to show that I could handle it (it was super clear those girls were watching us now), and at the same time feeling

---

[137] He could've stored a cask of moonshine in there.

[138] I'm sure we've all had a night when only whiskey would do the trick. I almost forgot to mention that Olivia kept a bottle of Jack Daniels on the low ledge of her bedroom window, adjacent to two small potted succulents and an even smaller ship in a bottle, as well as a framed picture that she'd taken with an outstretched arm of herself and her dad, smiling, just perceptibly gap-teethed (she'd had braces as a child, but their corrective powers could only do so much, since she'd come out of her mama with a mouth like a "shark," she informed me, in one of our relaxed post-coital moments on her flat boxspringless mattress), her dad unshaven and appearing to all extents and purposes like one of her Eastern European or Eurasian boyfriends who annoyed me to no end. When I asked her about the alcohol, she was like "That's not mine." And it's true, I'd never seen her drink any whiskey, or any so-called hard-liquor (see note 107).

[139] A wink is as good as a nod to a blind horse, as they say.

I'd overdone it because my esophagus clenched and reacted against a weird scalding hot corkscrew pain which traveled along my throat in the opposite direction of standard swallowing, the corkscrew-pain remaining hot and stubbornly lodged in the soft tissue of my alimentary canal despite my best attempts to bow my head and swallow some diluted bourbon-spit, which was all that remained in my mouth.[140] I shuffled forward one or two paces, still breathing out a whiskey aftertaste, and salvaged a wet smile for the taller girl.[141]

The tall girl smiled back. "You don't look so good," she said.

"It's OK," I told her, "I got beer."

She laughed "Oh. It's all better then. Michelle," she said.

We introduced.

"Nora," the other girl said.

I was like "This is Sean and Preston."

Nora went "Hi, Sean and Preston."

"Were you here to see Dag Nasty?" Michelle asked me.

I was like "Who're they?"

"They played first."

"No," I said. "We missed them."

Sean confirmed this with a nod.

"Don't tell me you liked Beta whatever?" Nora said.

"Hated them," Sean said. "Absolutely derivative."

"You're funny," Michelle said.

Sean shrugged and made a sort of uncanny Robert DeNiro face. "What can I say?"

"You missed the best band," Michelle said to me.

I was like "Sorry."

---

[140] Following the advice I'd once heard to get rid of hiccups: tilt your head forward, nearly upside down, so that you really feel the blood flood your ears, then swallow a big glob of saliva.

[141] I was kind of worried I spit on her, or sprayed her accidentally, the way you sometimes spray out saliva unexpectedly when you yawn.

"Are you all groupies or something?" Preston said.

Both girls kind of snickered. "We wish," Nora said. "Our lives are much too mundane for that. We'd be groupies if we could."

"If it paid," Michelle said.

Sean went "Ah, there's the rub!"

Michelle was like "He's a smarty pants, too." She touched me with her bare arm and didn't move away while I hurried down another sip of beer.

"I'm in publishing," Nora said, by way of specialized introduction.

"But please don't make any pitches," Michelle said.

Nora was like "It's the worst part of the job. I can't tell you how many people I've met, on the train, on the bus, just at the freaking park, who as soon as they hear I'm in publishing, just want to tell me all about their own little novel they've been hoarding in their sock drawer for nine years, two hundred eighty seven days, and counting. I used to smile and nod and be like 'Oh really,' but that never works. Now, I'm just like, 'I'm sorry, I can't help you.' It's so tiresome! Besides, I'm in children's publishing. Not like it makes a whole hell of a lot of difference. Then you get the real freaks. The ones who've got children's book ideas with like cartoon body organs. I should just say I'm a banker. Then they'll leave me alone."

"Or an ophthalmologist," Michelle said. "Then they wouldn't know what the heck you're talking about."

"Or think I'm an optometrist."

"You know," Preston said. "That's something I've always wondered about. What exactly is the difference?"

I was like "I don't know, but I think I need to see one," rubbing my eyes with the heel of my hand.

"Or maybe you should say you're a proctologist," Sean said.

"Ooh… too far," Nora said.

Michelle was like "Gross."

"Scratch that," Sean said.

"You've lost points," Nora said.

"Ha ha. You're an idiot," Preston said.

"In a weird way, that might turn people on," Nora said.

Michelle laughed. "So what do you do?" she said, pivoting to me. "I want to know all the typical stuff. Stable job? Gainfully employed? Are you a psychopath? I've been having bad luck."

"She means her ex," Nora said.

"Let's just say I've learned to read between the lines," Michelle said. "You never know, do you?"

"Her ex[142] was a fucking dick," Nora said to Sean.

---

[142] A moody and irascible, long-in-the-tooth hipster whose mutton chops were decidedly gray, and who insisted on preserving a flavor saver style tuft of hair on his chin. Beyond his most apparent flaws (his weird angst, his lapses into depression, his complete and utter snobbery, and egocentrism), he was also unaccountably determined to prove his heterosexuality, to the degree that all of a sudden, and out of nowhere, Michelle would turn around at whatever bar they'd gone to and find him flirting with a girl across the room, or even brushing some girl's neck hair affectionately, or laughing and telling jokes with girls barely out of their teens who still wore Lip Smackers and Body Fantasies (more than a fragrance!) and drank Smirnoff Ices. By the later stage of their time together, he was even bringing girls home, trying to pass theirs off as an "open" relationship and an invitation to all kinds of free-lovey bullshit, which Michelle had *not* signed up for, thanks but no thanks. Nevertheless, maybe in part because of her private suspicions[142A] re: Dean being a gay man trying to repress his natural instincts, Michelle did participate in one threesome with a horse-faced girl they'd met at a dive in Williamsburg. Michelle had needed an entire bottle of red wine before she felt comfortable and loose enough to get in on the action, by that point pretty lethargic and unremarkable anyway, and all she remembered from her one and only threesome was the horse-faced girl making cooing noses, kneeling in the papasan chair, while Dean lay on top of her (she was lying on her stomach),

and did what he usually did, without an audience. Dean's exaggerated heterosexuality marked the beginning of the end for Michelle and Dean, and she soon dropped him, after he suggested filming her together with the horse-faced girl who was "down for anything" (Dean's words). Only a long time afterward did Michelle start to consider possible ramifications of her actions, such as whether or not it had been wholly wise to have sex with Dean without protection. She'd already had a scare a week after their first hook-up, when an unaccountable red rash similar to the dermal explosion of scarlet fever broke out on her inner thighs and along her hooha. She was so freaked out she couldn't bring herself to get tested, and put it off, and put it off, sprinkling Gold Bond and applying cortisone cream to her thighs until the skin peeled in a secondary allergic reaction and the rash went away. She convinced herself it was nothing, just a fluke, and not like HPV or some syphilitic chancre sore or the like, which would inevitably develop into general paralysis of the insane. What really did it in for her and Dean, though, was much more mundane: it was his (in Nora's opinion) genuine dickiness whenever he found himself in a gathering of Michelle's friends. First off, he'd absent himself from the conversation not as an introverted person does but with a blatant show of impatience and condescension sure to ruffle some feathers, as if the whole lot of her friends were just so beneath him and not worth interacting with, in the same way Michelle's music was beneath him too—try mentioning Til' Tuesday without him flipping out and going off about the prostitution of modern music and corporate rock and Tom Waits and "How could you even call that art?"—and just remaining pissed off and angsty until he could hold it no more and he'd say something along the lines of: "You call that a chai tea? Wait till you've gone to Delhi and then tell me that's a chai tea," or "You call that rugelach? Wait till you've been in Jerusalem and then tell me that's rugelach," or "You call that blood pudding? Wait till you've gone to Iceland," namedropping all the places he'd gone to in his 47 years of free and easy living, thus killing the

I unintentionally (not by process of association, I'm not that mean) caught a look at Nick Amante, still conversing with his

---

conversation dead each and every time, and causing Nora, in a memorable parody, to say: "You call that bullshit? Wait till you hear what bullshit comes out of Dean's mouth at 12 o'clock at night." When they broke up the first thing Michelle did was book an appointment with the family practice.

[142A] Her early doubts were based on Dean's preference for Tommy Bahama second-hand shirts made out of silk or rayon, which he complimented—in colder weather—with light blue or light green blazers, so that he could have passed for an extra in *Miami Vice* or maybe *Columbo*, especially when you considered his faux-alligator shoes and his yachting cap. Then there were the long socks he said he had to wear for his "poor circulation" as he put it demurely, but which Michelle had an inkling he liked just for the texture, which was (in point of fact) sheer as pantyhose. His obsession with Marlon Brando's breakout films was likewise suspect, when viewed in a certain light, as was his delight in kitschy art films starring a half-naked Charles Bronson lookalike; and Michelle couldn't quite get over how long he took in the bathroom, doing God knows what—trimming his nose hairs (and he did own a specialty grooming kit)—every time they went out, fussing over his outfit with a concern for appearances way beyond that of the typical male (in Michelle's experience). She could excuse his facelift and some other plastic surgery he said he'd gotten on account of his age—he was indeed no spring chicken—and because he'd been in an accident: a bike ran over him at the Jones Beach boardwalk. She'd had her radar up for a while, but decided she'd misread him, especially since he seemed so genuinely, not to say obnoxiously, heterosexual whenever they were together, preferring to have sex in all kinds of non-missionary positions, and having a preference for sadomasochistic paraphernalia, which never struck Michelle as anything but heteronormative.

lookalike friend. Our group had fallen into a foursquare arrangement, with Preston as the odd man out.

"I'm sorry to hear that," I said.

"Why are you apologizing? You don't have anything to apologize for. I don't want to talk about him," Michelle said. "Tell me about you. What do you do?"

I was like "You first."

Michelle laughed, sipping her beer. "All right. I'm a librarian. I work for the New York Public Library—the Gerritsen Beach branch. What do you do? I can't help feeling like you're evading the question. Not a good start."

"Teacher," I said.

"No way." Michelle spun to Nora. "I told you he was a teacher."

"Soon to be," I said. "My program starts next week. Alternative Certification—through the city."[143]

"Oh." Michelle's face drooped somewhat. "We can't be friends then."

"Why not?"

"They rejected my ass."

"I'm sorry," I said.

"Would you quit saying that?"

"Sorry?"

Michelle was like "It's OK. Everything works out for a reason.[144] That's what I believe. I didn't get into that program so

---

[143] I'd applied for the mid-year New York City Teaching Fellows, but had been deferred until June. Anyway, I'd known about it for a while—since December—and Olivia was the first person I told. Her reaction was similar to Michelle's. She'd been turned down from AmeriCorps, I believe, and had an ongoing beef with all alternative certification programs.

[144] Sometimes we just don't know what's good for us. I mean, the entire time I was with Olivia I knew it wasn't working—and not just because she said, "I don't want a relationship, I just

that means I'm meant to do something else. Right now, I'm meant to work in the library. It's not what you think. I don't just sit there with granny glasses scolding people."

"Not what I thought at all."

"Yes you did. Everybody does. Check this out," Michelle reached into her purse and took out her clasp wallet. She opened it, ran her nail over a bunch of cards, and pulled one out: *Michelle Roberts, Super Librarian*.[145] "I run reading groups. I

---

want to take this casually, but I don't want a relationship" on our first date at Once Upon a Tart (a restaurant you can't really patronize with a straight face), the same time she told me about her fluent French speaking and showed me her huge edition of *La Reine Margot* by Dumas père, which she read at sidewalk cafes in the Parisian semi-shaded atmosphere of Thompson and Sullivan Streets above Houston. It was because we were never really there, never really part of each other, living life like an art film, more or less alone together—damn it! Just like the Daryl Throbhart song (note 16 etc.). Even in our most intimate moments, I was too scared to tell her anything deep (as in note 210).

[145] The email address Michelle provided on her card was legit. I emailed her about a week later, with my usual blather. To be fair I tried calling first (calling right outside the newly opened Mulberry Street Library as if channeling the good energy of this recently constructed library to call this librarian), but she didn't respond to my thoughtfully-composed voicemail which I handwrote on the back of a memo pad. A day or so later, she wrote back: "Your email was intriguing. I'm kind of surprised by how well you can write: it's almost the inverse of how well you can dance. Ha ha, just kidding. Anyway, your writing has won you a date, so that's something. I can meet you next Friday for drinks, if that sounds good to you." We arranged to meet in Flatbush after she got off work. But literally on the Thursday before, she wrote: "I'm afraid I have to cancel our plans. I've been seeing a gentleman (her word, not mine) off and on, for

do children's time. I go to schools. I'm already kind of a teacher. But it's laid back, you know? It gives me time for my own stuff. I write, too—I've written a novel.[146] Been there, done that. Another thing to check off the list. I asked Nora if she could put in a good word for me at Random House, but apparently our friendship only runs so far."

"It's nothing personal," Nora said.

"Yes it is."

"All right, it is."

"That's OK," Michelle said. She was so close to me that I could smell her breath coming in distinct, low exhalations, an artificially sweet but not completely nauseating smell, like she'd been chewing Laffy Taffys laced with white corn whiskey. "Next time Nora needs me to excuse her overdue library books, I'm going to be a real hardass."

Nora was like "Fair enough."

"I mean it this time," Michelle said. "I'm a very grudging person."

Maybe I made a face or something, because immediately she was like "No, I'm not. Plus Nora doesn't need me. Her company gives her all the free books she wants."

"Don't be bitter," Nora said. She'd moved farther away from us and was leaning in toward Sean.

"I'm not bitter either," Michelle said. "I would say I'm pretty even-keeled."

I was going to make a joke about 'even-keeled' and the fact that I was still holding two beers like they were ballast or something—one was almost done, just down to the dregs, but

---

about three months now, and we've recently decided to take the next step and become more serious. I had agreed to meet with you before this developed, and because neither of us was exclusive; however, now the situation has changed."

[146] Michelle's email, in fact, concluded with: "P.S. If you still wish to peruse my novel, I will gladly pass it along. Don't be too critical. I never claimed to be Chaucer. XXOO. MR."

the other had more than half, warm and scuzzy by this point with a grainy island-brewed flavor that stuck between your teeth like pumpernickel breadcrumbs.[147] Behind me, Sean was trying to get Nora to tell him the secret to getting published. She was saying oh how that was confidential, and swore him to

---

[147] I'm almost positive I had the same beer at Café Cubana on Bergen Street, that time Olivia told me that all her boyfriends were jealous of her because she had so much love to give—too much to be contained in just one relationship. I swallowed this bit of news and chewed my rice and beans adroitly, without stuffing my mouth, though I was hungry and tired, in that peculiar deplenished state that comes after idling around all day in the sun. We'd spent the afternoon traipsing across Prospect Park, through the end-of-day farmer's market with its stalls of sunflowers and Gerbera daisies, bright as lollipops, and one or two tents with lumpy loaves of brown bread and flies circling the stagnant flower water; we'd walked from there to Bergen Street, mostly downhill, lingering by art stores so Olivia could point out what was tacky from what was legit and what she could never afford from what she could produce herself if she just had the materials—if she could nab herself a sugardaddy to pay for it all. She was wearing a pink-patterned summer dress and had an enormous fake hibiscus clipped in a hairband and bright red lipstick which kept flecking the tips of her teeth, and she just kept smiling, not ashamed at all, despite the nearly dead tooth she had which she claimed her insurance wouldn't pay for (but when she had that sugardaddy··· just you wait). "What?" she said, taking my hand and squeezing it in her long fingers, sensing my disappointment which I knew I was telegraphing in spite of myself. "What?" Then, when I didn't say anything—just pushed my fork aside—she went back to whatever she'd been saying before about her trip to England and how there were no places to pee so she'd become a connoisseur of KFC restaurants just for the free bathrooms, and how her English friend had taught her how to curse properly: "'No, Olivia. It's not just *bollocks*. It's *the dog's bollocks*. There. Now you say it.'"

secrecy, and then started in on the last children's book they'd approved, some anime-manga allegorical number about a rabbit who learns Kung Fu.

"Rabbits," Sean said, amplifying his voice so we could hear it over the speakers.[148] "You hear that? Rabbits.[149] That's key."

"What's your book about?" I asked Michelle. I had the uncomfortable sensation that I might topple over at any time. We were already standing close. If I just reached out my

---

[148] They'd started playing something like The Misty's "I'll Never Make You Take Medication" and the volume had increased along with the distortion effects at the bridge of the song, adding to the general disorientation I (for one) was feeling right about now.

[149] Before Olivia got that rabbit, life was much easier. She could leave her bedroom door open for one thing; the apartment didn't reek like a pet store supervised by teenagers. I didn't come up the stairs only to see her sitting on the floor in a gray woolen skirt and a creamy blouse with Josephine, the rabbit in her lap like she was posing for a Norman Rockwell calendar. Before the rabbit, we could go where we pleased, watch *The Red and the Black* and then rush back to her room to make out, Olivia guiding my hands to her underclothes. We'd lie there and Olivia would tell me things like "I hate when guys don't finish what they start" (referring to oral sex). "I mean, finish your task. It's like you think it's a warm up exercise." Then I'd thumb the ridge of her hipbone. "I'm shaped like a '30s movie star," she would say. "24 inch waist, 36 inch hips. Childbearing hips. Though I'll never have a child." In a little while, she'd pace, fitting a bandana over her hair. "I mean, I might someday," she'd say, chewing on a piece of thread she'd pulled off her shirt. "When someone restores my faith in the world." "Is that all it takes?" I'd laugh. She'd come over, wearing a shirt but no pants, and stop in front of me. "Ian—you look so sad. And I really am glad I have you. You know that, right?" I don't know if I'd answer.

hands—or rather my knuckles since I still had those beers—I'd touch her hips.

"What?" She leaned in, and now I really did steady myself against her, purely for balance.

Maggie had rejoined Preston even farther back, and the two of them were both staring awkwardly in different directions. Preston was concentrating on the stage as if the accumulated shadows formed some kind of Rorschach test, which it was his job to decipher.

"You really want to hear about it?"

I shook my head: no. Michelle slapped my arm lightly. "You're wasted. Otherwise, I'd say you're being rude."

"I *do* want to hear about it," I said.

"Some other time,"[150] she said.

---

[150] And I did get a chance to read it, about a month later to be exact. Michelle sent it as a PDF because she didn't particularly care for my editing. *Tolbert's Tree*, still unpublished, deals with a family, the Mathesons, whose move to rural Pennsylvania goes a bit differently than planned. The family dad, Stu Matheson, is your standard okeydokey optimist, hoping he can save his marriage to the beautiful Allison (same name as Preston's wife, by the way) by whisking her away to some backcountry farmhouse and shouldering all the family finances on his own back (Allison has just been laid off when the story starts). Of course, no one's super thrilled about this whole back-to-nature/*Walden* experiment except for old Stu, who goes through his part with gusto, stripping the walls, painting, roofing in 90 degree weather, pulling poison ivy off trees with his own hands, fixing leaks, repairing faucets, plunging toilets, and generally making a ruckus and overexerting himself in every room of the house, not to mention the crawl space and attic—his trail of D.I.Y. projects leaving slipshod and potentially hazardous SNAFUs in his wake. How the house itself could have passed code is beyond Michelle's purview as a horror novelist (which is what she eventually becomes, though I'm not sure if

her original intention was such). Needless to say, the children, Cory and Bill are pretty much rolling their eyes for the first few chapters, while dear old dad tries to enlist their help and build up the sort of camaraderie you'd expect on *Land of the Lost* or *Swiss Family Robinson* or even *Growing Pains* or *Step by Step*. Cory, for one, is especially irritated at having to leave all her friends behind in the big city and move to some podunk town populated mostly by bonneted Methodists or Mennonites or she couldn't care less what they are, except that they remind her of certain Willa Cather and Laura Ingalls Wilder novels she skimmed through in junior high and never thought much of since they were boring as hell. Bill, off to college at the conclusion of the summer (*if he can only make it that long*) is more upbeat about the whole experience, and mostly lounges around in his boxers and a tank top, fixing PB&J's and fluffernutters at weird hours, as per usual teenage behavior. All this is well and good, and the story would be perfectly fine, except for one wee little detail: the obnoxious, hard-to-eradicate, part-shrub, part-tree that's been festering and basically bugging the shit out of Stu since the moment he set foot in the door. Clearly, such an ominous presence can be up to no good—the tree, and Michelle foreshadows this quite unmistakably, indeed functions as a sort of portal or door or pathway to an otherworldly realm, following the same strategy Stephen King uses with that enormous rock in "N." But Stu isn't going to take the tree's evil presence lying down. He cuts his hand open just trying to pluck a leaf and his decision is forged. He makes it his personal mission to pull the tree out, by hook or by crook, sparing no expense. By the end of the story, his monomaniacal obsession with the tree rivals Captain Ahab's in terms of sheer Shakespearean pathos, but it's worth pointing out that Stu reaches this pitch of excitement by degrees and doesn't emerge as a total nut until well into page 85, at which point Stu's wife Allison has totally lost her attraction and become something of a shriveled old hag (keep reading for more on that juicy development). It's also worth mentioning, that the story as a whole seems to mirror Michelle's

"You really think I'm rude?" I said.
"No. You're just a guy. I get it."

---

own relationship with Dean, such that the first 40 pages, taken by themselves, could be an entirely different novel, a sunny, almost upbeat comedy involving a dad as hapless as Tim Allen on *Home Improvement* whose great aim in life is just to have sex with his wife—not an overly ambitious aim, it's true, but at least something relatable and perhaps even commendable when one considers how many marriages end in a sort of abstinent stalemate. Even after all the rejections and the "I can't honey, I'm too tired"s, Stu is still entranced with the shape of his wife's buttocks, and fantasizes about mounting her supine body and just *doing his thing*, his sexual appetites unblunted by his wife's put-offs ("It was all he could do not to roll on top of her, and force his throbbing tool between her thighs" etc. etc.). Ironically, Stu's futile attempts to hack down the tree have resulted in the premature aging of his entire family, beginning with his better half, Allison, who in the midst of sex transforms into a "ghoulish… crypt-like Nefertiti, her skin flaking off her body, her pasty dark-veined tongue lolling to the side with abhorrent pleasure." This cursed botanical specimen has blighted the ones Stu holds dear. Even when the poor fellow realizes that his quest to kill the tree is literally turning his children into a couple of Rip Van Winkles, he still can't give it up—here's where the monomania kicks into overdrive. He purchases a chainsaw as large as the one last seen in the hands of Dennis Hopper in *Texas Chainsaw Massacre 2*, and gets to work. The tree gone, his children gone, the story ends with a perversely elated Stu falling to his knees and having a kind of orgasmic episode, which is interrupted by the arrival of an old farmhand who has come to re-shingle the roof and stumbles over the rotting corpse of Cory, the young daughter, who like the reverse of Benjamin Button (I.E. like Robin Williams in *Jack*) has aged at warp-speed and now departed, "shuffled off this mortal coil", and become food for worms.

We were turning in a circle now, not really dancing. When we turned toward the back of the room, I tried to catch Maggie's eye—I don't know why, it was a stupid thing to do given that I was now dancing with someone else in plain view of her—but she had a glazed-over expression; she shifted her weight from one leg to the other, with her knees locked, impatient, like someone waiting for the subway.

"I'd better throw these out," I said, pulling away my hands.

Michelle was like "Are those your friends back there?" She was looking at Maggie in particular, but I thought she might have been referring to Nick Amante (still there) on the near side of the room, hovering like a wallflower. He'd been in my line of sight the whole while we were dancing; I'd kept my eyes on him, while Michelle cuddled her head on my shoulder. His friend had left him, but he'd continued to stand by the stage, facing the door and the bar, as if expecting someone else's arrival. He still had the same brigadierish smirk on his face (bound to be annoying no matter what the occasion), but his hands were clasped in that friar-like gesture of benediction as if he were performing an extremely mild-mannered exorcism at the same time.[151]

"Sure," I said, verifying that Amante was in the exact same place as I turned away from him. "I've known them a long time."

"You work together?"

"Sure. We used to."

"But now you're leaving. You're going to be a teacher."

---

[151] Thus he'd remained standing there, for no good reason, looking smaller and more approachable now that he was on his own, and less like myself, although he still retained certain resemblances especially along the jawline and in the overall shape of his cranium, which appeared distressingly (not to say infuriatingly) square-shaped from behind, with a rounded hairline (as opposed to squared), just like me, tapering into a few stray neckhairs, not like me: those neckhairs screamed "Amante" all the way.

"That's right," I said. "It'll be wonderful."[152]

---

[152] What I didn't know then was this night would really be my last time with all these people since Sean would shortly move to Colorado, and Preston, hopes dashed at entertaining a workplace affair, would eventually settle into some semblance of domestic tranquility, replete with sweatpants-wearing Sunday football and an (initially) ineffective bout of couples therapy and the intervention of the family priest, a genial man named Jerome, whose fly-by-the-seat-of-his-pants evangelism lodged like an undigestable nugget in Preston's stomach where he'd mull it over and eventually come to the conclusion that religion was just another one of those obligations Allison had foisted on him, as unpalatable as an overdone salmon filet. All the same, since he was still ostensibly a family man, he would take one of the therapists many pearls of wisdom (which he'd derided at the time of the actual therapy, saying "if that's all it takes, I ought to be a therapist myself") and write a letter to Allison outlining his entire plight, which he then did, dutifully, glass of Maker's Mark by his side, chewing on his pen cap until it was as flat as those maple seed-helicopters (and wishing he could get away with chewing tobacco in his own home). He finished in the early hours after his wife's stomping had ceased to distract him, and presented her with a fair copy (edited no less) in the morning. To his surprise, and actual happiness, she started bawling, and hugged him, and then, packing the girls off to a friend's house for a late a.m. play date, led him straight to the bedroom and proceeded to do 2 out of the 8 "nasty" things he'd fantasized about right there in that letter, believing at the time that his words were the death knell of the marriage, since the shock of reading such filth—Allison had always categorized his run-of-the-mill sex fantasies as "absurd" whenever he squeamishly suggested such-and-such in the course of normal lovemaking—would surely put her over the edge once and for all and lead to divorce proceedings. Surprise, surprise, though, Allison was not the prude he took her for. The truth of the matter was, she was overjoyed Preston had actually taken the

time and effort to follow through on their therapy, which until that point she'd always figured he'd taken as a joke (he had, in point of fact), going along with it mostly so he could piss her off on the bus rides to and from the Dr.'s office by carping about the good Dr. and the runs in her stockings he'd happened to notice (although it was a minor miracle if he ever noticed a single item of clothing that Allison put on, not counting thongs or panties) as well as the Dr.'s annoying habit of never actually saying anything definitive, which Allison told him was a trademark of the psychological profession, the purpose of which was to get him to actually think for himself and try to reason out his own difficulties. Allison really believed Preston had no interest in solving these difficulties, and she nowhere in a thousand years even remotely thought the therapy would actually pay dividends and produce results in her admittedly dunderheaded husband, so that he would actually write something resembling—as she took it, at eight in the morning, when he lumbered into the kitchen with deep bags under his eyes and a nervous twitch in the hand that held the sweat-curled pages—a love letter, a sort of epithalamion (not that Preston would know the term) celebrating in, yes some carnal detail, a lot of the sex acts they had managed in their early twenties when Allison was more limber and Preston was about 50 pounds lighter and not as flatulent, and also pleading for more blowjobs and sex in the shower (these were the risqué sex acts which Preston had salivated over so adolescently) as well as an expanded use of costumes, ice cubes, dildos, clitoral stimulators, chocolate syrup and edible underwear, which Allison had to bite her tongue to keep from laughing over, because it all made her feel so unbelievably young again. This is all to say that in the end Preston himself played a part in resuscitating what all outside observers had to believe was a failed marriage, a doomed marriage, and for at least a year after the fact believed he was the luckiest man on the block; sprucing up his quasi-suburban (Carroll Gardens) row home with a gusto normally reserved for marketing whizzes or cutthroat bankers

"Don't say it like that," Michelle said. "I'd die for that job."

I studied her a moment. "Of course I'm happy about it."

"But you're too wasted right now."

"Something like that."

"I knew it!" Michelle stepped back. The music had changed again (it had changed before), the song was sort of familiar. It sounded at first like the 1980's remake of "I Think We're Alone Now," but then something, some part of the chorus or the instrumentals, made it impossible to be that song. "My favorite," Michelle said. "Nora!"

The two of them started hugging and singing, and then they were trying to get us to dance.

"I'm going to sit this one out," Sean said. "Bum knee."

"Oh, boo," Michelle said.

"You're breaking my heart," Nora said.

"No, seriously," Sean said. "My knee's swollen to the size of a cantaloupe."

"He's not kidding about that," I said.

"Gosh. I'm sorry," Nora said.

I glanced past the girls toward the stage and saw, to my surprise, and then disbelief, that Amante was gone. "Hold on a sec," I said.

In fact, the entire front of the room was empty, the last few people had migrated while we were dancing.

"Where'd he go?" I said to Sean.

Sean was like "Who're you talking about now?"

"Amante. The writer. Where'd he go?"

"Beats me," Sean said. "Maybe he's taking a leak."

"He was right there," I said.

Sean patted my arm. "Calm down. You don't even like the guy."

---

who grace their brownstones with abnormally fecund blue and purple hydrangeas. Preston was happy, that's all we need to know.

"He's all right."

"Take a deep breath," Sean said. "Maybe bourbon doesn't agree with you."

"What's that supposed to mean?"

"Preston said you drank his flask."

"It was half a flask," I said, "and he told me to drink it. I saved him some. Where is he anyway?"

"He said it was filled," Sean said.

"Some people exaggerate."

"Present company excluded, of course."

"Has he been standing there the whole time?" I said. I.E. in Maggie's vicinity. Preston had gone to get a new brew while we were dancing, and had generally made himself scarce, maybe even popped out into the lobby for a bit, but now he was back beside her like one of the Swiss Guard, shuffling in an extremely restricted circle, as if duty-bound to remain at his post.

"I feel bad," Sean said. "We ought to join them."

"What about your ladyfriend?"

"Girls in bars are sleazy," Sean said. "You know that already.[153] Come on."

"I'm not the same as you. My standards are much lower."

"No one's stopping you."

Michelle and Nora had lost all inhibition now and were belting, karaoke-style, air-guitars and everything, and

---

[153] Sean didn't need to remind me about his buddy Justin, whose girlfriend (he met her in a bar, of course) just *disappeared*.[153A] No explanation, no note, no forwarding address, certainly no goodbye. It was one of the pitfalls of dating anyone in NYC—the fact that your significant other, girlfriend, fiancée, dental hygienist, if they wanted, could up and disappear, *at any time*.

[153A] Like the "Hannah Sparrow" of *Inferno*.

eventually—through an extremely slow process of memory retrieval—I realized that I knew the song too: "Voices Carry."

"They're my favorite band ever," Michelle said. "Come on!"

"Their third album's much better," I said.[154]

Michelle shook her head, uncomprehending.

"Hold up a sec," I said.

Sean was attempting to detain Maggie near the door. "Let me buy you a drink," he said.

"I'm a little person," Maggie said. She thumped her fist to her chest and fake-burped. "I'm done."

I was like "Where you going Maggie?"

"I'm going to get a cab," she said.

"We'll go together," I said. She had the door open. "Don't you want to stay for the last band?"

Maggie lowered her voice. "I don't like being third wheel."

"Come on Maggie," Sean said.

"It's not like that," I told her.

Maggie crossed her arms. "Tell me what it's like."

"Her? You mean her over there?" Sean said. "They basically ambushed us. They're very nice people. She works in publishing."

"Fascinating," Maggie said. "I'm sure you have a lot to talk about."

"I'd rather talk to you," I said.

Maggie's smile was only half-sarcastic. "You are so full of shit."

"That's the spirit," Sean said. "See. That's what friends are for."

"I'm not going to be some third wheel," Maggie said, stepping out the door.

"The scene's getting old anyway," Sean said. "Where the fuck did Preston go?"

---

[154] Kind of an overgeneralization, but true in the case of 'Til Tuesday, I'm assured.

Preston had been meandering on the threshold of the conversation, rotating his shoulders like he was warming up for a race, but right when we needed him he was gone, slipping off as craftily as Nick Amante in his prime.

I was like "Check the bar."

"Good call," Sean said, patting my shoulder.

I followed Maggie into the lobby—it was more crowded here than inside the venue. I thought the signs had said "no drinks in the lobby," but no one was enforcing that rule (if they ever had been), and nearly everyone was supplied with something or other, El Presidente, PBR, dark drinks in short glasses plugged with lime wedges. Maggie was waiting for me about halfway to the door to the street.

"You don't happen to know where that writer went?" I said.

"What writer?" Maggie said. She crossed her arms. She was wearing her thin black suede jacket with sleeves that went three-quarters down her arms, and which, funnily enough, I hadn't seen her carrying the entire night so that its appearance now seemed almost magical.

"You know—the one with the glasses, the pit-stained t-shirt?"

"Your friend, you mean?" Maggie uncrossed her arms and pursed her lips. "Are you going to tell me what that's about?"

"He isn't in the restroom?"

"How should I know?"

I kind of did have to pee; to offset the feeling, I'd been stepping all crablegged from side to side, planting my feet as gingerly as a sandhill crane. "I'll be right back," I said, pointing my thumb at the restroom. "Will you be here?"

"Are you going to leave me with Preston?" Maggie said, relenting.

"No way," I said. "Will you stick around?"

Maggie leaned her head back and groaned. "Fine. Don't get lost."

"Stay here," I said.

For a second or two I forgot about Maggie and Olivia and everyone else and lost myself in communion with the urinal, scanning the hodgepodge of concert notices, stickers, graffiti, and other flimflam crusted to the walls. The urinal had a nauseous septic smell insufficiently masked by a blue flat disk of urinal freshener. The toilet flushed—I thought nothing of it, concentrating on the task at hand. I didn't want to be like one of those dudes who make awkward eye contact in bathrooms. Then Amante came out of the stall.[155] This Amante or pseudo-Amante walked right past me to the sink and fussed around, turning on the hot water and then the cold water, adjusting, getting the temperature just right, and then scrubbing his hands long enough for me to flush and still be waiting there, off to the side. I stepped closer.

He looked up at me, or not at me, rather through the glass at me. I guess it was obvious I was looking at him. He pulled the bows of his glasses, which he was now wearing, more firmly over his ears. "Oh," he said, instantly averting his eyes. "I'll be done in a sec."

"Take your time," I said.

The polite tone of his voice and the clear self-consciousness with which he washed his hands, somewhat anxious that he was holding me up, speeding up the process for my benefit—these were all telltale signs that this was indeed the real Amante. And yet, his face was less and less familiar. It was as if someone had taken an eraser and blended his features, dirtied up any direct references to the original. The eyebrows were the same, so was the hair, but the nose and something about his cheekbones didn't jibe with the Amante I knew. He shut off the water

---

[155] At least, I felt 80% confident it was Amante; I couldn't be sure. In a situation like this, I had to be certain. I didn't want to awkwardly introduce myself. Amante never made any sense anyway—for all I knew he could've left already and planted one of his decoys in his place. I wouldn't be surprised at all if that's what he'd done, just to throw me off the scent.

abruptly and pulled the lever for the paper towel dispenser. Even then, he held himself in a slightly defensive posture, shy and uncomfortable with the entire situation.

"I'm sorry, I think we've met... ?" I started.

He smiled at me, without opening his mouth, and was like "Huh?"

"Nothing," I said.

He glanced over, trying to place me. "Catch you later," he finally said.[156]

Then he was gone. I washed my hands in a hurry and went after him—now 92.5% sure that this was Amante, the one and only. He was headed toward the exit. I headed there too.

"Hey!" I called after him, but he was out of range.

The bouncer was on his stool, pontificating with this lanky white dude in a black leather suit like the first version of Jim Morrison. "Like a seal. That's what her skin felt like," the bouncer was saying.

"Far out," the other dude said.

I called after Amante again.[157]

"Nick!" the bouncer said, echoing me.

---

[156] That was also something Amante would say. He was always über-polite.

[157] Somehow it was imperative I confront him now and get it over with, whatever "it" was, say my piece and move on with my life. All night, I'd realized, I was coming face to face with this specter of success, this weird alternate version of myself who, despite one or two legitimate human-to-human interactions, had mostly eluded me and remained elusive, a slippery son of a bitch, lurking in the depths and popping out (as Preston would say) with the grotesque sneering of a moray eel, only to retract immediately and give me the slip, time and again choosing the precise moment when he could almost guarantee I wouldn't try to track him down or figure out what Houdini-like trick he'd utilized to evade detection.

"Yo, Nick," the other dude said.

I had him—he was on the sidewalk, hands in his pockets, heading north. I was just through the door when my pocket vibrated: Olivia. I stopped for a second and another dude behind me, who didn't take well to my hesitation, muttered "What the fuck" and skirted past me.

"Yo, yo," the bouncer said. "Pennsylvania. Come here."

His friend was lighting a cigarette.

"What do you want?" I said.

The bouncer was like "Hey. Who you think you're talking to?"

I looked over my shoulder in the direction Amante had taken. He was still within hailing distance, but farther and farther off, moving into that shadowy half-space, in and out of the streetlights.

The bouncer interpreted my gesture as a weak sort of nonconfrontation. "Ha, ha," he said. "You should see your face. Don't worry. We're pals."

I was like "That's right," still hesitating, pulled in two directions, and actually sort of mad.

"Where'd your honey go?" the bouncer said.

I was like "Honey?" For a second, I was sure he meant Michelle Roberts, *Super Librarian*, or (less plausibly) Olivia. I only realized he meant Maggie after he started giving me his own sad-sack dating history.[158]

---

[158] Not to get into particulars, but he was a devotee of OkCupid where his screenname was Bubbaloo Blue (and his corresponding avatar: a cuddly blue bear). He wished he'd had more good luck to report. He'd gone on a blind date at Tavern on the Green and totally screwed up his last "looking for a relationship" encounter, after he blew off his scheduled date and went and got drunk on Coors Banquet Beers with a random butch chick who'd hired him to move her couch. The butch chick was saucy and spiteful and wanted like all of her erogenous zones stimulated at the same time, which caused Bill "Quarter" Ray to cramp up and darn near re-aggravate a sprain in his

The leather dude was laughing at some private joke. He coughed abruptly, trying to get a hold of himself.

"What's your trick, anyway?" the bouncer said, ignoring his friend. "No, seriously." (I'd gone blank—as in, I was temporarily stymied and at the mercy of this overfriendly bouncer. I was still holding the phone, but I'd collapsed it accidentally before the message screen with Olivia's message appeared.) "I want to know. It can't be your looks."

More laughing.

I was going to tell the bouncer to fuck off and see what came of it (if worst came to worst, I was sure I could outrun him, it wasn't like he was Usain Bolt), but instead I was like "Beats me."

"It's a tough town to meet people, that's all," the bouncer said. "Hey." He must have sensed my attention drifting. "No hard feelings." He reached out his hand. I took it—his hand was almost gelatinous, no pressure at all, it slipped out of my grip with its natural weight. I didn't look at him the whole time.

"Nice to meet you, man. My PA brother. Where you from anyway? What city? Yo!"

I was retracing my steps to the lobby, about to read the message on my phone when Maggie just about jumped me.[159] "I'm glad I caught you," she said. "You ditching us all?"

I was like "Not likely. How'd I get home otherwise?"

I didn't want to confront Quarter Ray and his lanky accomplice any more times that night, so I backed Maggie into the lobby even though I was pretty sure she wanted to step outside. "I can't believe you," she said, digging in and refusing to back up any farther. "Leaving without saying goodbye."

"I wasn't leaving," I said. "Come on."

"I wouldn't put anything past you anymore."

---

wrist. He called and apologized to the date he'd stood up, but she didn't even respond—all he heard was her pissy breath on the phone.

[159] All Olivia's message said, when I read it, was: GETTING SLEEPY. By then, we were already heading off.

To be honest, it looked like Maggie had been about to leave too. She was holding her own phone—that bitty, purple Samsung model—and had her purse ready under her other arm. I was about to comment on this, when she was like "Find your friend?"

"What?"

"Your writer friend?" Maggie was close to me again, but not that close, and she was smiling, her hair brushed back like a boy's, shifting her weight on her heels. "Who you followed into the friggin' bathroom?"

I was like "He left."

"You're a weirdo," Maggie said.

"Thanks, Mags."

"You're really not going to tell me about him?"

I leaned against the wall and Maggie, like she was joined to me, stepped closer. Even now I'm not really sure why I said what I did. But, in a way, it wasn't a total lie. "He slept with my college girlfriend."[160]

---

[160] Anna and Amante met only once, so far as I know, outside a 2nd floor bathroom in Branford College, in that party suite known as "God Quad." As soon as I got to that party, running a bit late, and already somewhat sloshed from the Chevis Regal that my Canadian (but also Scottish) friend Nick (not Amante) McClean had procured from one of his humungous suitcases, I headed for the cooler, which contained some sort of everclear mixed with Kool-Aid, a surefire ticket to a blackout. According to Anna, I just stationed myself there, drinking cup after cup, even after she pulled one of my cups away, remonstrating. How she kept track of me was anyone's guess since she spent most of the night dancing with some peachfuzzy kid named Jeremy who she'd mentioned once or twice around the dining hall table, saying how he was "beautiful, but young." "Whoa, dude!" my pal Angie Zhou had said when she saw me with the everclear. "Drink water!" By then, I was already stumbling around and slurring my words and generally making an ass of myself,

attempting to pull Anna away from Jeremy and reciting romantic couplets that fell on deaf ears. Next thing I knew, I was on my knees in the bathroom, trying to scoop vomit out of the sink so the water would drain. That was my major concern: the water must drain. Angie was gone, her boyfriend Desmond (who had also—more successfully—removed another cup from my hand) was gone; Anna, so far as I knew, was gone, and there, right behind me, dressed in black like Laurence Olivier playing Hamlet, was Nick Amante. Drunk as I was, and in bad shape all round, I couldn't help wondering why Amante was even there, since the last I'd heard he'd checked back into some New Jersey clinic to treat his own drug addiction/mental instability, and had taken at least one year off from college. I was going to question Amante on this score, when duty called, and it was all I could do to heave whatever was left from my stomach into the sink. Amante walked over. He turned off the faucets, walked to the towel dispenser, and walked back. "Hey," I said. "Where are you going?" I clutched at his leg, but found myself slipping onto the tile. Then Amante's face was close to mine, and I felt his hand under my head, holding me up like he was about to perform last rites, and he whispered "Chin up, chin up. Don't worry, I come from a long line of drunks." I was shivering and shaking by this point, and dribbled spit out of my mouth, trying to form words, with the room spinning and Amante's five o'clock shadow spinning and the unmistakable sensation of falling into a pit and having everything close up over me in a cool, porcelain sheath; it was hugely embarrassing. Amante never let go. I closed and opened my eyes, really expecting Anna to be there—so what if we weren't technically dating? "Can you stand?" Amante said. He didn't wait for me to reply; in fact, I think we were already walking when he said this, or maybe that's how long it took for me to process his questions, which he put to me in a calm Jungian manner, with no trace of impatience or irritation or disappointment. We moved out, Amante whistling a marching tune, his arm around my waist, not minding that I stepped on his Bostonian shoes. Outside, I had to retch again, off in the

"Ah," Maggie said. "Shit. Sorry I asked."

"It's in the past," I said, trying to be dismissive.

"I shouldn't have asked."

I shrugged and motioned toward heading back inside the concert room door. Foot-traffic (I.E. new arrivals) was kind of moving in that direction, anyway. I could just hear someone at the microphone sounding pissed off and hoarse, the third act of the night. Then Sean strolled out, cutting across the crowd, not noticing us right away, patting the back part of his hair where he thought he might be going bald.

"Hey, Romeo," Maggie said. "Where's Tweedledum?"

"Oh," Sean said, surprised. "In the crapper. Why? Didn't you see him? I can relay a message if you want."

---

bushes, and when I looked up we were somewhere outside Branford courtyard, in an alley or street I'd never seen before, with dark fir trees and mulch (which smelled strongly of manure and induced more dry heaving) and some scraggly purple-streaked humps of winter cabbage. Anna was with us now, pacing back and forth. Her worried expression made me more worried—it's true that no pain is worse than the pain we feel for making another person feel pain. But Amante was talking to her, consoling her, and even then I had the weirdest feeling that she was laughing and brazenly flirting with him—with Amante—as if I wasn't even there. I had no doubt that in any other circumstance Anna wouldn't have cared a hoot about Amante but here and now, in my present deplorable state, it was as if they'd become bosom friends. And I was just sitting there, the whole time, crumpled on the curb, unable to move, as if all my blood had turned thick as corn syrup (which to my mind, explained the pounding around my temples) until I saw flashing red lights and felt Amante's arms around me again, lifting me up, and transporting me to the back of the ambulance, where the EMT gave me a jovial smile and said "You're all right now. You can stop pretending."

Maggie was like "No, thank you. Have fun. It's a party in the men's room tonight."

Sean went to the restroom door, turned to us, shook his head, and nearly missed colliding with some short guy in a beanie.

"What do you want to do now?" Maggie said. She was leaning into me again like this was sort of a casual thing, like she had to step out of someone's way or she'd momentarily lost her balance due to inner-ear jostling but don't you dare say she was remotely close to being drunk; she wasn't. I tried stepping away so there was an arm-length between us.[161] "What do you want to *do*?" she repeated in a modulated voice which left little room for interpretation,[162] especially as her somewhat downy forearm slid provocatively against the goosebumped skin of my own.

"I don't know," I said. "I'm fine just hanging out. I guess we're going to leave."

"And go where?" Maggie said.

I shrugged, noncommittal.

"Do you want to stay or do you want to go?" Maggie said right as the concert doors opened again, emitting the same husky voice, and what sounded like an amplified banjo. A few more people were calling it a night, heading out, or at least moseying toward the exit, among them a decent sized, athletically sculpted, dude in a button down shirt, with absurdly large biceps and a neck like a wrestler's. This dude separated himself from the rest of the crowd and approached us.

"Hey, Maggie," he said.

Maggie scooped at her hair as if in pain, and stepped away from me. Then—I wasn't sure at first—she put her hand on the guy's arm. "Ian, this is Paul. We met while you were dancing." She still sounded mad about the dancing.

---

[161] A la "save a little room for the Holy Spirit".

[162] I.E. there was no way it meant "Do you want to stay here any longer?"

"Nice to meet you," Paul said. We shook hands. "Not heading out?"

"Think so," Maggie said, though she didn't sound too set on anything anymore.

I was like "Yup."

"Can I convince you to stay?" Paul said. "I'm not leaving. I just had to take a call."

Maggie was like "Paul's one of the owners."

"Wouldn't think it, eh? I look like someone's dad."

"No," I said.

Paul was sort of drawing Maggie away, call or no call, and I looked over at the restrooms again, glad to see Sean and Preston had emerged and were loitering by the display cabinets. I pantomimed walking over there—to give Maggie some space and all—but Paul and Maggie weren't watching me, so I left all awkwardly, without saying goodbye or offering any parting words, or even pulling out some handy excuse like "I'm just going to go stop in the restroom," or "Be right back" (with obviously no intention of coming back), widening my eyes as I got closer to Sean. "The owner," I said.

I'm not sure if he heard me. He was half-looking at a montage of concert notices and bulletins and album advertisements: Regina Spektor, Nicole Atkins, Jess Peng, the Veronicas, Trespassers William, Not Your Mama's Radio, Goldfrapp, Cocteau Twins, The Lorgnettes, Camera Obscura, Ada Rebek, Santigold, Kiera Lynn Cain, The Misty's, etc., all behind the glass. "How do you feel about Neptune's?" he said, his attention divided between the glass display and his phone, which he'd taken out again. "You know, Preston went without dinner?"

"I thought you were fasting?" I said.

"Hell no," Preston said. "Liquid diet."

"Beer's like bread," Sean said. "Though, you'll never lose weight that way." He was rubbing his forehead with his fist closed over the phone.

"Is Neptune's that Polish diner?" Preston said.

166

"You been?" Sean said.

"Naw, man. But I could use a whole plate of latkas right about now." Preston held out an open palm. "Don't let me do it. All right? I really am cutting back. Aw, fuck it. What's it matter?"

"Latkas, that's health food," Sean said.

"Throw some sour cream on top and you got two of the major food groups," Preston said.

Sean was like "Right on. You said he's the owner. He owns this place?" He was looking directly at Maggie and that Paul guy now, though he spoke as if he'd just remembered her and was just sort of mildly interested.

I was like "Apparently."

"Good for Mags," he said.

We had to cut short any more speculating as to who was who, and who owned what, since Maggie was coming back.

"Well well well," Sean said.

Maggie put something in her purse. "Why do I always get the bald ones?" she said.

"You get his digits?" Sean said.

"I didn't come to get hit on."

Sean frowned and shook his head. Preston meanwhile had meandered over to the side of the lobby and was adjusting his belt, in an attempt at being inconspicuous.

"Anyway, I ran into him only because you two were AWOL, dancing with girls with bad dye-jobs."

"Don't change the subject," Sean said.

I was like "Bad dye-jobs?"

"Men!" Maggie said.[163]

"We're thinking of leaving," I said.

"Good," Maggie said. "I was ready an hour ago. About the time you were fondling your new girlfriend."

---

[163] My cluelessness had put her at a loss for words (a rare occurrence), though the follow up was clearly "You're so oblivious!"

"It's totally up to you if you want to go or not," Sean said. "No one's twisting your arm."

"*I'm* fine," Maggie said. "But don't let me tear *you* away."

"You don't mind missing the band?" I said.

"Are you friggin' nuts? Do you have eardrums?"

"That sound you're picking up on," Sean said. "That's on purpose, you know that."

Maggie was like "What about you?" She knocked her hand against my waist. "Will you miss 'the band'?"[164]

"Eh," I said. "I'll live."[165]

Maggie pursed her lips. She was on the verge of saying something else, maybe, I'm almost sure she was, but then the doors to the concert opened and Michelle and Nora came giggling out, and Maggie's face hardened. "Look," she said. "It's the blondies."

But they were only going to the restroom (the third set had injected new life into them) and they never even looked our way.

---

[164] She literally did these quotey things with her fingers.

[165] The morning after the ambulance, Anna came to pick me up from Yale New Haven Hospital. She held my arm as we walked along York Street back toward campus, through the sunlight that pinched my eyes, and it was like I was an old man, frail and infirm, and she was guiding me back to safety, her large and capable body more than supporting me as I tottered, sunspots in my eyes, sourness in my mouth. When we got to York Street and Broadway she was like "This is where I'll be leaving you. Don't ever do that to me again." There are many ways to say goodbye.

Book Three

In theory, we should have been able to walk to Café Neptune from Trash Bar without a hitch but Sean led us the wrong way and we got mixed up, falling into a quiet and deserted block which we initially assumed had been bustling with activity—albeit behind the scenes, in the manner of so many Williamsburg dives, which to all outward appearances look like Jiffy Lube garages or boarded factories or carnicerias or insane asylums but, in reality, are clubs and trend-setting lounges where female bartenders with hair like the Uma Thurman of *Pulp Fiction* serve ritzy cocktails on the order of sidecars and gimlets to the shoulder-to-shoulder, well-dressed, well-coiffed crowd. We'd approached a bodega that wasn't a bodega, and then we spotted a neon light, which turned out just to be some decorative tube wrapped around the fire escape of another derelict former factory building. This tube (or maybe it was some aborted artistic project of the Marcel Duchamp school) reflected the glow from a streetlamp and easily masqueraded as a legitimate sign for a bar. Of course, by now, Preston had to put in his two cents, like he was Henry the Navigator, and under his direction we went even farther adrift. Who knows where we would've ended up, if Maggie hadn't taken out her phone and plugged in the address and set us straight.

Meanwhile, I'd intentionally let them all go ahead of me and called Olivia again.[166] Three or four rings and her phone went to voicemail, like she had muted it on purpose, not wanting to talk to me, which meant I'd blown it, unless she was still preoccupied with her public health chums or whoever she'd

---

[166] Yes, I'd called last, but I couldn't help myself. It had been way over an hour—and I hadn't thought she would hold out so long. In other words, my resolution of three hours ago didn't last (see note 108).

ventured into Manhattan to see,[167] and—missing my opportunity to hang up and at the same time not prepared to leave a message—I kind of panicked when I heard the beep and became like an actor who knows with certainty he's going to flub his lines. I held the phone away from my ear for a sec, then said (with as much composure as I could muster, which wasn't much) "Hey Liv, it's Ian. Calling you back. Talk later." Short and desperate, the type of message I'd never in all my adult life wanted to leave.

I closed the phone unhappily and caught up with the others, who had just reached the diner.

It was possible we'd walked right by it: Neptune's didn't look like much from the outside. The florescent light that said: DINER was losing its oomph and the street we were on just blended in with the same old sleepy neighborhood we'd come out of, boarded up and shut down, certainly not welcoming or luring patrons or dressed up as 'urban hip' or 'industrial chic.' Still, for all that, the diner was packed. The place was literally overrun with mariachis. We couldn't hear their hubbub from the street, but we had our first clue they were inside when two mariachis in pink and robin's egg blue suits strolled out the door and down the steps, skirting past Maggie, who was leaning on Sean's shoulder while she unstrapped her heels and said the f-word under her breath.

Inside, the mariachis had commandeered a banquet table, which had become a cornucopia of dollar-store Mexican-themed knickknacks: maracas, burro piggy banks, Julio Inglesias bobbleheads, prayer flags, Dia de los Muertos festive streamers, glow-in-the-dark skulls, cactus and eagle statuettes, etc. A few more of their ranks were idling within the foyer, another couple went to join their pals for a smoke break as we came in. Even when I went to the bathroom, I had to wait my turn behind a disagreeable-looking mariachi—detachable Burt Reynolds

---

[167] It never occurred to me that she might've gone to bed by now. It was past 2:00, after all.

moustache all askew—who glared at me like I'd scuffed his shoes or done something else to offend him.

Sean had been unusually pissed off, annoyed no doubt by his limited sense of direction, but after he saw the mariachis he mellowed and became like his usual self.

"What's with the mariachis?" I said when I sat down. We had taken a booth by the large window facing the street, removed from the excitement in the center of the room.

Preston was like "Bachelor party." The casual way in which he said it—hardly diverting attention from a sugar holder he'd been fondling in his left hand[168]—made me feel like an idiot for not putting this together myself.

"Wild times," Sean said.

Maggie glanced across the table at Sean and Preston, as if this were old news. She yawned into the back of her hand, reading the menu.

"I don't get it," I said. I wasn't rubbing my eyes yet, but I was close to sleep myself, and I was fairly sure if I just put my head down I would've nodded off.[169]

---

[168] Preston was fond of pointing out how most of our sugar came from beets. He'd made this observation at least four times in all the time I'd known him, and I was just waiting for him to make it again tonight—but I guess he got distracted. Part of the reason I noticed his nervous habit was my dad does the same thing, only my dad rearranges his silverware—spinning his spoon and fork and setting them back in place, over and over again, without even realizing he's doing it, a trait I've inherited, though it manifests itself differently in me—see note 106, "I don't want to be marked."

[169] But I wouldn't have been able to sleep anyway. Why? I couldn't help thinking about Olivia, specifically Olivia taking out her phone and seeing my name on the screen and intentionally—yes intentionally—silencing her phone and then going back to whatever conversation she'd left off, as if I wasn't worth a second thought, or could just be deferred the way you

"Get what?" Sean said.

"How do you know it's a bachelor party?"

"Look at them," Maggie said.

They sure were having a roaring time, those mariachis, tipping their chairs back from the table, passing around carafes of sweet red wine, toasting indiscriminately. Of course, when you came down to it, they weren't *real* mariachis at all. Their pastel colored jackets and pants trimmed with black lace had a chintzy, inauthentic appearance, like they'd picked them up on the cheap from some specialty costume store in Midtown. Even their sombreros heightened the dubiousness of their *mariachi-ness* since they didn't match the rest of their gear (not in color, not in texture) and in some cases didn't even fit properly. But the wait staff was putting up with them,[170] and at this hour no one else was complaining.

"Too early for Halloween," Sean said.

Preston was like "Only in New York," and let it rest.

"Requests!" one of the mariachis was shouting, distinctly. A trumpet sounded, and then there was a general cacophony like the members of an orchestra before a concert.[171]

"How about 'Long Ago and Far Away,'" Maggie said.

---

defer a slight urge to urinate in the middle of some other engrossing activity like paring your toenails or watching reruns or chatting with a long lost friend. I was wondering how she could just ignore me like that, when this whole evening she'd been the one reaching out to me like she had something to say, playing this whole cat-and-mouse game, in fact initiating it, and even complaining about getting sleepy as if that were any fault of mine. She'd retreated back into that unreachable zone the two of us vied to inhabit and (if I was really honest with myself) I was just mad she'd gotten there first and now had leisure to toy with me.

[170] Perhaps the added gratuity (for parties over 6) sweetened the deal.

[171] It seems we couldn't escape from musicians that night.

Sean was like "I don't think they know that one."

"Pity."

"Requests!" they shouted again.

The mariachi's waitress—a short, stocky Polish lady with a hair net and a light blue skirt (pretty much the uniform of the establishment)—had come back to their table in the middle of the wood-paneled floor,[172] and was giving it a bit more

---

[172] This floor had also functioned as a dancefloor back in the day when this diner used to be Neptune's Ukrainian Wedding Hall. In most respects, the diner had retained its previous old world atmosphere, including the ornate lamp fixtures, a few swaths of deteriorating olive-gray carpet adjacent to our booth, the heavy faux-oak doors to the restroom, the imitation admiral's chairs, the formaldehyde-preserved marlin nailed to a huge slab of driftwood, an ugly tobacco-store era carving of a rimy mariner with an eye-patch and an outstretched hand displaying the mark familiar to any reader of *Treasure Island* (which was probably just mildew and/or mold, not part of the original conception). Even the smell of the place was a carryover from its previous days of debauchery and merrymaking, a rich suffocating aroma like biscuit batter and caramelized onions. But not every feature could stay. In the brief remodel, they'd replaced the gaudy chandeliers with subdued recess lighting and installed a long counter in front of what used to be a brick fireplace; the counter—in customary diner style—housed a refrigerated compartment which displayed all sorts of petrified custards and tapioca puddings in frosted glass goblets sealed with Seran wrap, as well as several dense loaves of day-old bread, which were collected every weekend and deposited in a trash bag out in the back alley, for the local homeless. They'd also done a shabby job painting over the fresco of undersea life, populated with as many weird denizens as a triptych by Hieronymus Bosch; the painters must have lazily applied one coat of seafoam paint thus allowing the previous incarnations to bloom through the top coat as if through a gauzy-green veil.

forcefully to the ringleader, this guy with a purple sombrero and an elaborate *Scarface*-style leisure suit. Meanwhile, a few mariachis had sauntered over to our table and, half-bowing, clearly inebriated, asked if we'd pick a song for them to play. Maggie winced and raised her eyebrows.

Sean was a lot more jovial. I didn't know how he'd perked up—if he'd downed another 5-Hour Energy or what—but he was suddenly the most alert out of all of us.[173] "How 'bout Pachelbel's Canon?" he said.

The mariachis were like "We can do that."

"He's being facetious," Maggie said. "Don't encourage them," she said to Sean.

The first mariachi started playing the opening measure of Pachelbel's Canon on his trumpet, pretty accurately all things considered, until Maggie cut him off, clapping. "All right. Bravo. Moving on."

"Gosh, you're no fun," Sean said.

"If they're going to play something, at least make it appropriate," Maggie said.[174]

The mariachis smiled back at us. "Ah! Appropriate, then. 'Gauntanamera'? 'Amorcito Corazón'?"

"'Cielito Lindo,'" said the second mariachi; he held a violin casually against his thigh.

Sean was like "I'm partial to 'La Bamba.'"

"Who's getting hitched?" Preston said.

"Our boy Tommy there," the second mariachi said, motioning to the table, to one of the sombrero-less mariachis, with light hair and a chubby, almost cherubic face, his cheeks totally red.

"Don't do it, man!" Preston shouted.

Maggie was like "That's nice."

---

[173] At least, for a little while.

[174] She herself would violate this stipulation soon enough.

"Yup. After three—how many years is it?" the first mariachi said.

"I think you're right, three," the second mariachi said.

"Three long years, he's finally going through with it."

"Three years officially—but how long they been sleeping together?" said the third mariachi.

"Two more."

"At least two more."

"They're making it legal, that's what counts," the first mariachi said. In between, he was limbering up his lips, and flicking his moustache with his tongue.

"Tying the knot," Preston said. "Pulling the trigger, eh?"

"She's a sweatheart—his wife—fiancée," the first said. "Whatever, she might as well be his wife. It's just a formality at this point."

"Well, it's more than that," the second said.

"Sure, whatever," the first said. "What'll it be? What song?"

"You'd be surprised how many we know," the third laughed—he seemed like the comedian of the group. He strummed some flamenco on his diminutive guitar.

"Thanks, but we're all kind of recovering," Maggie said.

"Recovering?" the second said. "Recovering from what?"

"Hearing loss," Maggie said.

"Boo. Boo," the mariachis said. "How often does this happen to you?"

"You're asking the wrong person," Maggie said. "I ride the subway. So, everyday."

"Ouch," the second said.

"Only, we're not asking for money."

"Totally free," the second said.

The third was like "Tips are optional. You may want to tip. But it's optional. Officially: no tips. We can't accept tips. We're not authorized to take your money. We don't have a permit. But if you want to express your appreciation... "

"I don't," Maggie said, looking across at Sean as if for confirmation.

"If only my moustache would stay on," the first said, pinching his nose.

"You seem like a nice bunch of guys," Maggie said. "Why not take your little instruments back to your table and put them in their cases and give them a rest? You can serenade Brooklyn later—much later."

"We've been serenading Brooklyn all night," the mariachis laughed.

"Serenade some other part of Brooklyn," Maggie said.

The second was like "Come on, Dave. It's a tough crowd over here."

"Last chance," Dave, the trumpeter, said.

Maggie was like "Thanks, but no thanks."

"Peace and love," the mariachis said. They squeezed out a few lines of "Cielito Lindo" but Maggie's glare effectively ended the trio's tableside performance.

"Godspeed, brother," Preston said as they were leaving. "I mean, to the groom-to-be."

I was like "Yeah, congratulations."

"Lots of luck," Sean said.

Maggie was like "I don't want to be a party pooper. I just don't want anyone playing a trumpet like right against my eardrum right now."

"It wasn't right against your eardrum," I said.

"Close enough."

Our waitress, who I think had been hovering by the hostess stand while the mariachis detained us, now darted in, apologetic, and asked what we were having. She was a bony blonde girl with a long face and impressive, multicolored bangs, some of which were embroidered, and she took our order with her right arm curled around, like in a defensive posture, as if one of us might snatch the ticket.

"Should I go first?" Preston said.

Sean was like "By all means."

"Then, here I go."

Preston was getting the Polish Sampler—meat pierogis, stuffed cabbage, latkas, and kielbasa—he really was hungry. I skimmed the menu again and when my turn came just ordered a Żywiec and a bran muffin.

"Olga," the waitress called to her chubbier counterpart, who was cashing out some dude in an EZ Rider jacket at the far end of the counter within the shadow of the marlin's tail. "We got bran muffins?"

The other waitress shook her head grimly.

"No bran muffins," the waitress said.

I ordered an apple pie instead.

"A la modey?" the waitress said, saying "modey" with no hesitation, with such definitive pronunciation that I immediately called my own into question.

"Sure," I said. "A la modey."

Maggie pressed my leg. "You really want that a la 'moodie'?"[175]

I was like "Don't be mean."

"You picked a very Polish dessert," Sean said.

Preston was like "Haven't you heard 'as Polish as apple pie'?"

"Just felt like it," I said. "What? Should I have got the rice pudding?"

"You're the boss," Sean said.

"Leave me alone."

Sean broke into a smile. "Sorry. Enjoy your 'modey.'"

"I don't see how any of you are hungry, anyway," Maggie said. "After those bratwurst."

"That was a lifetime ago," Sean said. "This is early breakfast."

"It might be my only breakfast," Preston said.

Maggie pressed her closed fist against my leg. "You must of worked up an appetite with your dancing."

---

[175] Her intentional mispronunciation set me straight.

Sean was like "He was dancing, not me."

"I saw what I saw," Maggie said.

I was like "Everyone knows I can't dance."

"Well, twinkle toes over here was giving you a run for your money," Maggie said.

"Save the ridicule," Sean said. "I've got to get my knee drained again on Tuesday."

My attention had wandered to my phone again, and without really watching what I was doing, I brought it out of my pocket and flipped it open, till the screen went onto sleep mode. I was sure I was being sneaky, until I felt Maggie's hand press my arm. Then I saw her glancing down at me.

"Got somewhere to be?" she said in a low voice.

"Nope."

"Who's on your phone?"

"Just checking our time," I said.

Maggie was like "Our time? Our time for what?"

Preston yawned mightily. "Fellows, I got to tell you. I haven't been out this late since—well—since I don't know when."

"How's it feel, Pres?" Sean said.

"Feels great, dude. Thanks for asking."

"How about the holiday party?" Maggie said. She was finally talking to Preston without derision.

"That wasn't late," Preston said.

"Not the actual party, the place we ended up."

"I remember where Ian ended up," Sean said. "He ended up getting us all tossed out of McSorley's."

"Don't remind me," I said.

"That was great," Preston said, breaking into imitation. "'Who me? I'm fine.'" He pantomimed me stumbling out of the restroom and then doubling over and puking. "'Get the fuck out of here,'" he said in an Irish brogue, imitating the bartender. "'Ya pansy. That goes fer the lot a ya.' I was like 'But, hey. I just started a fresh one.' No dice man. Thanks a lot. You owe me a beer."

"Let's not get into debts and obligations," Sean said. "You didn't have to nurse him back to health."

"That bad, eh?" Preston said.

"Worse," Sean said.

"We've all been there," Preston said.

"Sean was a hero that night," I said. "A real lifesaver."[176]

"*I can be your hero baby*," Preston mock-sang.

"We made the best of it, didn't we?" Sean said. "We met these girls on the ferry—this real hot girl, who was totally older it turned out. Remember?[177] Oh no, wait. You blacked out."

---

[176] For a representative sampling of my own "heroism," skip right over to note 201.

[177] The end of that evening found me on the ferry with Sean, unable to throw up into the Upper New York Bay. That's when this lady in her 40s and someone who I assumed (in my woozy state) to be her daughter approached us and started making chit chat. To further whatever plan he'd concocted, Sean convinced them that I wasn't sloppy drunk but rather seasick, and this won me some sympathy points from the older lady, who made me sit down next to her and started stroking my hair. Now and then Sean gave me a look that was meant to convey that I should *act cool* and just let him do his thing, since the younger girl had partnered off with him to let me and the older lady have some space. If I hadn't been so messed up at the time, I might have talked better. Instead, I was having some difficulty keeping myself from going permanently cross-eyed and not passing out on my new friend's lap. I played these symptoms off as seasickness for about five minutes, and I was mentally congratulating myself for my efforts, especially as I noticed that Sean was making the girl laugh and she wasn't even casting glances at her old friend or me anymore: a sign that things were going well. But I couldn't keep it up. The responsibility was too much for me and I made a grave error when I started telling the old chick how much I admired the character and temperament of Donald Rumsfeld, misjudging her political leanings—she was,

"Not my finest hour," I said.

Preston was like "But you had fun, no?"

"We ended up going to my place—me, Ian, and those girls," Sean said. "It would've been great, except Ian passed out in the hamper—you took the hamper down with you. The whole time this girl kept being like 'Shouldn't you check on your friend? I'm worried about your friend.' I mean, I turned him over, siphoned water into him. He was perfectly fine, just sleeping it off, but she was concerned. By that point, I don't think he had much liquor left in his system. He'd made a total ass of himself with her friend—that was hilarious. She was offended or something— what'd you say to her anyway?"

---

it turns out, a Republican and guessed (correctly) that I wasn't being serious. She'd probably been onto me before that, I mean the liquor was literally seeping out my pores, but some sort of mothering instinct in her had overruled her quite proper disgust at my shenanigans. Anyway, at some point in time, the whole thing was rather fuzzy, she stopped talking and stroking my hair—in fact, I distinctly remember her applying some Purell Hand Sanitizer to herself and scooting over to leave a seat between us. Despite all that, or maybe because of it (I.E. compared to me, Sean was a real "catch"), Sean persuaded the "daughter" to get a nightcap at his apartment which was a mere stone's throw from the ferry dock, and thus a perfectly reasonable suggestion. When I woke up, several hours later, the younger girl was peeing and Sean was reading a magazine, with Phil Collins playing lightly on his boombox. Remarkably, I felt as if renewed: no headache, no aftertaste of bile, no nothing, except for an overwhelming desire for fried food. And over donuts at our usual Staten Island donut joint, Sean told me he'd "made it" with the red head (I hadn't noticed her hair color or even heard her leave—I was in fact surprised she wasn't at the donut place too but she'd had an early morning dental appointment, impossible to reschedule). Evidently, Sean had a rather broad interpretation for what "made it" meant.

I shrugged.

"She wasn't *that* offended, really," Sean said. "She drove us over to my place. We would've been fine walking, but she thought we might've gotten mugged. I think she thought all the criminal element came out at night. She had an idea there was some meth ring in the community. Remember the drive, Ian? I didn't think so. We got back and everything was going great—we were talking (Ian was sleeping). The girls had a conference. The girl Ian offended drove home, 'cause she had to work the next day. Everything was lining up. Me and that red head really hit it off, I thought. We said goodnight to Ian—she was kind of a cougar, it was true, but I didn't find that out until later. Isn't it funny how the next morning everything comes into focus? Anyway, Ian kept coming between us—total cockblock—even in the other room. Every five minutes she was like 'He sounds too quiet in there.' I was like 'Sure, he's quiet. He's passed the fuck out.' She's like 'But I'm worried about him, is he OK?' Whenever anything got going, she was like 'Shouldn't we check on him?'"

"Bummer," Preston said.

Sean was like "She really liked Ian here. The next morning she was just sitting out in the living room, staring at him. He was just such a pitiful, crumpled sack of shit."

"Kind of creepy," Maggie said. "Watching Ian. Not going to lie."

"I'm going to point out," I said, "that I was one-hundred-percent fine the next day."

"She didn't want my number, that's all I know," Sean said. "Make of it what you will."

The waitress was back now with the food and I stared out the window, which provided little view of the outside other than the measly glare off the dying light on the side of the building and the brick wall of the warehouse opposite. I opened my phone. I was scanning Olivia's message GETTING SLEEPY. STILL AT BAR? and made up my mind I'd write one last time: CALL ME, in the imperative, an ultimatum of sorts, since it was possible my last phone call hadn't gone through or she'd been underground again, with no record of the attempt.[178] It took me a while to type out the message (I'd first spelled CALL ME, BAJM MDE[179]), but when I had it, I sent it, and went to work on my pie. I was kind of jealous of Preston's plate now that it was right in front of me, still steaming and fragrant—I really wanted a latka but Preston was chowing down. All Maggie had ordered was an Earl Grey tea. She held the cup with both hands like a kid, her elbows on the table.

"We had to take not one, but two cabs to South Ferry, because yours truly spewed his guts out in the first one," Sean said. "Anyone want fries, feel free."

Maggie acted like she was disgusted, but I helped myself to Sean's plate.

"Dick move, man," Preston said. "You do owe him."

"It's not like I did anything on purpose," I said.

Preston wiped his mouth. "You're a lousy drunk," he said. "Just admit it."

"Ian acts all innocent, but I think he charms the women," Sean said.

"Oh, I *know* he does," Maggie said.

---

[178] Yes, it would've been better to pretend she hadn't texted me at all, that first time; better to go back to that comparatively calmer time when I first got to the beer garden and I had my head on straight, knew this night was just about us celebrating—without complications—our boring years working together. Well, those years weren't so bad for all that. My entire relationship with Olivia was contained in those years working at The Fund, living in Soho, spotting Nick Amante every now and then like some lost soul, but I'd never told Olivia about him—he hadn't exactly made a favorable impression the only time they met (note 123)—God forbid he ever seriously infiltrate that area of my life.

[179] I still had one of those old fashioned flip phones where the letters A, B, and C were all on the *2* key, D, E, F were on the *3* key, and so on. So, another legitimate late night error.

I was like "Whatever." I kept my eyes narrowed on the placemat in front of me. The ice cream was melting into a sludge on the rim of my plate. Maggie was right. I wasn't very hungry. I could feel almost a high water mark in my stomach which made eating unpleasant—especially eating ice cream.

Sean was like "Guess who just came in?"

"Arlo Guthrie," I said.[180]

"Close. Look."

I was sitting with my back to the hostess stand and the door so I had to lean forward and look past Maggie, who had also turned. At the same time, the stockier waitress stepped around the counter (without a great show of kindness) and was motioning for someone to "sit wherever they liked"—there was a faded sign that said *Seat Yourself* though it was easy to miss on account of its proximity to a coatrack, containing several fuchsia mariachi jackets. Nick Amante (could it be any other?) stepped forward. He went right past us—of course he didn't see us—a bit self-conscious, on his own again. The thing was, now that he was *on his own again*, without friends, or beautiful women on his arm, I felt like I hadn't treated him fairly. Like Sean, I'd also cooled off and become more reflective, a result of my overworked digestion and the burgeoning awareness that I'd brought all this Olivia business on myself. I'd lied about Amante—that was on my conscience. I never had any evidence he'd really slept with Anna. And even if he had—that had been a long time ago—another epoch. We couldn't be the same people anymore.[181]

Sean was like "Lo, the conquering hero comes."

---

[180] I don't know how this name popped up. It wasn't like "City of New Orleans" had been on the set list at Trash Bar.

[181] I also should admit that it wasn't completely preposterous that Anna would've slept with him, despite his neck hair which she would have wanted to shave (knowing her obsession with grooming; in my opinion, a character flaw).

"Who is it?" Maggie said, rubbing her eyes and looking back at me. I was kind of surprised that she hadn't pegged Amante immediately, but her eyes were getting more bloodshot, and judging from the amount of times she yawned into the back of her hand,[182] she really was fading fast.

"Ian's writer friend," Sean said.

Preston was like "Did you text him or something?"

"Why would I do that?" I said. I was even more uncomfortable with the idea that Preston might have noticed me obsessing over my phone. He wasn't exactly the most perceptive man around, and that didn't bode well for my powers of discretion.

"They aren't even friends," Maggie said—and now *she* was talking casually, like Amante's appearance was a foregone conclusion, and—like Preston and the bachelor party—it was so obvious that Amante was here, and that he *would be here*,[183] she was surprised Sean had even bothered pointing him out.

"'Scuse me a sec," I said to Maggie.

"Are you serious? Bathroom again?"

Maggie hitched herself halfway out of the seat and gave me a weird half-frown, blowing her Earl Grey scented breath at me.

"Nope," I said.

I got out and went over to Amante's booth. He wasn't visible until I was right at him—and I had a sinking feeling (I'm not sure why "sinking," unless the alcohol was magnifying all my reactions and impressions at that moment) that he would have somebody with him, that he'd managed to smuggle someone else in with him, a very small person perhaps, or some unseen person had been waiting for him all along, that the real Nick Amante would never come to some fly-on-the-wall diner on the outskirts of fashionable Brooklyn just to nurse a cup of

---

[182] Causing me, by that proven scientific phenomenon, to yawn as well, without disguising it half so nicely.

[183] Where else would he be with the entire city of New York to roam around in?

coffee and meditate on life (real or fictional) without at least one companion or toadie to bounce ideas off of, or rather to fill the vacancy of Amante's protracted, philosophical glare.[184] But no. I wasn't disappointed. Amante was alone.

"Hi," I said.

"Hi," Amante said. He'd taken his glasses off and put them back on and was looking at me studiously like a naturalist or an ornithologist or something of that sort, but a *kind* naturalist, a *tender-hearted* ornithologist, someone who was inclined to feel pity and to commiserate with the birds he's spotted in his binoculars, in the spirit of a Romantic poet a la Shelley or Lord Byron, rather than a steely, cold-hearted sort of man who documents his bird sightings in a waterproof memo pad with indifference, as if by rote, without any emotion one way or the other.

"I'm Ian," I said.

Amante was like "Yes." He recognized me. That one affirmative "yes" was enough. Even though we were just acquaintances, we'd never really had a tête-à-tête, or enjoyed the favor of each other's company over noodle soup, or met up in some exotic hookah lounge, or expensive tea purveyor's with tea stronger than coffee, or undergone some wild peyote trip together in the midst of a Jack Kerouac inspired bender, or dropped acid and then visited a Salvador Dali retrospective at

---

[184] He'd worked that glare to perfection, I'd had occasion to notice, on other nights than tonight, such as for example, when I saw him reading his beloved *Lolita*, for the 15th or 20th time, by my reckoning, on the base of Claus Oldenberg's *Lipstick* sculpture in Morse College, whenever I made a late night run to Gourmet Heaven and returned to the little tower—where I was living—at some unusual hour, my junior year, while everything was going to shit, or as Anna used to post on her AOL Instant Messenger, thinking it was a hilarious slip of the tongue: *the shit has really hit the flán.*

the Guggenheim, we had enough back history that we didn't need to bother with formalities.

"Didn't I see you at the place?" Amante said. "Place" obviously code for "Trash Bar," in Amante's laconic vernacular.[185] Amante,

---

[185] Or Café Citron or Ferrara or Uniqlo or Atticus Book Store or Whimsels (now Ashley's or who knows what) or Sterling Memorial Library or The Yankee Doodle (the last four places in New Haven)··· the list goes on of all the places I'd run into Amante over the course of seven years. I'd probably even seen him at Neat Lounge that night I'd gone with Angie and Desmond for a change of pace, to get out of my own head for a while. I'm almost sure he snuck a peek at me coming in, sitting at the far end of the bar, moping (naturally) but also caught up in the general air of conviviality since it was our last year of college and all. And the time really was slipping away. Anyway, that same night, I soon found myself sitting next to Angie's friend Tammy, who was a lot better looking than Amante, and if memory serves, was wearing a black cocktail dress and already had achieved what Angie called "the Asian flush" though Tammy wouldn't admit it, and instead kept ordering more and more apple martinis for the two of us, the pace accelerating after Angie left to join another group of friends, warning me several times not to do something I'd regret with "*you know who*"—a warning I failed to heed. In my bedroom, very late at night, with the oppressive shutters walling us in darkness, Tammy whispered "Can I stay?" I was half-sitting and she was naked, her head on my armpit—not a comfortable position for the long term, though my arm hadn't yet fallen asleep. I was like "What are you talking about?" "My ex-boyfriend, Alex," Tammy said, running her hand down my stomach. "He preferred if I left." "He what?" "Nevermind," Tammy said—catching herself in the act of revealing some profound secret and attempting to laugh it off. "You're not him," she said. "I don't get it," I said, and I really didn't. Tammy flattened herself against me and spoke in a dry, inflectionless voice. "He made me leave. He didn't want me to stay with him." She shuddered; she did everything but cry. The

as I've said time and again, was given to these sorts of cryptic designations, a mark either of an extremely shy person, or someone who literally can't tell his right from his left and is only organized in writing, when the immediacy of speech is no longer a hindrance.

I was like "Trash Bar?" (Amante nodded). "Yeah, we were there. Anyway, we didn't have much chance to talk. I saw you come in here," I gestured around the diner, "and thought I'd say hello."

Amante didn't acknowledge my friendly overture, at least he didn't acknowledge it outwardly. But his redoubled smiling showed he was touched, in his own genteel way. "Lively here tonight," he said.

The banquet table had erupted in laughter again and this time the waitress was just letting it play out. But the mariachis weren't slowing down, if anything they were rowdier than ever; the ringleader was calling for more wine and the trio who'd broached our table (now a quartet, they were joined by an accordion player) were making the rounds again, circling the diner counter-clockwise with an attempt at circumspection,

---

next day she went behind my back and asked Anna all kinds of particulars about our relationship in order to gauge if I was "relationship ready," and texted me that she wasn't sure about me, she'd have to think it over; then, an hour later, she texted and said disregard her earlier text, she thought it might work out after all; then she called me to break up, then called three times between 1 and 2 AM, and when I didn't answer texted me "WE'RE FINISHED." The next time I saw her, she was wearing an argyle sweater and had just finished shopping at J. Crew on Broadway. "Hello, Ian," she said cheerfully. "What do you not live in the 21st century? Do you not return calls?" I apologized, in a generic way, but she wasn't even mad. She kissed me on the cheek, in greeting, then went "What I wanted to know is—do you want to go to the YSO performance of Mozart's 40th symphony?" I was like "Uh··· "

avoiding a surly looking Eastern European gentleman in a colorless raincoat, hunkered down at a single table by the door to the kitchen, mashing his slightly raw fries like they were cigarette stubs and downing shots of vodka from a ruby red shot glass.[186] The accordionist was completely blitzed, though— a circumstance the others hadn't taken into consideration while they tiptoed past the shady vodka dude. Without waiting for the go-ahead, he started in on "Bella Notte" from *Lady and the Tramp* and his comrades had to shuttle him into the hall toward the restrooms, barely suppressing their own laughter which came out like wet sneezes and snorts.

"Watch out for those mariachis," I said.

"They aren't really mariachis?"

I was thrilled Amante was as clueless as I was as to the credibility of the mariachis. I was like "No. It's a bachelor party."

"Ah!" Amante said—the truth of the matter dawning on him with the same suddenness as it had for me. These little similarities in the inner-workings of our respective brains were less offensive to me now that I was actually conversing with Amante and he wasn't trying to avoid me or slink down into his seat like Incognito Mosquito.[187]

"Quite a send-off," I said, my language indistinguishable now from Amante's own.

"It's something," Amante said, noncommittal.

"I'm not sure how the staff feels about them."

"They'll take the business," Amante said.

"It's not like they're driving people away."

---

[186] I knew what Sean would say if he'd seen this cantankerous vodka swigger: "mobster." He had his back to him, though. And yes, Sean applied the Mafioso label way too liberally—which didn't make it any less applicable to Preston's father-in-law, by the way.

[187] *Incognito Mosquito*, a series of children's books by E.A. Hass, which nurtured my pre-adolescent love of detective stories—compare Amante and "Italian folktales" pages 211-212.

"Maybe they can play here every Friday night. Make a gig of it."

"But they're fake mariachis."

"Yes. They don't quite pull it off."

The waitress—our waitress not the bossy one—was grinding her teeth at the edge of Amante's booth. I glanced at her. "I'm keeping you," I said. "You know. You want to join us? Me and some friends from work?"

Amante raised his bushy eyebrows. "I wouldn't want to impose... "

"Not at all!"

"But really—I wouldn't... "

"Come on," I said.

Amante nodded and got out of the booth, the waitress watching us with a dejected face, as if the entire matter were out of her hands, and she was just a passive spectator.

"Hey," I said to Maggie, Preston and Sean. "This is my friend Nick."

Amante saluted and shook their hands and then I scrunched in next to Maggie and he took the edge of the booth next to me.

The waitress came to our table and started scratching notes on a new slip. "Are you... together then?" she said. "Separate checks?"

"Yes, thank you," Amante said. He ordered a coffee—black.[188]

"So," Sean said. His perkiness of a few minutes ago had all but dissolved—he was back to looking frazzled—although of all the diners in Brooklyn, Manhattan, or the greater New York region, this one had some of the most flattering lighting, in terms of toning down blemishes, dark under-eye circles,

---

[188] This was a small difference between us. I never drink black coffee and all through college I avoided it. In fact, when I was with Anna, I didn't drink coffee at all. There's a first time for everything, though, and it's hard to thrive in the big city without some form of stimulant.

stained teeth, and overt frumpiness. "You're a writer." This declaration was an even more blatant sign of fatigue, since Sean was never so blunt during regular office hours.

Amante hitched his shoulders like he was preparing for the backstroke: an embarrassed affirmation.

"His book is good," I said. "I read it a little bit ago."

Maggie glared at me. "Flip-flopper," she said.

I could feel myself getting kind of hot. I was like "Well. I mean, it's a little morbid."

"That's all right," Amante said. He was speaking to the table, but I was sure he was trying to reassure me. "You don't have to like it. I'm more concerned about people being honest."

"Truly?" Sean said.

Amante did his shoulder-hitching thing again. "I hope so," he said.

"So, you mean, if someone really gives it to you," Sean said, "a critic or reviewer. They just lay it on, no mercy, you're fine with that?"

"All press is good press," Amante said, with his cryptic smile. The waitress set down his coffee, and he put his hand around it, pulling away—it must've been too hot.

"That's maybe true," Maggie said.

"For a writer, at least," Sean said.

Preston, who'd slunk into the corner of the window, with his head literally against the glass as if he'd suddenly gone catatonic, revived with a badger-like snort and a revving sound in his throat. "What kind of stuff you do?"

"Me?" Amante said.

"Yeah, man."

"Books," Amante said. "I write books. And short stories. An article or two," he added, as if just reminded of the fact. "A play," he said. "Or, no. Two plays now. One's going to run at Theatre Source. On Macdougal. I have a friend there who asked me to adapt something for him. It's not technically my play."

"Still," I said.

"Plays, eh," Preston said, leaning forward and inadvertently knocking Sean's beer. "Sorry," he said. "What about screenplays?"

"Sorry?" Amante said. "Oh. Screenplays?"

"That's right. Screenplays."

"I haven't done any," Amante said. "I guess I could."

"How much would you charge to write one?" Preston said.

"Well. I don't really know. I've never worked that way, really. But I could."

"'Cause I got something, floating around up here," Preston tapped his head, significantly. "It's a doozy."

"Really?" Amante said.

"Yeah. Big bucks," Preston said.

"Megamillions," Sean said, nodding at me. "He's told us all about it."[189]

Maggie looked at all of us like we'd gone insane. She was like "What's your book about?"

"Who me?" Amante said.

"No one else here's written anything," Maggie said. "So far as I know."

"No. You're right," Sean said.

"Can you copyright an idea?" Preston said.

Sean was like "I think you have to write it down. Don't quote me on it."

"That's the thing," Preston said, more subdued now, because Maggie had shot him a doubtful look. "I can't write for shit."

"Obsession, I guess," Amante answered Maggie.

"Your book's about obsession?"

"Among other things."

---

[189] See pages 131-136.

"It's not a very happy book," I said, wanting to redeem myself with Mags.[190]

Maggie went "Sounds right up my alley."

"What is? The obsession or—the other?" Amante said. "It not being a happy book?"

Maggie shook her head slowly, forced to spell out her sarcasm. "What I meant is—it's not something I'm interested in."

"Come on," I said. "Obsession. Who isn't interested in obsession?"

"When I read a book, I read for pleasure," Maggie said. "I don't want to read some depressing story about depressed people."

Amante was like "Fair enough."

"Don't you feel obsession's been overdone?" Maggie said.

I had an impulse to poke her, like she'd poked me all those times before, not because I particularly relished defending Amante, but because it didn't seem fair to invite him over and then interrogate him like the poor deposed Martin Luther at the Diet of Worms. I would've poked her too, only she was wearing a skirt, and somehow the presence of her bare legs, made the gesture seem more inappropriate than it was, even if I managed to poke her on the fabric of her skirt.

"I don't know," Amante said. "By whom?"

"Um. Every writer in the twentieth century?" Maggie said.

"I guess I just wanted to do my own version," Amante said. He had a kind face, I'd give him that as well, especially with those glasses which lessened any sharpness in his eyes.

"Your view of literature is depressing," Sean said to Maggie. "Anyhow, congratulations," he faced Amante, and beamed with what appeared like genuine enthusiasm. "I do plan on reading your book soon."

---

[190] And the book does end unhappily, in despair, with numerous examples of rigor mortis, suicide, occultism, and unpunctuated masturbatory dream sequences, et al.

"I gave him my copy," I said.

"Thanks," Amante said, clasping his hands, back to imitating a friar.

"No prob," I said.

"After you're done," Maggie said, "leave it on my desk. Maybe I'll look at it."

"I'm flattered," Amante said.

"I'm not saying I'll actually read it," Maggie said. "If I don't like page one, that's it. Life's too short."

"I agree with you," Amante said. "Never force yourself to read anything."

"Thank God you're not in publishing, Mags," Sean said. "Who'd want to send their shit to you?"

"I would," Amante said. "Compared to the wolves out there."

Maggie was like "How old are you, anyway? Same age as this youngster?"

"Maybe," Amante said. "We were in the same college."

"Yeah, yeah. Heard all about *that*," Maggie said. She smirked at me in passing.

I was like "What goes on in college… " but didn't end the thought.[191]

---

[191] It took my friend Angie a solid week before she forgave me sleeping with Tammy Gao—and even then I think she only relented when she saw how harried and disheveled I'd become, almost overnight, on account of Tammy hounding me to death with her contradictory text messages and libidinous late night phone calls. "You've got to help me," I said to Angie, but she clicked her tongue. "No, Ian, you got yourself into this doing exactly what I told you not to." Tammy had already gone on a sort of stakeout of Morse College, pouncing on me when I left— inviting me to piano recitals, chamber music concerts, folk festivals, all because I told her I liked *The Magic Flute*. I was paranoid I'd run into her again. I sought safe harbor in Green Hall, the art building, where I added gratuitous stippling over previous contour drawings, just to avoid her. I was 40% flattered

"See no evil, speak no evil," Amante said.

"You're at the wrong table," Sean said. "Here, we only speak evil."

Maggie was like "What he means is, we're despicable people." On the heels of that (and maybe to forestall Amante's lame "no, no"), she said "It must feel good to publish a book at twenty-five or whatever."

"I don't look at it that way," Amante said. "Yes, it feels good. But, the book just came out of me. I felt like I had very little to do with it. It would have gotten out one way or another. I'm glad it's gone."

"Sounds very out of body and all," Maggie said.

Sean was like "I've heard of that. I've heard of writers saying that."

"If it was still inside me," Amante said, "I'd probably be dead."

"Not a great plug," Maggie said. "But I'll give it a fair chance."

"Please do," Amante said.

"I'm not saying I'm going to like it."

"I'd rather have your honest opinion," Amante said. "What I meant—about being dead—is that a book's sort of like a parasite after a while. It just sits there, leaching off you. You need to get it out. That was the way *Inferno* was. Not all books are like that. The book I'm working on now, in fact. It's the complete opposite. I don't know a single word I'm going to say, until I sit down and type it. *Inferno*, I knew every word I was going to say. I could feel them inside me. I knew the whole book from beginning to end. Line by line."

---

by the attention, but enough was enough. Finally, Angie came to my room one day on the way to dinner and announced that Tammy had a new boyfriend. "Oh, thank God," I said. But all of a sudden, for no rational reason, and with a gut-wrenching sense of irreparable loss, I became jealous. I went "Wait? Who?" "Oh no," Angie said. "Take my advice and drop it. Just move on." Then she said: "You need a hobby."

"It does move fast," I said.

"Listen," Preston said. "I don't get what you're saying. But let's say I give you the rough idea for a movie. How long, ballpark, do you think it'd take you to write it?"

Amante was like "Hard to say."

"Would you pipe down about your friggin' movie," Maggie said. "When'd you become a cinematographer?"

"Just a hobby," Preston said. "Something I do in my free time."

"Which you have a lot of," Maggie said.

Sean was like "Now, now."

"Just saying," Maggie said. "Some people could stand to do a little more work. Real work."

Instead of flushing or blushing, strange white spots like fingerprints appeared in Preston's cheeks.

"That's unfair Maggie," Sean said. "No one at this table does any real work—except maybe Mr. Amante."[192]

---

[192] Say what you will about him, Amante was a disciplined kind of guy. He'd been producing who knows how many literary snippets for small scale publications, a horror story here, a grotesque character portrait there, ever since he was in high school, when he'd sent a short essay to *The Paris Review* about his experience reading *Portnoy's Complaint* as a first grader. And then of course, yes, *Inferno*, the talk of the alternative literary world, enough to make him a celebrity among the crowd reading rags like *The Village Voice*, *Grand Street News*, *The New York Press*, *National Post*, *Fray Quarterly*, and *Downtown Express*, the book itself, with its unenviably cheap binding and weird cover photo depicting what I can only deduce is the inside of a plantation outbuilding for curing tobacco circa 1789, coming in at a full 229 pages. Amante, so far as he had ever vocalized such a statement, lived for his writing. That was part of what used to infuriate me about him, his sort of casual disregard for anything other than writing, including his own health and wellness. What did it matter if he pushed himself beyond all

"Not true," Amante said. "I do the least of anyone."

"Yeah, well writing a book I guess can be qualified as work," Maggie said. "But only if it's published. Can I help you?" she said, holding her eyes wide and blinking strenuously[193] at the band of mariachis who'd made it around the circuit to our table.

---

endurance, drinking 40 cups of espresso each morning like Honore de Balzac, and burning an ulcer the size of a grapefruit through the lining of his stomach? What did he care if he never got out of his chair some days and developed lesions on his buttocks as well as all forms of joint and muscle aches and cramps and carpel tunnel syndrome up the wazoo, and needed as many or more eye operations as Joyce and a kidney replacement too from lack of water, and ended up a dropsical, lumpy, Quasimodo-like invalid with eyes like Sloth from *The Goonies* and internal organs in as rough shape as Mickey Mantle's after forty years of hard drinking? It was all for writing! That was all that mattered to him. Even his strange perambulations throughout the city seemed to serve some literary purpose, as if he was sleuthing about in search of his next story, the consummate observer, and nothing but an observer, never really a participant in anything—until this night at Neptune's, I guess—never joining in anything, either. Maybe he really was some forlorn beatnik. Maybe it wasn't just a pose, his habit of poking his head in other people's windows while they were about to make love (note 121), turning up God knows where and when, and immediately tramping down the road, chewing on the remains of a poppy seed bagel and musing on the fresh denouement to his next story. How can you deal with a man like that, with this sort of shadow man with no substance? Well, there you have it. That's what got me: the fact that he was only an observer. An observer through everything. An observer to the last.

[193] Each one of those blinks was so exaggerated it was like she'd just applied Visine—Seasonal Healing and Redness Relief.

"Tough crowd, tough crowd," the guitarist said, remembering our last encounter.

But the accordionist was undeterred and up and launched into some Parisian or Venetian street tune that made me think of gondolas. While he was playing, Maggie leaned forward, bracing her arms like someone about to freefall or skydive. She stayed absolutely still and the accordionist accelerated, the dude showing great manual dexterity, though the instrument itself confused the hell out of me, like a bagpipe, and I was caught up trying to decode its construction and all the weird buttons. The actual notes (which I'd stopped listening to) ran too fast even for the accordionist, in the end. He fumbled and stalled out about three-quarters of the way into the piece, and out-and-out stopped playing, looking extremely embarrassed.

"You get the picture," he said.

"It's the alcohol," the trumpeter said. "Neil never messes up."[194]

The accordionist was like "Let me make it up to you."

"Don't worry about it," Preston said.

"Even so," the accordionist said.

Amante hadn't put down his coffee this whole time and was sipping it now and then, his arms drawn in like he was guarding a basketball. He'd jostled my beer by accident so I figured now was as good a time as any to drain a little more off it. I managed another small sip against the best wishes of my stomach which had ballooned uncomfortably above my belt.

"Why mariachis?" Sean said, easing himself to a sideways position in the booth.

"Why not?" the trumpeter said.

The violinist was like "Groom-to-be goes to Julliard."

---

[194] Alcohol had precipitated a similar failure my first night with Olivia (note 107) but she never held it against me.

"That's a great school," Amante said under his breath.[195]

"Fuck yourselves," Sean said, grinning so the mariachis didn't have time to misinterpret him. "You're talented."

"Some of us are," the violinist said. "If you notice, I've never played anything. This is just a prop," he said. He held his instrument loose by the neck, like he was weighing it. "I don't even know how to hold this or what it's for," he said, waving the bow.

"But the rest of you..." Sean said.

"Yeah, we're all right," the guitarist said. "Even him," he hung an arm around the violinist. "He's being modest."

"More wine for me," the violinist said. "Liquid courage."

"Watch your back," I said, noticing the skinny waitress behind them.

"Sorry ma'am."

The accordionist was doing some kind of finger exercise in the air. "Ah-ha," he said. "Motherfucker. Now I have you."

"Do you know any Irish music?" Maggie asked.[196] She'd slumped back in the booth, but was still more or less eyeing the accordionist.

"Oh, wait," the trumpeter said. "Requests?" He stared right at me for a sec as if I was the one requesting their services, his eyes somewhat inflamed and rather probing.

"Did you say Irish music?" the guitarist said. "Is my name Shannon O'Rourke?"

"Do you know 'Siobhan McGriel'?" Maggie said.

"I think I knew her in eleventh grade," the guitarist said.

The violinist was like "You and me both, bud."

"Can't say I do," the trumpeter said, thoughtfully dropping his eyes. "You, Neil?"

---

[195] Apparently this was one of those stock phrases Amante liked to pull out (see note 123, "Oh, that's a great school. That's a great school.").

[196] See note 102.

The accordionist shook his head.

"I didn't think so," Maggie said.

Sean was like "Why don't you go with something more mainstream, Mags?"

"Michael Bolton?" the violinist said. "We know his entire catalog."

"Here's an easy one," Maggie said. "'By the Rising of the Moon.'"

"Come again?"

Maggie didn't give them any time to confer. She went "'The Hussar's Wife'?"[197]

"Nope."

"Nope."

"Come on," Sean said. "You don't know 'The Hussar's Wife'? What kind of mariachis are you?"

Preston was like "I knew 'The Hussar's Wife'... " but stopped right there.

"I feel like I should know 'The Hussar's Wife,'" Amante said. "You?" he asked me.

I was like "Naw."

"So much for Ivy League education," Amante said.

"We're not Celtic instrumentalists," the trumpeter said, giving Maggie an almost full-body scan with his eyes. "I mean, look at us."

Maggie was like "Shame."

"But we'll try anything once," the guitarist said. "Maybe if you hum it, we'll get the gist."

"I'm all out of ideas," Maggie said. She was wrinkling her nose—a rare facial expression for her—and she looked like a kitten, cuter than usual.

"'I Said I Loved You, But I Lied,'" Preston said.

Maggie groaned.[198]

---

[197] An instrumental song, I glean.

[198] Could this have been one of the songs on her CD (note 4)?

"Wait," the accordionist said, without looking up, as if he'd been carrying on a conversation with his instrument. He unslung the accordion and handed it to the trumpeter. "Wine," he said, or rather ordered.

The violinist went to get him a carafe.

Maggie was like "What? Are you singing?"

"Just… I need a moment," the accordionist said, loosening his shirt collar and coughing.

"I was kidding," Maggie said. "Please. You don't have to go through with it."

I was suddenly cheerful. "What song are you going to sing?"[199]

---

[199] I realized later that it was seeing Tammy Gao in *The Magic Flute* that made me like her—that's why I was so intrigued with her that night in Neat Lounge—seeing her in that crazy black Maleficent dress with a background of summer thunderstorms playing out on the projector screen. Yes, she could hit the high F and all, she sang all the arias in the shower, I was told. She was super talented and that gave her a mystique I've never really known—I mean, I've never been with another performing artist. Toward the end of our senior year, she went back to her old boyfriend, Colin So; rumor had it she basically ran his life, though she wasn't a complete diva; she didn't sing Cat Stevens songs while walking barefoot down Elm Street like so many other musically-inclined undergraduates, like that Jeremy scoundrel Anna slept with and swooned over at parties in Branford or Berkeley College. Tammy could also speak five languages fluently, including Mandarin and Cantonese; she read Sanskrit; she was a senior editor of the *Yale Daily News*, a member of Mensa, Phi Betta Kappa, Summa Cum Laude, president or at least a vice president of the Yale Entrepreneurial Society, a member of Yale Carillon, an amateur cellist, performing some piece by Strauss for the Master of Timothy Dwight College, and now (three years out of college) was a financial brainiac based in Malaysia. Despite these multiple

The violinist handed the accordionist a pretty full carafe and the accordionist slammed it, gulping it down like a bear. Who knows what else he would've done—behind us the mariachis clanged their wineglasses and someone yelled "Bravo! Bravo! Encore!"—if he hadn't suddenly lost his balance, stepped sideways, feinted left, then fallen into our table, breaking his fall at the last minute with a stiff arm. The coffee and tea mugs clanged and my beer tipped over, inundating all our plates. Then the accordionist was back on his feet, waving off his friends, and the stocky waitress was honing in on our skinny waitress, who had returned to our booth just in time to witness this performance and was smiling crookedly.

"Hey now!" the others shouted. "OK, fella, let's take it easy."

The stocky waitress was berating (in Polish) her skinny colleague, probably blaming the accident on her. She shooed away the violinist and the trumpeter whose instruments permitted them to pull the accordionist by the armpits.

"Please excuse him," the guitarist said. "It just got sort of weird."

"Did it?" Amante said in a very soft voice.

I smiled at him, his attempt at a joke—sarcasm too. Right then, there was thunderous applause from the mariachis' table—the stocky waitress had demanded some assurance that they keep themselves under control, emphasizing bluntly that so far as any of the diner's décor was concerned (she was especially worried about the marlin), you break it, you buy it.

The guitarist was like "He's well, the thing is, Neil's socially awkward."

---

accomplishments, she was generally distrusted (especially in college), considered somewhat fake, and had a reputation for burning bridges, making men cry, betraying close confidences, etc. Angie Zhou always greeted her with a cold, condescending wave in circumstances where she couldn't cross the street or hold up a copy of *The Economist* and pretend she'd never seen her at all.

"You're fine," Sean said. He held his beer and I stacked the plates as the skinny waitress swept a rag over the table.

"He hides it well," the guitarist said, wincing at his comrades.

"Have a good night," I said.

"We will," the guitarist said. "We have been."

"Hey," Preston called as he was heading back to his table. "Send the groom over. Let's make sure he knows what he's getting himself into."

Maggie was like "Don't" and Sean laughed over his shoulder.

"Sloshed," the guitarist said, turning away.

"Eh—none of you will remember any of this," Preston said. "That's what it's all about, boys."

"Probably for the best," Amante whispered to me.

"Maybe so," I said.

Sean was still laughing and shaking his head at Maggie. "You're a real heartbreaker tonight, eh Mags? What kind of black magic did you pull on that guy?"

"Some people just don't know how to drink," Maggie said.

"Yeah, but did you see what he had?" Sean said. "He was drinking white zinfandel."

"Church wine," Amante said.

Maggie was like "Exactly my point. Some people shouldn't be drinking."

"Well, I felt a connection there," Sean said.

"Go for it," Maggie said. "It's probably been a while for you."

"Between him and *you*," Sean said.

"Hey, I forgot," Preston said, leaning toward Amante. "What happened to that chick you were with?"

"You mean Jenna?" Amante said.

"Sure," Preston said. "Was that her name?"

"We're not together," Amante said.

"What?"

Even Maggie was staring at him now.

"We broke up," Amante said. "Right there. Wasn't it obvious?"

"Not really," Maggie said.

202

"Dude, you'd totally taken over the show," Preston said. "She stopped singing so she could make out with you."

I was like "They did stop playing music."

"I got to be honest," Maggie said. "It was a little juvenile."

"Sorry," Amante said. "I can see that. I can see how it would've looked that way to you."

"That was a break up?" Sean said. "Are you sure?"

The mariachis were cheering even louder now; it might've been because their waitress was walking back to the kitchen, apparently giving them one last chance.

"I'm positive," Amante said. "Jenna is a fun time, but she's hardly the type of girl you bring home to your parents." Amante got kind of red, maybe realizing he'd just made a value judgment—something he normally avoided. "Not that my parents would've minded. Just, she's not the sort of person who'd make them—anyone—happy. She's unsettled, is what I mean. My parents would prefer someone... to be settled. I guess. I'm unsettled myself, so it's a double standard, I admit. I'm chronically unsettled."

"With lines like that, I wonder why," Maggie said. "I'm teasing."

"Maggie sounds a lot harsher than she is," Sean said.

"You'll get used to it," Preston said.[200]

"I call it like I see it, and if I see an idiot, I call them out," Maggie said.

"I hope you're not saying... " Amante started.

"Don't worry, hon," Maggie said. "You're not on my bad side, yet."

Maggie put her hand on my arm and I patted Amante's arm, as if giving Amante a vicarious pat for Maggie. Pretty soon, I was going to have to use the restroom, but I didn't feel like it was an emergency yet.

---

[200] A bold statement, all things considered.

"Maggie's bad side's pretty nebulous," Sean said. "We don't always know where we stand."

"Don't push it," Maggie said.

Sean was like "I wouldn't dream."

"So you're not with that crazy chick?" Maggie said.

"Jenna?" Amante said (unnecessarily, it seemed to me; we all knew who Maggie meant). "No. Not anymore."

"But you left it open, no?" Preston said. "You can't just examine a girl's tonsils—you get me—and expect things to end quietly. You had to have left the door open a crack?"

"No. Closed. End of story," Amante said.

Sean was like "Sounds definitive."

"It is." Amante set his coffee on the saucer. "I couldn't keep up with her anyway.[201] I guess I'm getting too old."

---

[201] Ditto me and Olivia. Sometimes I wished I could've been a hero to her, but that never happened—unless you counted all the times I dropped whatever I was doing to make sure she was OK. Like the night she called me, nostalgic and unusually needy, while I was playing Trivial Pursuit with Rebecca Fershleiser and our roommate Lizzie and Lizzie's boyfriend Jon, who was miffed because Rebecca's old edition of Trivial Pursuit still had Leningrad instead of St. Petersburg, causing him to forfeit a decisive victory. I took her call; I didn't let it go to voicemail. "Who is it?" Rebecca said. I cupped the phone and went "Olivia." "Who's Olivia?" Lizzie said. Rebecca was like "That's Ian's girlfriend." "Shh," I told her. "Ian has a girlfriend?" Lizzie said, parodying a junior high gossip. "She's pretty," Rebecca said. "Don't take too long, Ian." Lizzie was like "You should invite her over." "We're not dating," I said, listening to Olivia and going "mmm-hmm". "She wants to meet at Ben's pizza," I said. "John's is better," Jon said. "Are you going to go?" Rebecca said. "Because if you are, I'm taking your turn." I was like "Should I?" "Go!" Rebecca said. Then she was talking to them, like "Every day I come home he's watching *Girlfriends* and *My Wife and Kids*. His mind is turning to mush. If he doesn't get laid soon, I

"Old!" Maggie said. "Yeah, you're real old. Give me a friggin' break."

"I mean… " Amante was out at sea for a sec.

"Too wild, eh?" Preston said.

---

think I'm going to void his lease. You hear that, Ian?" So I went, and over pizza Olivia informed me of her recent, off-the-cuff plan to live abroad. She was like "Korea. Or maybe China. Or Ecuador. I can't decide." I patted the grease off my mouth with a napkin. "There's so many places," Olivia said. I nodded. "Sounds fun." Olivia was wearing the same gaudy makeup, slacks, and a blazer—she looked like some cabaret singer or magician's assistant. The red pepper flakes burned my lips. For a second or two, I wondered if she wanted me to say "No!"—a definitive "No!—if she was trying to get me to put up a "fight" for her or if she just wanted to goad me into fighting, like before when I'd said I didn't like her seeing other people and she had been like "Well, I don't really care if *you* like it. It's not *your* choice." It didn't matter anyway. If she went abroad or didn't, if she dated ten guys simultaneously or didn't—she'd always be the same slightly scared, provocatively dressed girl, with the bold smile and the gray eyes, the girl who had whispered in my ear that first time we kissed (note 15) "Why'd you wait so long?" And I felt like, yes, maybe I had waited too long, and it was too long, waiting for Olivia to love me. But to put that into words—that was another thing. So I made myself agreeable and recited all the meaningless minutiae I could recall about Korea and kimchi and soju and Seoul and China and Ecuador too, ready to expand my rambling to any country on any continent if need be, until I could see that Olivia hadn't really thought through the idea of living abroad, and she eventually dropped it, like any other worn-out conversation, and asked if I wanted to accompany her to Phebe's—some bar on 2nd Avenue—where she was meeting Anton Kolnikov, her soon-to-be-boyfriend (note 7), and some compatriot friend of his, who turned out to be more like a bodyguard (note 225).

"You have no idea."

"Do tell," Sean said.

"Don't," Maggie said. "We have a couple of sex obsessed maniacs over here."

"I thought you agreed not to mention that," Sean said.

I was like "Me too."

Maggie's smile was only half in jest. "You're detergent compared to the other side of the table."

"I'm glad I'm on this side, then," Amante said.

Maggie was like "You should be."

"Don't listen to her," Sean said. "What you should be doing is grilling this one over here for story ideas—he's lived the life of a buccaneer."

I couldn't help laughing at Sean. I almost had to bite my tongue to stop since there didn't seem to be any occasion for it. I'd forgotten to ask Preston the rest of his Belize story which, according to Sean, was pure fiction, just your typical "I got laid on the beach" type story, with an undercurrent of gracelessness and despair.[202]

Preston roused himself and looked around. "I won't deny it, if it's me you mean."

"Yeah, he's been a real Captain Nemo," Sean said. "Isn't that right, Pres?"

"I've seen some sights," Preston said, his neck falling back into his shoulders. "Haven't read that many books, though."

"Good for you," Amante said. "You don't want to be in thrall." He met our blank stares. "Avoid books as long as you can."

"Weird advice—coming from a writer," Maggie said.

"Really?" Amante said. "I thought it was my best advice all night."

"To not read," Maggie said. "Yes. That's priceless."

"I suppose I would like some people to read," Amante said. "I'd like to get paid."

---

[202] Not all stories need to be told.

"It's your constitutional right," Preston said. He sounded as if he were gearing up for a stump speech, his chin propped in his hand, but he just closed his eyes and assumed a vacant expression.

Sean went "I don't know about that."

"What I mean is," Amante cleared his throat. The waitress returned and he nodded for another cup of coffee. "Books aren't the same as living."

"More... beer?" the waitress said to me as if she were translating for an extremely old person. I shook my head—to be honest, I was glad that mariachi had knocked my beer over and I didn't have to drink anymore.

"We know that," Maggie said. "That's why I won't read the bad ones. They remind me too much of real life."

"I'm beginning to be afraid you won't like *Inferno*," Amante said.

Maggie was like "You never know."

"Your version of bad," Sean said to Maggie. "It's just hit me. I think some people call it 'realism.'"

"I don't care what it's called," Maggie said. "I don't care for it."

Sean was like "That's your prerogative."

"Not everyone likes realism," I said.

"It's her constitutional right," Preston said, latching onto that phrase like a crutch.

"I'd like to hear from the real writer," Maggie said. "No offense. You still haven't let me read your story yet," she said to Sean.

Sean rubbed his forehead. "Not finished yet."

"In other words: never," Maggie said.

Amante was sipping his coffee, eyes averted, this whole time.

"This guy's actually done it," she said.

Amante raised his eyes, innocently, as if to say "Done what?"

"I don't feel any pressure," Sean said. "That's been my biggest downfall."

Maggie narrowed her eyes and looked back at Amante. "He's been sitting on some story for seven years—is that right? What would you say to him? Lost cause?"

I was almost positive Sean had never shown his paranormal romance story "Aunt Gretel"[203] to Maggie—but hearing her speak like this, with the authority and frustration of an agent who had staked her whole career on Sean's literary output, I wondered if maybe—in some ways—Maggie knew Sean better than I did. And if that was true, then maybe Sean knew Maggie better than I did too.[204]

Amante made a strained face. "I wouldn't say that."

"But what *would* you say? What would it take to light a fire under his ass? How do you motivate yourself?"

"With me it's different," Amante said. "If I didn't write—I'd probably be dead. Or locked up. It's a case by case basis."

"That's just what I've been saying," Sean said. "I enjoy my life too much, and therefore I can never get anything done."

"That's pretty piss poor," Maggie said. "If you ask me."

"Life interrupts your work, certainly," Amante said. "But what else is there to write about?"

"Got me there," Preston said.

Sean—with a sleepy burst of inspiration—went "Animals. You can write about animals. You can write about rabbits."[205]

I was like "That is what sells."

"You two have lost your friggin' minds," Maggie said.

Amante was like "No. What I meant to say before is—live life first, then write about it."

"That's from *A Moveable Feast*," Sean said. "Isn't it?"

"Don't start name dropping," Maggie said. "I don't get the reference."

---

[203] See notes 31-32.

[204] Those two insights, for whatever reason, struck me as depressing.

[205] Referring to Nora's children's book (see page 147).

"Hemingway," Sean said. "He wrote it."

Maggie was like "Depressing."

"I've been always meaning to wonder," Preston said. "Is Hemingway related to that chick who gets it on with Jeff Bridges[206] in that movie *The Mean Season*?"

"I think so," I said.

"Let's not go there," Maggie said. "What are you talking about?"

"OK. This'll help," Amante said. He sipped his coffee, and for a second it was like he meant the coffee "would help" *him* gather his thoughts. Then he was like "When I was a kid I had really bad asthma. I was sick all the time. I got pneumonia in the winter." He took another sip of coffee. "I know it can't be true," he said, "but I feel like I was in bed for an entire year. That can't be right, but that's how it felt. My room faced a hill and that year we had a blizzard. I remember waking up and I'd see the snow, and it looked fake, it was so big, it couldn't be real snow. It was like my dad was shoveling for days. I'd wake up to the scrape of his shovel, scraping, scraping, all day long. Another thing I heard was kids sledding, on the hill out back. I don't know how long the snow lasted, but to me it could've been months. I wanted so bad to be out there. All I could do was lie in bed. I could feel my lungs working—like there was a limited amount of air, and if I used it all up I'd drown. So I'd lie there and try to build up a surplus, my thought being: hey, if I can store up a big enough surplus then I can go outside. Hearing those kids sledding out there—it was more than just missing sledding. Fuck sledding. I was missing everything, everything that was important to me in my seven-year-old mind: my entire world."

"Raw deal, man," Preston said from his corner.

---

[206] He meant Kurt Russell, but easy mix up.

Amante moved his coffee from his right hand to his left so he wouldn't elbow me while drinking.[207] The space was tight and I'd done my best to ignore his inadvertent encroachments; nevertheless, with Maggie's flirty fingers patrolling the booth by my right leg, I found myself in a bit of a 'Scylla and Charybdis' type situation—though my situation was obviously not so dire.[208]

Amante kept going "That's how I felt. It was even worse back then. Those days lasted forever. The only way they passed was when I stepped outside myself. I'd be lying there, all frustrated and angry. I literally wanted to pick a fight with my own body, like my body could detach from me and if I kicked its ass hard enough it would start following my orders. I guess I didn't think too much about lungs back then, but I thought about my throat—which was always tight; it was tough to breath. I'd imagine my throat, like it got ripped out of me. To me, it looked like a long string of beef jerky. That's how much I knew about human physiology, back then. I'd stand in one corner of the ring, and this beef jerky throat would stand in the other corner of the ring, and the bell would ding, and we'd go at it, and I'd just pummel it. I'd lay it on. I'd whip that thing into a patty and then pull it back into its original shape (like they do in cartoons when an anvil falls on a character) and my throat would be all humble and contrite and promise to do a better job next time. That's what a kid imagines."

"A sick kid," Maggie said.

"Exactly. I was that sick kid," Amante said. "Or do you mean, sick in the head?"

Maggie shrugged. "No. I get it."

Sean frowned at Maggie and made as if to drink his beer. None of us really felt like drinking anymore—Sean and Preston's beers were still pretty full. The waitress, probably sensing

---

[207] As with all extremely polite people, accidental body contact mortified him; you could see it in his eyes.

[208] We don't reenact Greek tragedies, after all.

things were winding down, had made herself scarce, following a siege-like strategy of cutting off service so that we had no choice but to request the bill and pay up whenever she reappeared.

"I'd think about other things too," Amante said. "My dad used to read me Italian folktales, but when he wasn't there, I'd make up my own. Very basic, full of clichés, really, but enough to keep me occupied. I entertained myself. What else could I do?"

We all sort of collectively shrugged—this was the most I'd heard Amante talk, up close, in a Charlie Rose-ish interviewy way. Even Maggie was listening, without her usual commentary, like she was really interested, albeit her attention seemed to go in and out, like someone in the back row of a class lecture.

Amante treated us all to a shy grin, apologetic almost, but also swept away by the moment.[209] He went "It was a way to pass the time. But it wasn't all fun. My plan was to write all my stories down, as soon as I could, but each day I'd forget one or two. I'd tell them over to myself, in this prearranged order. I think I had a pneumonic device for them, I don't exactly remember. But if I started with twenty stories on Sunday, by Monday I was already down to nineteen. I couldn't figure out what story I'd left out. I'd wrack my brains. I'd come up with nothing. So I'd invent another one, and I'd be back to twenty, but then on Tuesday, I'd be down to eighteen, and I know I'd lost a couple more."

"But you got better?" I said.

"I got better," Amante said.

Sean was like "Good for you."

"You still got asthma?" Preston said.

"Not so bad anymore," Amante said. "Back when I was little, it seemed like it took months to get better."

---

[209] I could relate—there's something about telling a story that drives you along, even when you notice your friends yawning and checking their watches and responding belatedly to texts which all of a sudden have become pressing.

"How many stories did you write down?" I said.

"None," Amante said. "The first day I could go outside, I walked along the hill. The snow was melting. The ground was all patchy. I could only walk a little while. I was still 'being monitored,' I think the phrase is. But the cold, in and of itself, wasn't bad and I was bundled like I was climbing Everest. I sweat a lot. I was better though; I'd passed some crucial point. The doctor was saying encouraging stuff to my parents. Anyhow, I'd missed out. I cried but I didn't want anyone to see. I was healthy enough to bawl. I didn't even think about the stories until a while after, when I made this determined effort to write them. That's when I found out they were gone. I wrote out a table of contents, with just numbers, and turned to page one. Nothing. No name, no title, no characters, no 'once upon a time.' Maybe 'once upon a time.' But that was it. It was like my head was a rock. Everything was gone."[210]

---

[210] Leaving Amante to tell his own stories, I'll admit that there was one night when I came close to telling Olivia how I felt about her—that (apart from my attraction and all that, nothing too unusual there) I found myself oddly inspired by her—that it was more than a few large-scale crayon drawings (see page 106) which I'd drawn just to impress her and get in her pants—no, it was more than that. It was in the morning, how I'd unfurl my memories of the night before, how I'd hold onto single moments with her and develop them over and over again like still photographs. No amount of simplistic similes could ever lessen the appreciation I had for her, the pain I felt whenever she went away. I wanted to tell her that she drew everything out of me, that when she put her hands on me, I could have narrated my entire life, I would have, willingly, that everything, each episode from my past seemed destined to reveal itself to her, she was the one who resurrected everything, made it live again, brought it out—and that was what I missed most of all. I didn't miss talking with Olivia—I missed the words I'd never said, the opportunities I never took, which never left me. Yes, I

"Shame," Sean said.

"It didn't bother me so much then, but I've drawn some conclusions about it," Amante said. For the last few minutes he'd been taking sips out of a near-empty coffee, too polite to bother our timid waitress, probably thinking no one even noticed. "First: without exercise your creativity plummets," he said. "It atrophies and when you need it—it's unresponsive."

"Sure," Sean said. "Need to get the blood flowing."

"Is that your medical opinion?" Maggie said. "Dr. Sean Lucy, MD."

I was like "No, that's true, Maggie."

"My parents always wanted me to be a doctor," Sean said.

Maggie was like "Look how that turned out."

"Everyone's parents want their kids to be doctors," Amante said.

---

would have told her, tried to tell her at any rate, except Olivia was in one of her own painfully reflective moods that same evening and she just went off about how she had no home (her perennial theme), how her Clinton Hill bedroom, small as it was, contained all she had in the world, since her mom had sold the house right from under her and that was it, her childhood packaged and lotteried off; she couldn't even go back to Savannah anymore without a blind rage taking over at her mom's impulsive and unkind decision to sell her stuff without asking, and that meant that she had no home, she wanted to make it very clear exactly what that meant and how different we were because of it, and could I understand: she had no home, home was just the place she happened to be at the time. She fell asleep telling me about some play she'd read, Euphrates' *The Suppliants*, Greek tragedy, and I wanted to say: our life isn't quite a Greek tragedy, we aren't actors in some Greek tragedy (I.E. note 208), but her Euphrates tripped me up. I was like "Euripides?" And she laughed too, and said "Ha, what was it I said?"

Preston went "Not mine. My dad took me aside, and said, 'Listen, son. Not everyone's cut out for those highfalutin professions. Can't fly on borrowed plumes, catch my drift.'"

"Sage words," Sean said. "Sounds like Aesop."

"He was just being realistic," Preston said. "But, yeah, he got it from Aesop."[211]

---

[211] On the subject of Aesop, I can't completely pass by the fable (of sorts) that Olivia's dad once told Olivia—in a moment either of extreme cruelty or tenderness. Olivia told it to me on one of our outings—maybe the night we ate dinner at Café Cubana (note 147), which will be significant again in a moment. I never forgot it. In fact, one morning, when she was getting dressed in my little room in Soho, she plopped down onto the bed next to me and said, "You know what would hurt me more than anything? If you left, without saying goodbye." I studied her eyes for a moment—she had gray eyes, but they sometimes looked green or hazel, eye color being relative. "Don't worry," I said. "I'm not the shadow father." She was embarrassed. "You remembered." Her dad's story (a bedtime story, mind you, which he told her one night before he skipped town, the first time), centered on a king, who strikes a deal with an old witch: you make me happy (I.E. find me a "hot" woman to marry) and I'll give you my firstborn, the usual spiel. Everything goes according to plan: the king gets married, and a few years down the line, he and his token-hot fairy tale wife have a baby girl. Of course, the witch comes back, and the king tries to buy her off, but no dice, deals with witches never come off as easily as you would like. So, the king decides to deny the witch and kick her off the premises. He goes a few steps farther: bans her from the kingdom, sets up an embargo on witchy merchandise, gives orders to shoot the old crone on sight, suspends the writ of habeas corpus, etc. The witch, fuming, but living life on the run, in daily danger of being peppered with buckshot, casts a spell on the deal-breaking king which turns him into a shadow. The days go by, and the king becomes shadier and shadier, until

Sean was like "I'll drink to that."

"Hear, hear," Preston said. "Though, you know, I'd never tell my kids something like that. 'You know honey, not everyone's meant to be a doctor or lawyer. Some people are meant to work a cash register at Chick-fil-A.'"

"Course not," Sean said. "Never say that. Dream big. Especially when you're young."

"Just don't expect me to shell out one hundred thousand dollars for private college," Preston said.

"That's what scholarships are for," I said.

"Exactamundo, brother. Scholarship or bust."

"Could you father-in-law maybe lend a hand?" Sean said. "With the educational expenses?"

Preston's eyes went to the window. "He hasn't made any promises."

"What else were you going to say?" Maggie asked Amante.

"The other thing? When a story dies, it never really dies," Amante said. "It just turns into something else and stays inside, until you figure out a way to flush it out."

Sean was like "You need a laxative—in a sense."

"Nice," I said.

"Don't judge us based on him," Maggie said, pointing her eyes at Sean.

But Amante wasn't shocked at all. "Precisely," he said. "Laxative. A way to expel it."

"Whoa, big words," Preston said. "You really must be a writer."

Maggie was like "What's the big word, 'laxative' or 'expel'?"

"Come on Maggie," Sean said.

"Big for me," Preston said.

---

finally he just disappears into the ether. He doesn't even get to say goodbye since the mechanism of speech is denied him due to extreme attenuation of his voice box. Hence, he (literally) becomes a "shadow father."

"So what's the trick?" Sean said to Amante. "How do you get the story to come out?"

"Damned if I know," Amante said.

Sean was like "That's not an answer."

Amante nodded. "I know. You just have to wait."

I had my own thoughts and opinions on the subject, and I was about to offer them,[212] when my phone started vibrating. "Excuse me," I said to Amante.

"You've got the world's smallest bladder," Maggie said—unware, at least at first, that I had a phone call.

"My curse," I said.

"Ian can have the outside seat from now on," Maggie said.

But Amante didn't mind standing up—he was actually quite limber, vaulting off the bench like he'd just concluded a regimen of squats for quadriceps strengthening.

Shaky as I was, I moved quick toward the bathroom, opening my phone a couple paces before the actual hall—I didn't want it to go to voicemail and I didn't know how many rings I had left. I put the receiver up to my ear and was like "Hello?"

The sound on the other end was staticy, like heavy breathing, and at that precise moment the mariachis started up again, playing some cacophonous Birdland jamboree in unison.

"Hello? Hello?" I said. "Goddam it. Goddam you," I said to the mariachis.

The hall where the bathrooms were had one of those old style pay phones attached to the wall, as well as a corkboard advertising the Kiwanis, Rotary Club, other clubs of that ilk, Boy Scouts, a Polish festival in Greenpoint, Maine Coon cats for sale, a lost Doberman, Suicide Prevention Hotlines, cleaning services from reputable Brazilians, Casimir's Laundromat, a bunch of crap really. An especially glib mariachi was loitering by this phone, as if expecting a call, like he was Dick Tracey. I gave him a dirty look and he walked away, but right then another

---

[212] E.g. note 210.

mariachi with a shirt like Zorro[213] and pantaloons to boot, took his place like sentinels relieving each other.

"What's up?" the new mariachi said.

I nodded, curt. Then, trying to give myself as much privacy as possible, I closed my phone and opened it and pressed redial. The phone went "Brring brrring brrrring. Your call could not be completed as dialed. Please hang up and try your call again."

"Piece of shit," I said.

"Poor reception?" the mariachi asked.

"Yeah," I said, with an accidental Austrian accent.

The mariachi was like "Fuck technology. What're you going to do? Can't survive without it… "

Right then the payphone rang and the coatless mariachi, shaking his head sympathetically, but also like he was puzzled and somewhat amused, went and answered it. "Yello," he said. "Hi?" He hung up. "Odd," he said.

"You weren't expecting that?" I said.

"No, no," he said. He'd resumed his slouching, upper back against the wall. "A friend of ours is in there." He bobbed his head lazily toward the bathroom. "Not pretty."

The mariachis in the dining room were shouting "Boo! Boo!" One of them was tinging his wine glass with a dessert spoon. Now I heard distinctly, "Pass the carafe. No, not that carafe. The full carafe. Yes, that one. The carafe. Yes."

"It's rosé," another of the mariachis said.

"Wonderful. Good for the soul, then."

I scrolled down the contact list on my phone and hit Olivia's number. This time the phone rang properly. I steered away from the payphone and hunched over, squeezing my phone to my ear without even realizing the amount of pressure I was exerting.

"Hello," said a man's voice.

"Olivia?" I said.

---

[213] The Antonio Banderas version.

"Mmfffold on."

I held the phone away from my ear. "Excuse me," I said, turning around. I was worried the coatless mariachi was snooping over my shoulder, but the hall was now empty; he must have gone back into the restroom to help his pal. "Hello?"

"Hello," Olivia said.

"Liv? Where are you?"

"I'm home."

"Home," I said. "Then who just answered the phone?"

"That was my roommate."

"Your roommate?"

"Yes Ian, my roommate. Remember, I have roommates. Where are you?"

I told her.

"Why didn't you call me?"

"I did call you."

"No. Before. Not when you were at the bar. I wanted you to call me. I think I know why you didn't."

"What? What are you talking about?" I said.

"I told you, it's not like that anymore."

"What? Not like what?" I was back to digging the phone up against my ear, and I realized I was infuriatingly repeating everything she just said.

"Like before," Olivia said.[214]

---

[214] If you look at a rough chronology of our "relationship," you might see why I was confused as to the meaning of "before" and any other time designations:

Nov. 2006: met Olivia (note 123)

Jan. 2007: first date, Once Upon a Tart (note 144)

Mar. 2007: first slept together (note 107)

Aug. 2007: 1st "breakup" (although we weren't dating)

Oct. 2007: back together

Nov. 2007: 2nd "breakup"

Nov. 2007: back together

"Who's this roommate?" I said.

"Jackson."

"Is that your roommate, or a town?"

"Just forget it, Ian. I can tell you some other time."

"No, wait. I'm sorry," I said, leaning back against the empty part of the wall, right beside the payphone. "What's up?"

"I wanted to tell you in person," Olivia said.

"Tell me what?" I said.

Olivia yawned into the phone—I heard that clearly enough. "You want to meet in Soho this week?"

"It's OK. You can just tell me now," I said.[215]

"OK," she said. "It's super exciting." Her breathing was audible now, like it hadn't been before—either that, or I'd been listening too hard. I'd always loved that personality trait, her heavy breathing on the phone. "I'm going to be an aunt," she said.

The bathroom door opened and the coatless mariachi backed out like he was pulling a gurney, followed by the sick dude, a green looking blonde kid still in full dress, with fake epaulettes and frogged coat buttons. He was familiar in an indistinct, might have met you on the street way, but beyond that I couldn't place him.[216]

Nov. 2007: 3rd "breakup"

Dec. 2007: I answered Olivia's call (note 201)

Jan. 2008: still not together

Mar. 2008: Olivia's b-day (note 7)

April 2008: on speaking terms

May 2008: Olivia resumed needy phone calls

June 2008: present-time

[215] Why postpone the inevitable?

[216] Unless he reminded me of myself all those years ago, when Amante performed a similar fraternal service (note 160).

"A what?" I said, forced to do a version of the foxtrot to avoid the plainly inebriated mariachi who—when I got a better look at him—may or may not have been the groom-to-be.

"An aunt," Olivia said.

"What are you talking about?"

"Well, not exactly an aunt. My dad's girlfriend—she's having a baby. She's due end of January. But it sounds too weird to call her my sister. She's my niece. I'm going to have a little baby to take care of. I'm so so happy. For someone who's never going to have kids, I'm finding myself going ga ga, and I mean she's only the size of a plum. Currently."

"Wait," I said. "I thought you wanted to meet up."

"I did," Olivia said. "My dad just told me. I went out to dinner with him and Kara, and he told me. You're the first person I told."

"Thanks," I said.

"You should feel honored."

"I am," I said, but I'd kind of gone numb too, and I was shivering a bit. Another mariachi burst out of the bathroom, a plump, high-waisted dude who I'd definitely never seen.

"Yikes," he mumbled, scooting past me. "I wouldn't go in there if I was you."

I waved him off. He was readjusting his pants before stepping back into the dining room. "Hey, yo, Bernard," he shouted, his pants wedged unattractively into a butt shape as he moved away.

Olivia was like "Do you want to come and help pick baby clothes?"

"Sure."

"It's OK. I can tell you're not enthusiastic."

"No, that's not true. What are you up to?"

"Going to bed. It's late, Ian. I figured I'd try one last time. My roommate and I shared a bottle of Bordeaux and we've been nodding off listening to the new Bob Dylan: Connor Oberst. You heard of him? You didn't have to avoid me. I told you I don't want any of that weirdness."

"You're right," I said. "I'm happy for you."[217]

---

[217] Sometimes, when I look back on it now, I regret how my topsy-turvy time with Olivia put a strain on so many other relationships. For instance: Rebecca Fershleiser, my erstwhile roommate. I wish I'd left things better off with her—but as I said (in note 26), we weren't really getting along by the end. In the weeks after I gave my one-month's notice, Fershleiser barely talked to me, except one day when some douchebag in the apartment next to us left a humungous polyester living room set sitting right in front of our door. I came home from work and about burst out laughing just at the absurdity of this ensemble, especially the plastic wrapped loveseat, which was within six inches of our door, sitting cockeyed on its head, with the legs up in the air. I had to negotiate this thin wedge of space and was mentally congratulating myself for my dexterity when I ran into Fershleiser on her way out. This wasn't unusual. We had different hours—and Fershleiser, should she choose, could always work from home, since her jobs were all freelance and computer-based. I indicated the door and said something like "Watch out," and Fershleiser shook her head not comprehending, with her usual sardonic puckered lip that I'd long ago stopped taking personally, and then she swung open the door. "What the fuck?" she said. "Are you fucking kidding me? Is this a joke? Whose chair is this?" She was speaking to me with her hands on her hips, her hips cocked, a pale beige colored purse with that fake reptilian skin slung over her shoulder. I was just like "Uh." But Fershleiser bore down on me as if I was the guilty party. "What—you're just going to let them leave this in front of our door and just go on in like it's nothing? What if there're bed bugs? Did you read the label? It says: 'Treatment' and there's a picture of a fucking bug. Inconsiderate assholes. No fucking way. Whose shit is this?" "The neighbors, is my guess," I said. "Well, knock on their fucking door and tell

them to haul their shit out of our hallway," Fershleiser said. I shrugged and sauntered to the door. "Forget it," Fershleiser said before I could squeeze past her into the entryway. "Assholes." She went over and knocked, and some slick kid in Buddy Holly glasses and a brown plaid shirt came squinting over, apologizing. Behind him, from the open apartment, we could hear the seductive trumpet music of vintage Harmon mute Miles Davis, which made me think we'd maybe interrupted more than just a logistical impasse over how best to arrange the furniture. "I want these away from our door, if you don't mind," Fershleiser was saying. The kid was like "I'm sorry. They've all been treated. We had the whole place bombed. They're completely clean. You could eat off them. We never actually saw a bed bug, if that makes you feel better. It was just a precaution. My friend had them and well... We wanted to be safe. They're fucking shit to eradicate." "No shit," Fershleiser said, not smiling. "When I saw that picture, I was like, 'Are they leaving their bed bug infested chair right in the hall?'" "I know. That picture is pretty twisted. I should've taken it off. I will. I'm really sorry about that. I completely understand why you'd be upset. I would be too. I am so so sorry." He was already dragging the offending loveseat, or more like pivoting it on its axis without making much headway. "Get a hand here," he called back into his apartment. "My girlfriend and I," he said. He called again and this stick-thin girl with enormous hands red as boiled lobster in a gown and slippers stepped out and she was also profusely apologizing, until the two of them became one united apologetic voice, bowing from the waist like English butlers as they dragged their enormous plastic wrapped furniture back into their domicile, the girl making pretty much minimal effort to get a good grip on the seat's sides with her long French-tipped nails, so that in the end the kid pretty much moved all the shit by himself. "Did you see the girlfriend? Jack Sprat could eat no fat," I said when they were out of range. Fershleiser, still unamused, for all eternity convinced of my uselessness, went "I'm going to be late for work."

"And Ian," she said.

"Yes?"

"I love you. You know that already?"

"Yes," I said.[218]

"But it's—a different kind of love. You know what I mean." The way she said it, like it was a foregone conclusion—or maybe she was just sleepy and not enunciating the same as usual— made the words even more final and depressing, as if we'd both agreed to certain terms and conditions long ago, like two generals after a hard-fought fight.

"Sure," I said.

"I count on you, Ian."

"I don't know why."

"Yes you do. I want you to remember the best of me. You remember everything else." The last bit came out like an accusation.

"That's not true," I said.

"Don't bullshit yourself," Olivia said. "When we went back to Soho that night, remember? You knew exactly—verbatim— everything I told you about my mom and dad, everything I told you about that freaking dollhouse my mom got me (for crying out loud!), that J.G. Ballard book[219] that changed my life, all that stuff I told you at that Cuban place on Bergen Street.[220] Do you remember we missed the F train because it ran way up the platform and we ran after it—that night. I know you do."

"I remember," I said, sullen.

"Then think: what I told you that night, when we were about to go to sleep."

"'Goodnight'?"

---

[218] She had, as she said, "so much love to give" (note 147).

[219] *The Kindness of Women* (in which the love of the narrator's life dies slipping on stone steps).

[220] I couldn't deny that I remembered that (see note 211—and 147 again).

"Ha, no. I told you that you were like a vaccine—you know what I mean. That I'd just gotten out of a relationship with Garrett—I don't even want to say his name. That thanks to you I was finally able to cut him off like the gangrenous limb he was."

"Sure. So?"

"So—that's why I said I'm always thankful for you."

"But not too much."

"For fuck's sake, don't make me cry about it. You can always call me. I'll answer. It doesn't matter what. OK?"

"OK," I said.

"OK?"

"I said 'OK.'" I'd moved back. I was leaning against the now mariachi-less payphone—I accidentally knocked the phone off the console and just let it dangle, beeping. "Well. Goodnight."

"Goodnight, Ian. Try to be happy for me, will you?"—that was the last thing she said.

I closed the phone, not even perplexed anymore, as if all sorts of doubts and worries and concerns had just evaporated, leaving the inside of my head like an empty shell that had been picked clean by birds or some other animal that eats shelled animals.[221] I walked right through the band of mariachis, without hearing them, a low humming noise (totally disconnected from reality) in my ears. I sat down on Maggie's old seat, not even seeing anything, except a sort of mesh-like cocoon that covered my eyes all of a sudden, like a cataract or macular degeneration, brightened by one or two little sparks like the after-glare from the sun.

Maggie and Amante were gone.

"Hallo," I said. "What happened to the gang?"

Sean was like "Outside smoking."

"Really?" I said.

---

[221] The term "crustacean" had definitely slipped out my recall for the evening.

"Apparently Maggie has a soft spot for successful novelists," Sean said.

Preston was looking out the window, his face a fleshy blob against the glass, except for the vaguely dark reflection of his eyes and goatee.

"As for us, old boy," Sean said, "we're discussing next moves."

"I could stand another drink," I said.

"I like your style," Preston said.

Sean was like "Żywiec?"

"No can do," I said. "Coors Light from here on out."

"Pssh," Preston said. "Tap water beer."

"It's your funeral," Sean said. "But you're the man. I'm at your disposal."

Preston was like "I second. I do got to clean up the house a bit tomorrow, though. We're building a kind of arbor thing, and I promised Allie I'd chip in. She also wants these fence posts that cost like $1,000, 'cause they're wood even though the plastic ones will last longer and don't need to be touched up every season but oh well. The lady wants what she wants."

Sean was like "What a man, what a man, what a mighty good man."

"Hell. I don't got a curfew," Preston said. "I'm down for anything."

The waitress only brought one check (she claimed she forgot) but Maggie had left enough for her tea—more than enough—and Amante's $1 coffee wasn't worth squabbling over. I put a twenty dollar bill on top, asked for change, and went out the door.

Maggie and Amante were on the sidewalk, Maggie pulling on a cigarette with a kind of desperation.

I went "Since when do you smoke?"

Maggie turned to exhale downwind. "You think I tell you everything."

"Like whatcha mean?"

"My bad habits," she said. "You think I'd tell you those?"

Amante, standing close enough to hear all this, had absented himself as tactfully as possible and was making every conceivable effort to look like he had a major interest in the old warehousey building across the street, which blocked the view to the loading docks along the river.

"Not making any poor choices, then?" I said.

Maggie stepped up to me. She smelled like cigarette and her eyes had wrinkles on the side and her hair shone bright against the light. "I'm almost thirty-four," she said. "I'm not making poor choices anymore."

"Fair enough," I said.

A cab was pulling up along the curb where yesterday's rain had gathered the remains of old newspapers and clumps of black sludge that used to be leaves. Whether we'd called the cab or not didn't matter; there was no one else around. "You OK?" she asked. It was difficult to tell if she was really concerned anymore or just resigned to my continuing to make a fool out of myself. She stepped closer to me and I hugged her like I was hugging a cousin, in a proper sort of way. I might have even patted her back, but I wasn't sure (if I did pat her back my brain immediately obliterated any trace of it), though I caught a weird almost unbelieving sneer forming on her mouth[222] as she backed away, looking up at me with her small face with the sharp nose and the beveled chin, and her hair cut like a boy's, falling over her ears, yet still catching the wind because it was so thin.

"Don't do anything stupid," she said. "I can say that to *you*." She stared at my phone, which I'd never put away. I was still holding that phone like an ignoramus.

"Sean's here, he'll keep an eye out."

"Yeah right."

---

[222] Exactly the type of sneer a woman would sneer if a man she was attracted to patted her back like she was one of the bros, like we'd just concluded an intramural basketball game and were wishing each other "great game, bro!"

Sean and Preston had ambled over and Sean approached, checking his own phone. "So," he said, making as if he was distracted, eyes on the screen.

Maggie was like "So."

"That's it?" he said.

"I'm about to crash," Maggie said.

Nick Amante opened the cab door, gentleman till the end, and stepped to the side.

"Catch you later, Maggie," I said. "See ya!"[223]

---

[223] I've seen Maggie a few times since—coffee at Graindaisy, brunch at the Maritime, a stroll through Chelsea Market, that sort of thing, always with Sean and one or two other friends from work, or a couple of Maggie's Tenafly buddies (yes, she had some female friends), women who like to plan trips, whose cellphones chirp constantly when they receive emails, who tolerate me even if I'm like a kid. The last time I saw her was for Sean's going away party, at some Mongolian restaurant off Astor Place. As we were leaving—Sean chatting with a girlfriend from Jakarta—she held up an unrecognizable copy of *Inferno*, my own copy, the one I'd lent Sean. I was like "Don't tell me you've read it?" Maggie nodded quietly. "I forgot to give it back to you." I was touched, somehow, by the gesture, in spite of the book's worn, dog-eared condition—the pages were stiff, blistered and wavy with serious water damage. "I didn't think that guy could pull it off," Maggie said, standing on her tiptoes. She'd been drinking a lot of vodka. "Nick Amante?" I said. Maggie's feet collapsed into her heels and she was short again. I was like "What? You didn't think he could write?" Maggie teetered but found Sean's elbow (he was facing his friend). She went "No. He sure could write *this* book. Forget it. I don't know what I'm trying to say." I was like "It's OK." I was feeling a weird tenderness for Maggie, like I'd never see her again and this was our final, unambiguous goodbye. Maggie regained her footing. "God, do you remember that whitetrash girl he was with. I mean, *not* with. That bullshit story he gave—he was with her, but he

"See ya!"

"Bye, Mags."

"Bye."

"Bye, Maggie!"

Amante closed the door. He shook my hand. "It's been a pleasure," he said.

I was like "Nightcap?"

Amante shook his head. "I'll walk with you all if you're heading that way, but I can't drink."

"Oh," I said. "Right."[224]

"Where to, young buck?" Sean said, clapping me on the shoulder. Preston was a step behind, listening to a voicemail from his wife.

I shrugged. We were walking up the street following the taillights from Maggie's cab. My phone felt cold and lifeless, like some dead artifact I'd discovered. I had to open it again to

---

wasn't with her—they 'weren't' dating." I said sure, I remembered, though of all the details from that night Amante's pseudo-lover hardly stood out for me. Across the Bowery, a troupe of college kids swayed past. They were young (younger than me), dressed as if for Mardi Gras, with boas and beads, tiaras and eye masks. They moved as a unit, arms linked, almost synchronized, every few paces a shoe getting stuck or someone breaking stride, and everybody giggling, screaming at each other to get a move on, hurry up, slip that shoe back on, then a collective groan as the phalanx shuffled on. The energy had gone out of Maggie's face. "Well," she said, "more power to him." She turned to Sean before I could reply, like Sean was the one she really wanted to speak to and she was just buying time talking to me. That was the end of that conversation.

[224] I'd completely forgotten that Amante had cut back and almost eliminated his drinking, ever since his college meltdown (see note 33 "a total basketcase").

verify that Olivia really had sent me that first text, that I really had talked with her.[225]

"I know a bar close to here," Preston said, muffling his phone. "It's divey, and the clientele leaves something to be desired... "

"Sounds great," I said.

"Lead on, Pres."

"Gentlemen," Preston said, hanging up. "Follow me."

---

[225] Anton Kolnikov was already at Phebe's Bar when Olivia and I got there—along with a friend, Stefan Grigorievich (or maybe I made his name up—I probably did). Kolnikov was flabbier than I'd expected, his chin a full circle the diameter of a plum, set in his bulging neck. Grigorievich was the opposite—every angle of his face was crystalline and he had hair like some late '70s rocker; Grigorievich's English also was not as good as Kolnikov's and for most of the evening (we wound up at some Russian bar farther uptown where sorrowful, hollow-eyed waitresses served us Baltikas and flirted with Grigorievich, whose resemblance to Roger Daltrey or Peter Frampton intensified after every drink) he stared at me hostilely as if telegraphing some secret message, which in the language of *The Brothers Karamazov* could very well have been "I understand you are here at the invitation of the lady, but your place is quite clearly elsewhere. Outside··· where there will be weeping and gnashing of teeth. Hee, hee, hee! Oh, believe me, sir, I understand you. I un-der-stand you perfectly!" Kolnikov, on the other hand, was unprepossessing and spoke candidly about life in his adopted country—he was an exchange student, milking the system, considering any available bureaucratic loophole to avoid his motherland. He shared his Baltika, discoursed on American architecture, commended our national love of peanut butter. When we were alone, he invited me to drink vodka with him, Russian style. "To Olivia," he said. "Olivia," I said drunkenly. Kolnikov wiped his mouth close enough to kiss me. "So," he said. "How do you know her?"

About the Author

Will Clattenburg was born in Philadelphia, Pennsylvania and attended Yale University, graduating with a BA in English. He has taught in public schools at the elementary level for over ten years, first in Brooklyn, New York then in Albuquerque, New Mexico. For the 2020-2021 school year, he taught "live" from his bedroom, using his eight-year-old's art easel in lieu of blackboard. His short story collection, *The Art of Fugue*, was published in 2020, and several of

Photo: Michelle Douglas

his stories have appeared in journals and books, most recently *The Best Short Stories of Philadelphia* and Crack the Spine's *The Year* Anthology. He received an MFA in Creative Writing from New Mexico State University and lives with his family in Albuquerque.

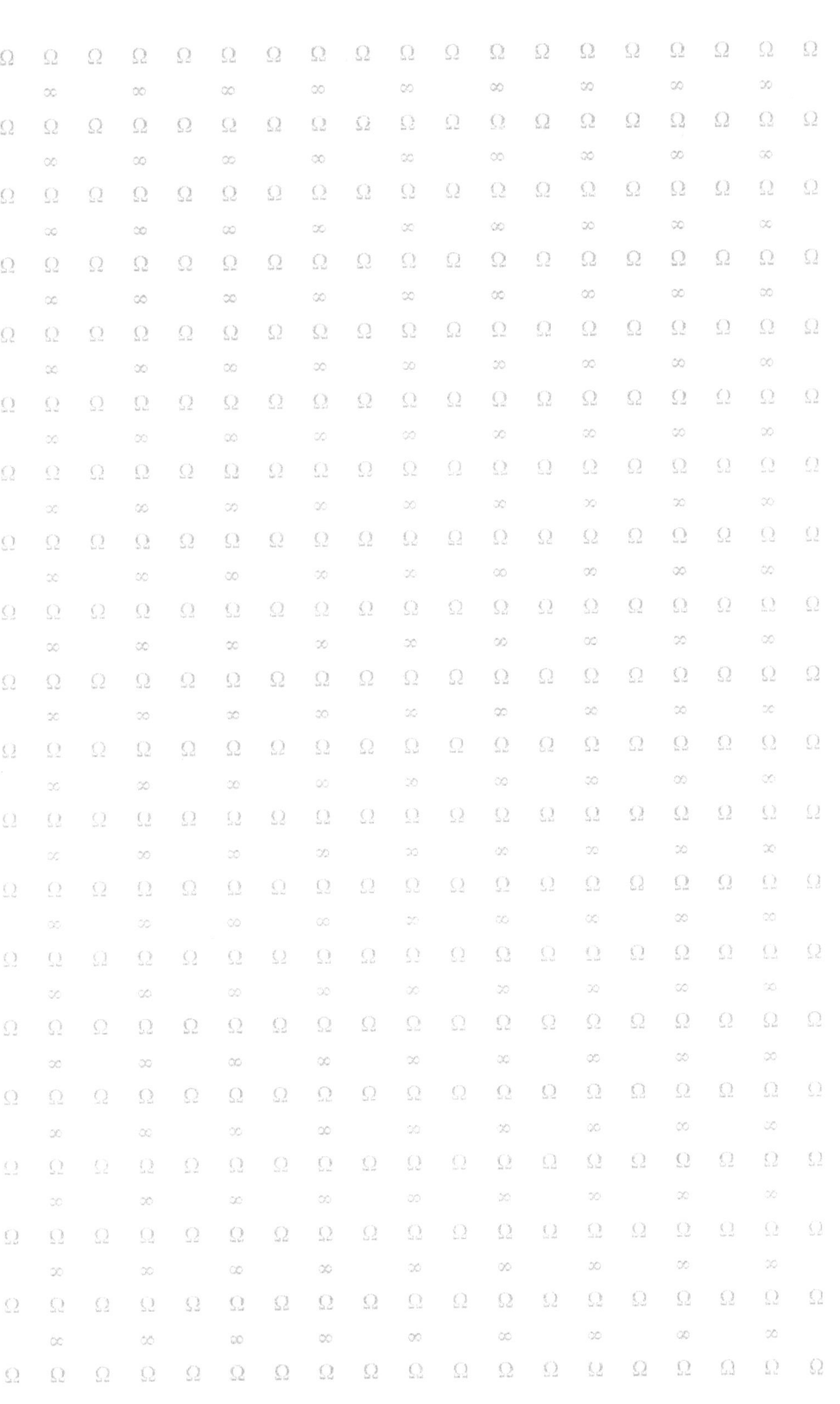

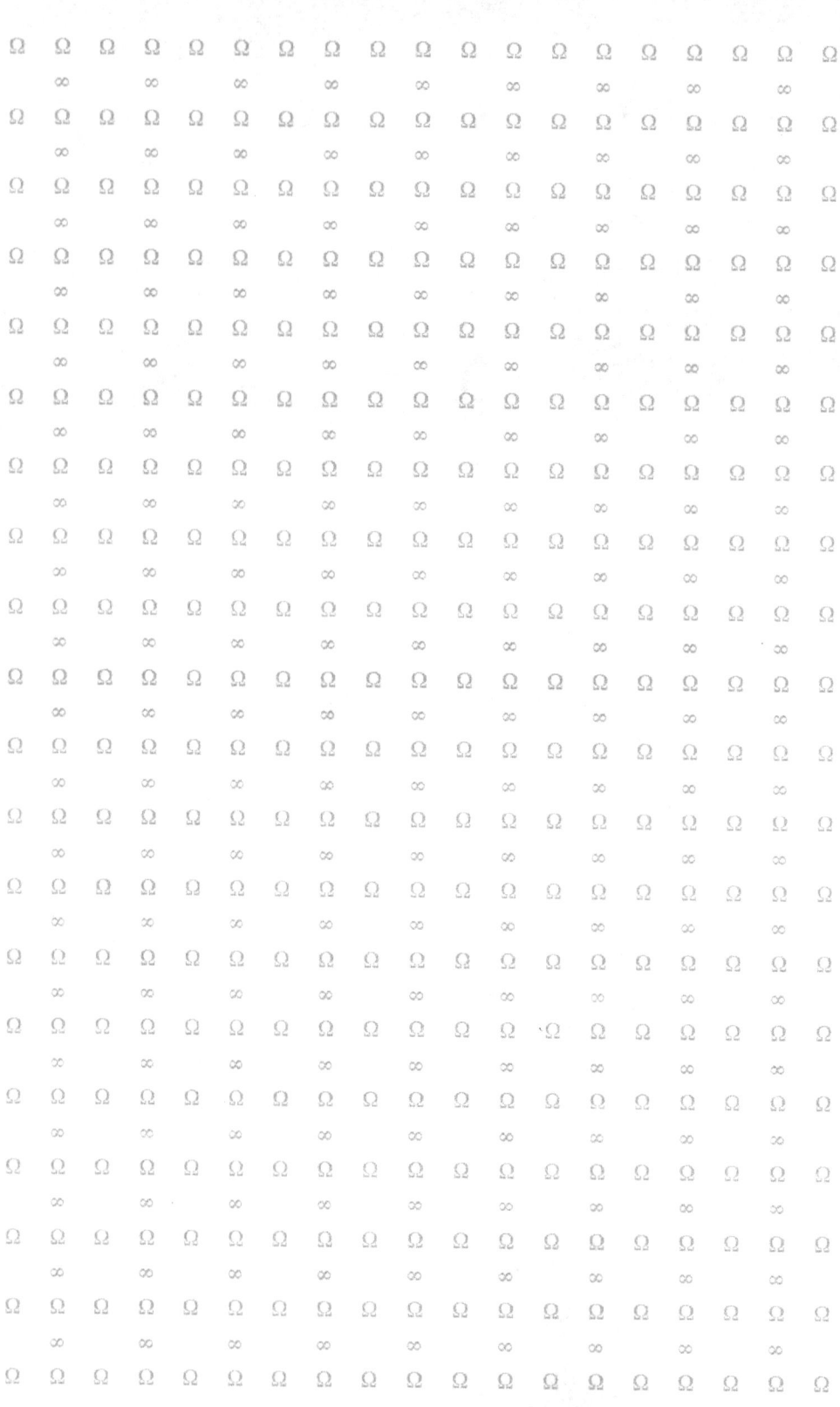

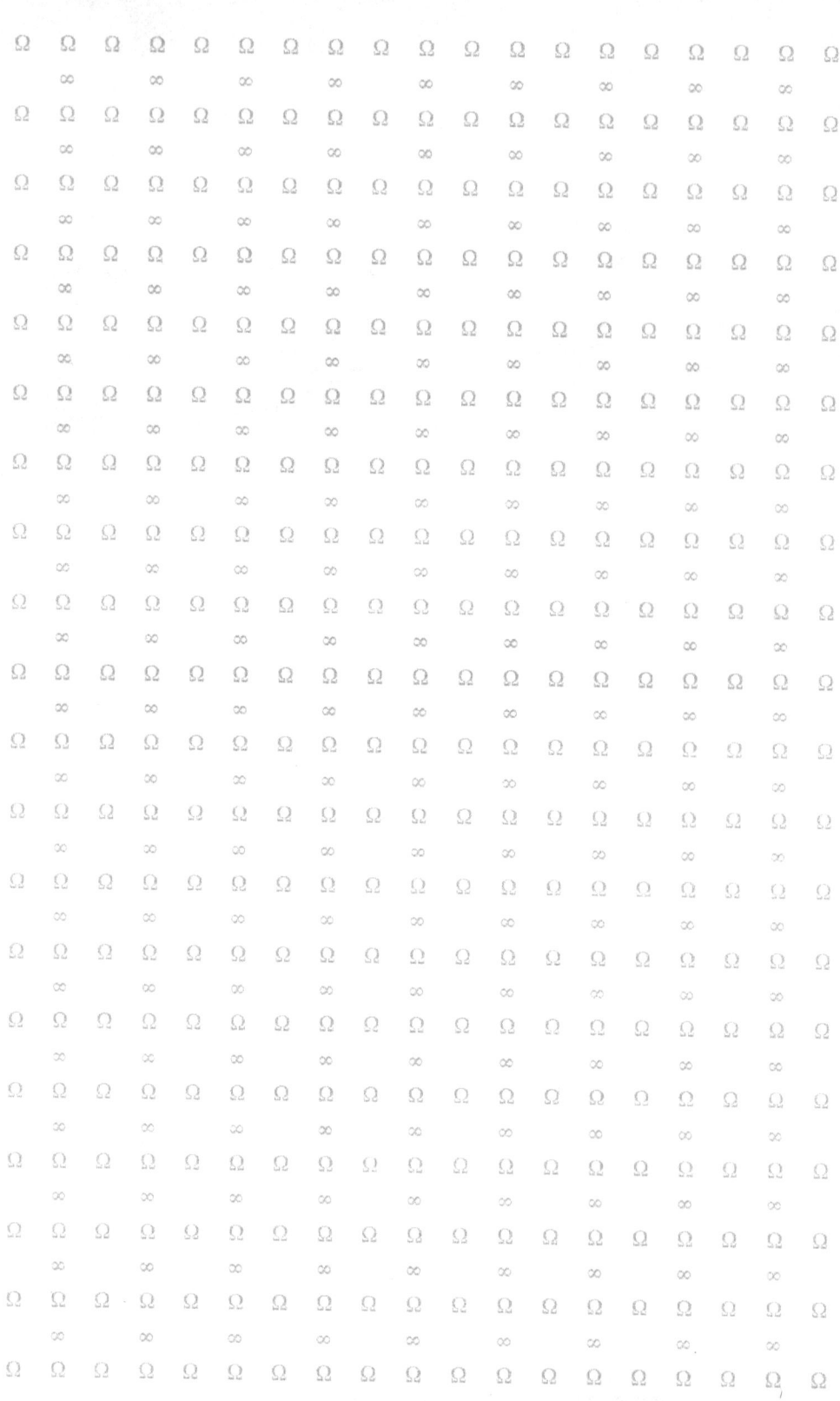